Also by J.

Girl on th

The Butterfly Trap

Jack's Story

KATUMBA

J. V. PHAURE

A CIP catalogue record for the book is available
from the British Library

Cover Design by
jasonpowell-design.co.uk

ISBN 9781915787255

Typeset, Printed and Bound in Great Britain by
Biddles Books Limited, King's Lynn, Norfolk

Dedication

To My Parents

About the Author

J.V. Phaure is a British author, best known for her novels Girl on the Beach, The Butterfly Trap and Jack's Story.

Writing has always been a passion of hers and she takes her inspiration from the people she meets and the countries she has lived in. She loves nothing more than to sit on her village beach and people watch and write. When she's not writing she enjoys windsurfing locally to her.

She lives in North Essex with her family.

To find out more about the author you can visit her website or find her on Instagram, Twitter and Facebook.

www.jvphaure.com

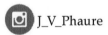 J_V_Phaure

 @JvPhaure

 Facebook.com/jvphaure

Acknowledgements

Thank you to all those who have made KATUMBA the story that it is.

With heart-warming thanks to my wonderful editor Caroline Petherick.

"To be called a refugee is the opposite of an insult; it is the badge of strength, courage and victory."

Tennessee Office for Refugees

Chapter One

A small body lay on the cracked rubber floor of the battered dinghy, gently pushed by the ebb and flow of the water as it washed towards the brown gritty shores of the derelict coastline. The greyness of the skies merged with the deep murky waters which were snatched momentarily by the foamy crest of a wave that carried in its swell a slimy layer of scum and remnants of discarded plastic bottles and soiled paper. Amid the sombre colours of the sky and the sea the bright orange dinghy bobbed on the shallow surf, rocking unevenly with each breaking wave as it made its way closer to the shallows, where it caught on the grit, scratching at its torn hull. The filthy water swirled, forming a deep pool in its centre. One of its sides collapsed; the air from it had now gone, and it was as lifeless as what it had carried – or tried to. It pushed up against the shore with each frothy swirl of seawater until it finally caught on the small pebbles beneath it and rested there.

Her hair was caught in tangled beaded braids, some of the beads chipped, and their once vibrant colours washed away by the salty water, the beads smudged up against her cheeks, leaving small indentations where they had pushed into her skin. Her lips were cracked, and her hands had scratch marks from other hands that had gripped at them. There were friction burns on her wrists caused by the tension of those grasps, those vain attempts to stay in the boat that could only lead them to their own deaths. Where the final gasp was

1

taken from them and the fear in their eyes, the last she would ever see. A frozen frame of an innocent soul now swallowed by the depths of the ocean. They were escaping a land that had brought only danger and persecution, and they were running into a danger that would engulf them whole, and yet it was their hope – it was their only hope. In her clenched fist she clasped a silver locket, the chain broken, its tiny hinge bent, and inside it a small piece of leaf and some fragile bits of bark. The grating sound of the shingle against the rubber caused her to lift her body from the floor of the bashed and half-deflated dinghy. As her hand leant against the side of the boat it sank into the squashy rubber, and the air wheezed out as if letting go of the breath of those who had clung to its sides. Her eyes cut a striking icy grey against her deep brown skin and beaded hair.

The gulls wheeled in the sky, their piercing screams penetrating the quietness surrounding her. Their frenzied dives lurched down to a red and blue mound on the pebbles, and they bashed their sharp beaks against it, their webbed feet clawing at the redness of it, squawking at each other as they'd dart down again to take another jab – daring, too daring.

'No! Get away. Stop …' she murmured as she pulled her body out of the boat. She fell onto the sand, the grit of it sticking in her nails, the salt stinging the open skin, her locket still held tightly in the palm of her hand. The corners of her mouth were dry, with a white crust sticking to them. She could barely utter the words 'No. Go. *Leave!*' that she called again, but in vain. Her body was weak and weatherbeaten. She crawled across the shore towards the shrieking seabirds. The gulls' eyes glared menacingly at her as she pushed her body closer. They screamed and wheeled above her, a frenzy of grey-and-white feathers coming at her, attacking her, her cries going unheard. Silent. She collapsed by the mound of red and blue.

She lay still, allowing her eyes to become accustomed to her surroundings. The figure of a person walked past her in the distance; she could barely make it out.

'Please,' she murmured through cracked lips. 'Please.' The figure disappeared. The girl blinked a few times, trying to focus on whatever was around her. She pushed herself up from where she was lying, pushing away the soft quilt that rested over her. She swivelled herself to the edge of the sofa and slowly and gently made her way to the window where the light shone through, catching its rays on the crystal beads that hung from the lampshade on the windowsill and casting a twinkling shadow against the wall. Her bare feet were cushioned on the thickness of the rug, her toes curling as they sank into its soft woollen touch. It was unlike the simple woven tapestry rug that stretched across the earth floor of her home, which she'd beaten daily against its outside wall. Where the dust from the matting would roll like dancing specks through the air until it joined the tracks that would lead to the well, where the women would carry huge urns of fresh water on their heads, their feet bare or protected by simple sandal-like shoes or moccasins made from the hide of a goat, or shoes given by the Red Cross.

She peered out of the window, making out the road that wound around and over the coastline; like a leather belt, it was grey and cracked with age. A land full of nothingness, yet calm and with an abundance of colour she'd never seen before. Even though the sky was grey the land had a tone that was deeper than the brown land she was used to, where the sun would beat down and bake the soil, snatching at any moisture, but most of the time leaving an arid dusty landscape. Now she watched as the sea crashed against the rugged coastline, its deep greyness uninviting and cold, so unlike the water she used to swim in, catching fish with her bare hands. To her, fishing by swimming underwater was as easy as breathing, yet now the waves she was faced with carried a weight in them. The souls in each wave, returning over and over as an aquatic heartbeat.

'You're awake?' She turned to see a man standing by the door. In his hand he held a small china plate of food. 'Pilchards on toast,' he said, placing the plate on the table, with a knife and fork. She looked at the silver-coloured objects, the knife like a spear or knife for cutting a goat carcass that turned over an open fire in her village, but smaller and not pointed. The fork was like one she'd used on the fields where she'd laboured with the women, only it was smaller, much smaller, and less sharp. She turned them on the table, not knowing what to do with them.

'D'you speak English?' he asked gently, taking up a chair opposite her.

She nodded. She had been taught some English by the kind doctor who was from a country where football was played, and her villagers knew of Manchester United and cricket. The kind doctor had the same pinky-pale skin and long thin nose as the man who sat opposite her. She had sat with the kind doctor and learnt some English words – mostly long words that she would never need, which had come from a medical journal. She remembered those words on the front of the British Medical Association's journal, the *BMJ*. *One day*, she had thought, *I'd like to be a part of that association*. The kind doctor had also taught her simple words and sentences in English, and whilst he worked within their village, she learnt that she would like to be like him. She had thought that many times. She too would like to be kind and intelligent and learn more about cricket and Manchester United.

'Where are you from?' this man asked, leaning forward, resting his hand under his chin.

'Africa,' she said, pushing the tomatoey fish into her mouth with her hand. The silver objects still lay on the table unused.

He looked at her quizzically and a slight smile gently broke across his face. 'Africa's large. Whereabouts in Africa?'

'Eritrea.'

He cocked his head and smiled. 'How many of you were there?'

'In boat? Was twenty–' she stopped and pressed her finger on each finger of her right hand, 'and five.'

'Twenty-five,' Tom repeated back to her. '*Was*?'

She creased her eyes as she looked at him. Although she knew he had said the word *was*, she didn't know its full meaning, so she continued: 'The seas took them. We too many for small boat. Fear took them, they drowned, the storms, the big waves, we had no chance, but we took our chance for a better life. To reach the land of hope.'

Tom watched her as she said these words. A sentence she had perhaps learnt, whose words came in the right order. 'And the boy?'

'The boy?'

'On the beach.'

She cast her look to the ground, remembering Amanuel's smile and the dances he would perform to the elders of the village at the firepit. If the sea had been a track, he would have galloped along it like a gazelle. 'The small boy my brother, but he was washed on beach, the birds of the sea fed off him. I tried …' She turned her hands in on themselves and her eyes stung with tears.

'He's here.'

'He's under the ground?' A tear fell from her eye.

'Buried? Why would I do such a thing? He's alive. He's sleeping in my room. God knows how he's alive, but he is.'

'He's alive, my brother's still with me? You saved him too? Please tell me you speak true words.'

He tilted his head to one side and a gentle smile crossed his face, 'I do speak true words.'

'Please let me see for my own eyes that he is with me, my Amanuel.' She cast her glance back to Tom.

'You need to eat, at least try to. Finish your fish and then I will show you.'

She wanted to devour the food in front of her, but each mouthful stung her lips and her stomach cramped as she swallowed. And it didn't look much like fish to her, at least not the ones she knew. These fish had no heads.

'Please let me be with him.' She pushed her plate toward the pile of books in the centre of the table. He nodded and led her through the hall and then up the stairs to the room where a small body lay on a bed, tossing and turning in his sleep. The pillow was drenched by his perspiration as the fever ravaged through his tiny body, seemingly giving him no chance of staying alive. The short fuzz of his hair still glistened with particles of sand that had caught in it. His black skin had beads of sweat clinging to it, and his chapped lips trembled.

'Amanuel, Amanuel,' she whispered.

He murmured in his restlessness.

'It's me, Abrihet,' she said in Tigrinya. 'Can you hear me?' She brushed her hand against his forehead. Then in English: 'He's burning, he has fever, he needs medicine.' She didn't turn to the man who'd brought them into his home for shelter, but just let the words fall from her lips. She had learnt these words from the kind doctor, words she'd heard him say daily.

She hadn't the slightest clue what medicine Amanuel needed, but she knew when the fever came and ravaged through their village the children would be shielded by nets that the people would bring in their van, a white van with a red cross on it. And then the kind doctor would give medicine and the nets would help. She didn't know how, but they seemed to stop people getting ill.

She heard the man leave the room. Abrihet listened as he made his way back down the stairs. She sat alone on the bed beside her brother, his arms bearing open sores on them where they oozed red, and a clear liquid wept from them, the sharp beak-like marks where the gulls had pulled his open flesh from his small body. He was dressed simply in a red short-sleeved t-shirt and the brightest of blue shorts. A pair of battered sandals lay by the side of the bed.

'Amanuel,' she whispered softly as he stirred a little, his eyes fluttering open and closed until they stayed open and rested on his sister's face. She smiled at him as she stroked his cheeks, and again in Tigrinya: 'We're safe for a while.'

His eyes seemed to smile a little and he held her hand. 'And our friends?' he whimpered.

She shook her head.

'What would you do?' he mumbled.

She looked at him, her hand stroking his bewildered face. 'What would I do?' she questioned softly.

'What would you do?' he said again.

'What would I do, Amanuel?'

His eyes as deep and velvety as melting chocolate stared back at her, fixed. 'If I died.'

'Carry on,' she said.

7

They heard a door clicking shut and the footsteps of the man outside, going away from the house. The room they were in was a warm one, and a large box rested on the floor with small boxes inside it. She had not seen these before; they were made of wood, a honey-coloured wood that gleamed in the light. On top of the box rested a lamp and pictures, pictures of white people smiling, and a sailing boat. A sailing boat with the whitest of sails outspread and a man standing at its edge, grinning broadly, with a golden dog by his feet, and a woman, a white woman in shorts and a t-shirt, beaming too, cuddling the dog. It did not look like the dogs that lived in her village. Its fur was thick, and its face smiled. Abrihet's eyes scanned around the room. The floor was covered in a softness that was the palest of greys, almost the colour of the silver moon that would shimmer on the pool of water where she used to swim for fish. Strange white wooden planks flanked the windows. They looked a little like ladders – but why would white people hang ladders on the wall for no obvious reason? She gazed in wonderment at the room. Never had she seen such a place. The light that hung from a silver pendulum bore no resemblance to the light that buzzed and flickered in the kind doctor's room, where the metal beds with nets were. Here, the bed where her brother lay was perhaps as big as four of the kind doctor's beds if she had pushed them together. The top of this bed was golden brown like the wooden boxes, and the covers on it were a silvery grey, like the soft floor. *This must be the land where Manchester United were from and where cricket was played,* Abrihet thought. *This must be the land where our kind doctor was from. The land of hope.*

And now this place was where she had travelled to across oceans and seas, trekked over dangerous terrains, to reach this land of hope. Where the sounds of gunfire and shooting ceased. Where the dense smell of burning grass roofs no longer lingered in the air. Where no longer would the men from outside rampage through the small huts of her village, kicking the women to the ground and grabbing them by their vibrant-coloured headscarves. The sound of their screams and pleading from them to stop, begging them to leave, to just take their money, the little money they had. Their pleas ignored as the terrible men tore away the women's and girls' garments and penetrated them hard and with force, and when they'd finished, they'd leave, laughing and jeering. They'd boot the scraggy dogs so they'd howl, and then they'd kick over the brownish water that boiled on the fires – the only water that the villagers could drink.

'Boiling it will clean it,' the kind doctor would say. And so that's what the villagers used to do. And now, all that was left for Abrihet and her younger brother, Amanuel, was a place she did not know, a place that her parents had probably paid weeks of earnings for, to give them their spaces on a boat that would bring them to safety. A place on a boat that would take them to a land that would give them a better life, that would stop the torture and rape, that would allow the two children to become like their doctor – intelligent, wise and kind.

The door clicked once more, and Abrihet listened to the footsteps as they approached. Her breath held. Her eyes stayed on the man as he entered the room again and walked toward the bed where she still sat, holding the hand of her little brother. She stared at what was in the man's hands. There was no net, just a box with pink and red writing on it. She tilted her head to read the letters that ran across it – *Cal… pol* she mouthed. She stared curiously at the picture of a white boy on the front of the packaging, who didn't look as sick as the children from her village beneath the nets or even as sick as her own Amanuel, who cried out intermittently.

The man sat at the head of the bed and took from the box the bottle of pink medicine. It smelt like a sweet fruit.

'How old is he?' he asked, tipping the syringe out too.

She counted on her fingers once more and hesitantly replied, 'Eight?' She was a little unsure why this question had been asked. She watched intently as the man took the syringe from the box and allowed the thick, gloopy medicine to trickle into it. And then he gently lifted the boy's head and raised the pillows to cushion him a little.

'Here, open your mouth a little,' he said, opening his own mouth to show the boy. Amanuel opened his mouth and a crack of blood wept from the soreness of his lips.

'This will make you better,' said the man in a hushed voice. He laid the boy's head back down, and brushed his hand through the short fuzziness of his hair. He left the room once more, returning moments later with a small square blue bag. He unzipped it and took out a small pipette with a clear solution in it, some white padded gauze and micropore tape. He broke the small tube and allowed the liquid to run over and into the wounds on Amanuel's arms and legs. Amanuel whimpered with the shot of pain, it stung more than if a swarm of wasps had attacked him. And yet he let the man aid him.

'I'm sorry, it's almost done.' He stopped and looked at the small boy, his face breaking into a reassuring smile, appeasing for a brief moment the child's discomfort and fear. 'My name is Tom, Amanuel, I will make these better for you.' He gently dabbed at the open sores until the flesh was no longer a deep red raw wound but instead a clean soft pink. He folded the gauze and placed it over the wounds and secured it with a strip of micropore tape, and then he pressed it down gently. 'There,' he said taking the box and the empty wrappers and pipette, and placing them on the bedside table. Then he got up to leave the room once more.

As he reached the door he paused and turned with a smile of reassurance. 'You've made it.'

'This the land of hope?' she said faintly.

'Yes.' And then he left.

Abrihet allowed her eyes to rest on the door where he had stood, where he had said those words, *You've made it.* They had. They had made it away from the village to a shore that brought them hope – but what about their parents? When would they arrive? Would they *ever* arrive? Until then, Abrihet and Amanuel were alone.

Although they weren't.

And they would learn that too.

Chapter Two

Tom's mobile vibrated on the kitchen counter. The name on the screen flashed *Kate Mb.* He took the glass of wine he'd poured and pressed Answer.

'Tom, have you got the telly on? Have you seen the news?' He placed his wine on the counter and picked up the remote control for the television, which was mounted on the wall. 'That's the beach, d'you see? A boat's been found, but the passengers are missing, possible sightings, feared drowned. Refugees again, Tom. Thought to be African.'

'I'll call you back,' he said, closing the call. He increased the volume on the television.

The reporter was standing on an Italian rescue boat surrounded by African people, wrapped in silver and gold foil blankets, some crying, some shivering, others silent with a fear that they'd be taken back to where they'd come from.

'There are tough questions to be asked …' Tom pushed the volume up. The reporter continued. 'As the sun sets and if you're the person bailing the water out of the sinking boat it amounts to *don't let me drown in the dark.* At night the situation becomes critical, radio messages bristle with panic. Migrant boats are sinking all around us. More than 800 people have been packed onto that boat in the distance. The boat's called a double decker, where migrants hide on the top and bottom decks. Bodies crammed in. At least 200 people have been drowned after capsizing in small dinghies. Rescue efforts are being made as quickly as they can, all in the dead of night.

When the motorboats were out taking people from the sea, there is a strange window of trauma and quiet. Just the rustle of the gold and silver foil blankets. This crisis is complex, and perspectives are different. Frederik, a carpenter from Holland, has volunteered to help. He has pulled eight dead bodies from the water already, one a child no older than six.' "I'm just a carpenter," Frederik cries. "Why won't Europe help us?" 'His emotions are visible, his perspectives are different to the men in suits calling crisis meetings, closing borders, turning boats away. In the corner of the rescue boat an African woman sings. Her faith is what has kept her alive. In her arms is another small child, clinging onto the warmth that is life. A child who has not drowned, one of the lucky ones. This is Robert Foster, reporting from the *Mare Bellito*, BBC News.'

Tom paused the television, leaving the frozen image of a child whose eyes stared straight at him, penetrating to the back of his skull. He took a large gulp from his wine glass and then pushed it to one side. He could feel his heart pounding. He left his mobile on the kitchen worktop and went upstairs to check on the children.

They were lying together on the bed, Abrihet cradling her younger brother in her arms. There was no net around the bed.

Amanuel's tossing and turning from the fever had subsided – the Calpol had eased his raging temperature. The white gauze padding was still in place, shielding the wounds and jabs inflicted by the seabirds. Now with a shot of red oozing through them, Tom would dress them again later. He walked over to the bed and pulled the silvery-grey chenille throw over the children, gently tucking it in at the sides in a cocoon-like way, simply allowing it to rest on them. He brushed it down a little and stood, with a semblance of a smile, watching over them.

Tom sat down at the worktop and stared at the frozen image on the television, chilled by the deep, dark eyes that gazed back at him. He felt as if they were watching his every move, yet they were still. He picked up his glass of wine. Did he need to go back to the beach? The girl, Abrihet, had said there had been twenty-five people in the boat. He needed to know if the two children were the only survivors. But he knew that if he went for a run he might find more people washed up on the shore clasping to their last breaths, waiting in the dead of night, clinging to life, hoping that they too might be found. He dragged his hand through his hair, his mind in a quandary. He kept telling himself that the two children were the only survivors and they were now safe, and that any more would have been reported on the news.

The sea would soon spit out the bodies it had taken, and they would rest, lifeless, on the sandy shores of Kent.

He opened the screen on his phone and pressed Last Call.

'Tom – did you *see* it?'

'Yeah, I did.' He breathed heavily. His leg trembled. He balanced his foot on the footrest of the high stool, and his leg stopped trembling. 'Kate, you need to come over.'

'What? Now?'

'Yup.'

'Okay, I'll be there soon. What's up?'

'I'll explain when you get here.' He closed the call and stared at the television screen, the eyes of the African child still fixed on him. He opened his laptop and waited for a few seconds whilst the screen came to life, then googled "African migrants". He scrolled through the stories and reports until he came to an article. A story he knew he would find. He bit the skin at the side of his finger, his eyes never leaving the screen.

He squinted as Kate's headlights dazzled him through the window. He closed the laptop and waited for the car to beep and the indicators to flash before he opened the front door.

'Hey,' Kate said, 'I've brought wine.' She thrust a bottle of Côtes du Rhône at Tom before kissing him on the cheek. He closed the door behind her and went into the kitchen.

'So come on, Tom what's the urgency?' she asked as she watched him pour her a glass of wine.

'I need to show you something. But you have to promise, Kate, you have to promise not to tell a soul – and I mean *nobody.*'

'Okay, I promise. Brownie promise.' She cocked her head and scrunched up her nose, and the corner of her eyes creased.

'Seriously ...'

'Seriously, come on. Don't keep a girl in suspense.'

'Follow me, but shhh.'

Gently he eased the door handle down. Kate gasped. He placed his finger across his lip, silencing her.

Kate looked at him and shook her head. 'What the f---?' she said in a hushed voice. She sighed, silently flicking her eyes from the bed where the two bodies lay back to back. *Don't say a word, you'll wake them,* he telegraphed. Kate raised her eyebrows.

Tom closed the door and went back downstairs.

'Fuck,' Kate said taking a gulp from her wine glass. 'Where were they?' Her eyes moved across his face, looking for the answer.

'On the beach. I found them early this morning when I was out for my run; they were pretty much clinging to life.'

'Shit, Tom, did anyone see you?'

'No, it was way too early.'

Kate exhaled. 'What are you going to do?'

'I dunno. Help them – I guess. I haven't thought that far ahead.'

'My God.' She paused. 'Where are they from?'

'Eritrea.'

She threw him a look as if to say, *but whereabouts?* 'Jesus Christ, how the fuck have they made it here and still alive?'

'I dunno, but they have. The boy was pretty much half-dead when I found him. I had to get him medicine.'

'Medicine? Tom, you don't have children. People will ask questions. Shit.'

'He needed medicine – he was almost fitting with his fever. I couldn't just not get him any and leave him to die in my bed. Then what? The girl would have been taken and placed in some unknown immigration centre; the boy buried some place away from his parents in some pauper's grave. Questions would have been asked. What was I supposed to do?' He pushed his hands through his hair as he leant back against the work surface.

She touched his hand tenderly and allowed it to rest there. 'Nothing. You did the right thing. But now what? They've got no family here, there's bugger all reason why the Home Office would let them stay. Jesus Christ, we're dealing with a country that's closing down its borders, where a stuck-up arsehole's calling for immigrants to be deported. You don't stand a hope of keeping them, and neither do they stand a chance of staying. They have no papers for a start. They're illegal immigrants! You're harbouring illegal immigrants – shit, fuck, bollocks.'

'I can't *not* try. I can't stand by and watch this happen in front of me, in front of my own eyes. What does that make me? I have to try, and I need you to help me. They have to stand a hope, because, Kate, that's what the girl said: *It's the land of hope*. They'll have sat in a boat for days, and another for weeks, God knows. They've crossed waters we don't even paddle in, scared shitless in the dark on the seas because this *is* their hope. Travelled halfway across flipping Africa and Europe – and I'm not going to run past them and say some coastguard can clear that up. Am I hell!' He thumped his fist down on the counter.

Kate stared back into Tom's eyes. She pushed her fringe away from her eyes and buried her head in her hands. She sighed, and sat staring out of the window into the darkness. 'Have you thought this through, Tom?' she questioned shaking her head without her own doubt consuming her, but wondering what she was signing herself up to if she agreed. Her mind raced with uncertainty. She could lose her job – worse still, be struck off the medical register. It was unethical in every sense of the word, harbouring immigrants. She took another gulp from her glass. 'This is mad, Tom. It's mad.'

'Kate. You know why I'm doing this? You know I can't give up. They're from *Eritrea*.'

'I know,' she swallowed, and her eyes stung. 'But Eritrea's huge.' She knew all too well the significance of the country, and the reason why Tom couldn't give the children up now. She cast her eyes to the television where the face of the African child still remained, etched on the screen, etched in their own minds. 'Okay' she said, shaking her head in disbelief. 'Okay, I'll help,' her voice almost lower than a whisper.

'Thank you,' Tom said as he pushed himself away from the worktop and squeezed her shoulder before retrieving the bottle of wine. She covered her glass with the palm of her hand.

'I'm driving,' she said.

As they sat together, neither of them heard the footsteps on the stairs and across the hallway, and it was only when Abrihet was standing at the door that she gasped: 'Sorry ... Amanuel ...'

'Is he okay?' Tom asked, concerned.

'He has ...'

Tom shot a look at Kate and hastily made his way up the stairs, unsure of what Abrihet had been about to say, terrified that he would have to give up after all. That he now had a body to deal with.

He went to the bed and closed his eyes. 'Thank God,' he said under his breath.

'Tom, is everything okay?' Kate asked as she approached the bed.

'Yeah, everything's fine,' he replied, his voice hushed.' He's just wet the bed, that's all,' he sighed. 'He's just wet the bed,' he said again, relieved that soiled sheets were all that he had to contend with.

'I'm sorry,' Abrihet said her voice low, her eyes cast to the ground.

'Hey,' Kate placed her arms around her. She lifted Abrihet's chin, to see her eyes full of fear and like sunken hollows. She turned her hands in hers and glanced at them; the girl's nails had a reddy-pink discolouring to them. 'I have some things in a bag, I'd like to see if you're all okay.' She smoothed her hand across Abrihet's forehead and brushed it down through her beaded hair. 'Tom, I'm just going to get my bag from the car.'

He nodded.

'I'm sorry,' the girl said again.

'Don't be sorry, it's fine.' He smiled at her as he left the room to find clean dry bedding.

The front door clicked shut. 'Everything okay, Kate?'

'Yep, just thought I'd give them the once-over. Her eyes are sunken due to dehydration and her nails are discoloured.'

He and Kate returned a few moments later with freshly laundered linen from the airing cupboard. Abrihet watched as he scooped Amanuel up from the sodden sheets and beckoned to Kate to open her arms to hold him. His body was light in her cradle. He opened his huge dark eyes and stared up at Kate's face, and she smiled down at him.

'Hey,' she said and scrunched her nose in a smiling kind of way. 'I'm Kate.' He stared back at her, his eyes growing larger as he tried to make her out. And then he smiled. Kate gave a sound that comes only from the warmth of a smile.

'D'you think you can stand while I get these wet clothes off you? We can wash them and then you can put them back on in no time.' She beckoned to Abrihet to come forward. 'Here, stay with your brother whilst I grab a towel. You got him?' She took Abrihet's hands to show her she meant her to hold him. 'You got him?' she said again.

'I got him,' Abrihet repeated. She stood, allowing her brother to fall into her a little, wrapping her arms around him, keeping him safe and warm whilst she waited for Kate to return. She cocked her head to one side and stared at the charcoal-grey towel that Kate carried in her hand. It was large, and as soft as the floor she stood on. She'd never seen such a piece of material, nor one that smelt so sweet. It exuded a fragrance similar to that of the medicine this kind man had given her brother – sweet. As sweet as the lush rose-blushed mangoes that swung from the trees like fragrant lanterns in her village. It smelled remindful of the white woman who now cradled her brother. Abrihet helped peel the wet shorts

19

from Amanuel's small body, then he lifted his arms whilst Kate eased the red top over his wounds and over his head and left them next to her in a small pile.

She took her stethoscope from her bag, cupping the diaphragm in her palms for a few moments, then placed it on Amanuel's chest. Instinctively he took slow deep breaths. 'You've done this before. Good boy!' His bare stomach protruded. 'Good,' she tickled his tummy and turned him, and again he breathed deeply. 'Perfect, and again. Gosh you're good at this.' She turned him back to her and tweaked his nose.

'I'll take a peek at these too,' she pointed to the dressings, then she wrapped the towel around Amanuel's tiny frame and lifted him in her arms and carried him back over to the freshly made bed. She gently laid him down. She smiled again as she plumped the pillows behind him. She rested the palm of her hand on his forehead. It was cooler. He smiled back. The beads of sweat had now gone, and his eyes, as deep and dark as a volcano that lay dormant, searched her face. Leaving him briefly to get her bag, she placed it beside him on the bed. Trying not to hurt him, she peeled away the dressing from his arm. The wound oozed.

'Does it hurt?' She made a face that expressed hurting. He nodded. 'Thought so. It's a teeny, tiny bit infected. Now what have I got here to help?' She delved into her bag and took out a package, ripped the top and laid it out on the clinical sheet, then put on the rubber gloves before tearing open the sterile gauze wrapping. Then she tipped the saline solution onto the gauze and gently dabbed at the wounds on his arm. He winced and pulled his arm back a little.

'Hey, almost there. You're going to need some antibiotics for this,' she said, taking his arm and patting it dry before placing a sterile dressing on it. The blood began to soak through, so she added another dressing and applied a little pressure. She did the same for his knee, only this time she gently pinched the flesh together and applied four steristrips and gauze padding.

'There, as right as rain,' she said, scrumpling up all the used gauze and rubbish in a clinical waste sheet. 'Are you hungry?' she asked, taking her hands to her mouth as if to mime eating something. Her voice was soft and warm to his ears.

He nodded.

Kate turned. 'And you, my lovely, are you hungry too?' She made the same movement, with her hands to her mouth, to Abrihet.

'Yes, I hungry.'

Kate left the room, taking with her the soiled bedding, the medical rubbish and the small bundle of clothes. Tom joined her moments later in the open-plan kitchen, where she busied herself making sandwiches.

'I've made peanut butter sandwiches for them,' she said as she cut the bread into four equal squares with the crusts removed. 'All children like peanut butter, don't they?' She had no idea really, but she knew her two nephews did, and her sister always cut the crusts off their sandwiches. The two African children would probably have eaten the crusts, though. They weren't like white English children.

'Probably safer than Marmite,' Tom said, with a hint of a smile.

'So, what now, Tom? I need to get the boy some antibiotics. He's got a slight wheeze on his chest – maybe an infection brewing – and he definitely needs something for his wounds. They'll need clothes too, you realise that, don't you? They have nothing. And how do we even let their parents know they're safe, that they've made it? They must be going through hell not knowing. I mean to put your child on a boat because that's the safest option for them. Like, it's mad for a parent to be in a place where the open sea's safer than the land, safer than their home.' She turned to him, holding the plate filled with a simple supper. 'It's mad, Tom.' The tears stung her eyes.

'Hey, I know, don't get upset, they're gonna be okay. I promise you. And clothes and stuff, well I'll just go further out, nobody needs to know that bit. You can get the odd medicinal stuff, can't you? I mean it won't look odd for you.'

Kate sighed heavily and shook her head slowly. 'Antibiotics, I don't know … I can't start faking people. Did you see his face, Tom? Oh my God, his eyes, his small body. I can't bear it. Now I know why …' She stopped. The words didn't come. But a memory of what used to be came flooding back.

As she took the sandwiches upstairs Tom watched her with a deep-rooted instinct of why she was helping. She had the same memories after all.

She took a deep breath before she entered the bedroom. She brushed her free hand on her jeans and tucked her hair behind her ear, as if she needed to snatch those few seconds to compose herself and not let the children see she was as scared as they were. She knew the consequences of harbouring immigrants. She knew that with no real knowledge of English, they'd be taken, be all alone again. But this time their hopes shattered. She brushed her eyes and put on a face that said Cheerful Kate. *You've got this, Kate. Think positively, Kate.*

'Hey,' she smiled. 'Look what I've got you both.'

The two children tilted their heads in unison and peered at the perfectly formed white squares with no crusts. They each took one and held it with one hand before biting into the doughy centre. They smiled a little as they tried to dislodge the sandwiches from the roofs of their mouths. They had never eaten a sandwich before, or tasted the creaminess of a paste that tasted like peanuts, which, with the soft white bread, caked the roofs of their mouths.

'Is it good?' Kate asked.

They nodded. They thought they'd understood what she had asked and her face was kind and smiley, and her head nodded vigorously when she said those words and she did things like the kind doctor. They took another bite of their sandwiches and Kate winked at them as she pushed herself up from the bed.

'I'll get you some water.' She left the room to go back downstairs.

The children sat on the bed with the plate and their food. Amanuel peeled the sandwich apart and licked the peanut butter off the bread. Then he placed the perfectly formed square back on top of the other one. His sister watched and smiled at his eagerness to devour the food. It certainly tasted good, a taste they would never forget. It was their first taste of hope in the country where Manchester United were from and cricket was played. They imagined that Manchester United and the cricketers would enjoy these perfectly square sandwiches with peanut butter too. One day, they would learn that cricketers would delight themselves in perfectly formed sandwiches and much more.

Kate returned with two glasses of water. The children took the glasses tentatively and pressed them against their lips. They had never tasted water so clear as this, or so cold – ice cold. Amanuel made a slurping noise as he tilted the glass up. Some of the water trickled down his chin and fell onto the covers, leaving a small wet patch. As the water slid down his throat his stomach gurgled with gratitude. Kate took the unfinished water and placed it next to the medicine on the bedside table. They watched her as she pulled the shutters across the windows. *So that's what the ladders are for, to take away the moonlight,* Abrihet thought. Kate took the empty plate from the bed and left the room, gently pulling the door to.

Kate was a good person; the children would soon realise that.

'They must have been starving,' she said as she returned to the kitchen. The washing machine beeped loudly; she pulled out the laundry and handed it to Tom. 'Here, you'll need to dry his clothes, and I'll come back in the morning with some bits. Keep them watered and fed; they're both suffering from dehydration and malnutrition. Keep an eye on Abrihet's nails, lots of vitamins and nourishment, and Amanuel too, he has a pot belly. Peanut butter, little and often, and full of protein. I'll grab some vitamins from the wholefood store. I'll love you and leave you. I've a few evening house calls to do.' She took up her keys before Tom led her out to the front door. 'Call me if you need anything, I think they'll sleep through the night.' She kissed Tom on the cheek before turning towards her car.

'Kate.' She turned back. 'Thank you.'

She smiled. 'See you in the morning, gorgeous.'

Tom stood at the door and watched until the rear lights of Kate's car had disappeared into the night. He closed the door behind him and turned the double lock and pulled the security chain over.

The rumble of the tumble dryer whirred in the background, breaking the silence in the house. Tom poured another glass of wine and flicked up his laptop lid. He scrolled down the page and hovered the cursor over the article. He stared at the screen and the headline that glared at him – *Eritrean villagers raped in front of children.* He swallowed before he allowed his eyes to read through the article. Every line filled his stomach with a sinking feeling that made him retch. He held his breath as he read the next line: *A man ran with a young boy on his back and a girl in his arms to the safety of a Red Cross van, then was shot in the back. Killings and rapes were witnessed by those two children.* Tom cast his thoughts to the two who now lay sleeping in his bed. Two children who had probably witnessed the very same haunting images. Images that for him were lines on a page of a computer's screen. Lines that he could shut down and walk away from and never revisit. Never to read again the chilling story of a man saving others' lives being killed in cold blood. For a split second he had questioned in his head whether what he was doing was right, whether Kate was thinking more rationally than him, whether having two illegal immigrants in his house was worth the risk, was just too much pain to bear. But Kate had agreed that she would help. God knew how, but together they would protect these children. He owed it to the murdered man.

'Jesus Christ,' he said out loud, pushing away his wine away from him and pouring himself a Jack Daniels.

The shrill sound of the tumble dryer broke his thoughts. He took out the bundle of lilac-scented laundry and shook out the small blue shorts and red top. The label in them popped out: *M&S*. Someone cared enough, at least, to send their children's unwanted clothes to a charity shop. Someone, somewhere. He folded the laundry and left it on the worktop before turning out the light and going up to the spare room. As he passed his room, he poked his head around the door. The children lay fast asleep, soft snuffling sounds coming from the small boy accompanied by the odd whimper. Tom smiled faintly and closed the door.

They were safe now.

Chapter Three

His Apple watch buzzed on the bedside table with a 6.30 a.m. alarm. Tom turned it off. On any normal day he would have gone for an early morning run. But this wasn't a normal day. Firstly, because he wasn't in his own room where his running kit was and secondly, because he had two strangers in the house who he couldn't leave alone. He threw back the duvet, tilted the slats on the shutters and allowed the morning light to peek through. He left the mountainous heap on the bed and padded across the landing to the main bathroom. The steam from the shower misted the screen, and he stood naked below the pelting hot water. Today was a new day with a different focus.

The Nespresso machine buzzed as the steam funnelled up from the espresso cup beneath the black spout. The aromas of chocolate truffle-infused coffee wafted through the kitchen. He switched the television on as he sliced a banana into a bowl with natural yoghurt and a handful of mixed berries from the fridge.

Piers Morgan and Susanna Reid filled his screen as they sat together on a couch. Next to them Rupert Everly, the Home Secretary, squirmed uncomfortably on the daytime television sofa as Morgan fired unwanted questions at him. Tom took a grape from the fruit bowl and let it roll around his mouth before pushing his teeth down on it and bursting through the skin and chewing on the sweet fleshy centre.

'How's the government tackling this crisis?' Morgan snapped.

'Well, it's not quite as straightforward--'

'It's never been straightforward,' Morgan smirked.

'Listen--' Everly spluttered.

'What are you doing about this crisis? It requires an honest answer,' Morgan interjected.

'The government is in talks about it and it's not straightfor-ward ...' rambled Everly.

'You keep saying this though, don't you? Don't you think it's time the government began to lead with a backbone?

'Well, yes, but--'

'There are no buts. You'll have viewers, and the United Kingdom's population seeing those harrowing pictures. Hundreds of bodies have been hauled from the sea. I'm a father myself. Have you seen this image of the dead boy on the front page of the papers? Is that what you want to see when you wake up with your coffee and perfectly poached egg in the morning?'

'I *have* seen it, and I too am distressed, but—'

'But what? - it's not our problem? Is that what it boils down to?' Morgan pushed.

You either liked Morgan or you hated him, but you couldn't take away his drive to nail a politician down and get answers.

'It's complex. It's not that simple,' Everly responded.

'Easy to eat your poached eggs, is it? How d'you like them, Rupert?' Morgan sneered.

'As I said, it's more complex than that.'

'Really?' Morgan said the cynicism dripping from his mouth.

Tom waited for Everly to try and excuse the failings of the government. 'Bloody idiot,' Tom said aloud. He'd seen enough, and directed the remote control squarely on Everly's face as if the infra-red light would extinguish him as well as the television. Tom's phone pinged in an alert tone.

Hey you! I'll be over at 10ish with some bits after my house calls x

He responded with a thumbs up emoji, then swished his wrist and caught the time on his watch: 7.45 a.m. He tilted the slats on the shutter, allowing the morning light to creep into the room before sitting at his glass drawing desk, where he filtered through his work and brought out a huge sheet of paper with the drawings he had designed for a client. He didn't notice the kitchen door push open a little and Abrihet standing there, a little haphazardly. Then from the corner of his eye he caught the slightness of her figure watching him, and he looked up from his work.

'Hey,' he said. 'Did you sleep well?' He motioned with his hands together under his ear like a pillow.

She nodded. She thought it would be the right thing to do.

'Would you like some breakfast?'

She tilted her head and frowned.

'Hungry?' he asked taking his hands to his mouth.

She nodded. 'Excuse me, please,' she said, 'I lost.' She took her hands up to her neck.

Tom creased his eyes a little.

'I lost,' she continued. 'On boat, I lost.'

Tom shook his head, 'Your necklace.' He took his hands to his neck the same way she had done.

She nodded again.

'It's here.' Tom went over to the kitchen worktop and handed her the broken locket. He took her hand and let the intricate piece of jewellery drop into her palm. 'Your necklace,' he said again, this time more slowly, as if teaching her the word for perhaps the most precious thing she had escaped with, other than her brother.

'Yes, my neck–lace, thank you.' She opened it and gently brushed her finger across the contents before closing it and holding it tightly in the palm of her hand.

'Yep, that's right, necklace, it's pretty. The pictures? Are they your parents?' he motioned to her and the pictures that were perhaps inside. 'Your parents.'

She nodded. She hadn't understood him. There were no pictures inside it.

He smiled gently. 'My mum had a necklace just like that.' Abrihet didn't understand him. But she listened anyway. 'Are they still there, in your village?'

She shook her head.

'I'm sorry.'

Her head dropped down, and she stood without saying another a word. She watched Tom as he went to gather the laundry, then took Amanuel's clothes and pressed them down with his hands again before handing them to Abrihet.

'Here, they're all nice and clean.' Abrihet took them from him and smelt the scent that they exuded and then she turned and left the kitchen and went back upstairs. This time in her hands she clasped the silver locket. Tom went back to his desk and drew his hands through his hair. Even communicating with the girl was hard. *How will I ever manage this?*

But he would.

A red van pulled up outside his house and the cheery sound of the postman as he whistled up the street delivering the morning's post could be heard. Tom went outside to retrieve the letters from the mailbox by the gate.

'Morning, Tom,' the postman said between whistling.

Tom tilted his post in a saluting kind of way, locked his mailbox and went back inside. The charcoal-grey door clicked shut, and from the corner of his eye he sensed two pairs of eyes on him. Abrihet and Amanuel stood at the top of the stairs and peered down at him. Their bare feet curled on the soft floor beneath them – they were a little uneasy about what they should do.

Tom smiled up at them, his face coaxing them down with a gentle hint of reassurance. 'Hey, come down,' he said gently, his smile warming them.

They had slept well, and Tom seemed like the kind doctor, although he hadn't said much. But his face was friendly and they felt safe, and he had made Amanuel better without a net.

Amanuel slipped his hand into his sister's, and together they began to descend the stairs. Amanuel had never walked down such a beautiful staircase before, and he took each step with trepidation, gripping his sister's hand tightly. To this small boy the descent seemed like a sheer drop, as if he was standing on the grass roof of his village hut whilst he helped prepare the worn-out reeds with his father.

Amanuel could see from the top of his roof where the ends of the reeds on each rooftop met in a bundle of twine. Where the women sat in huddled groups, cheerily nattering whilst they stirred the maize in a pot and cooked pieces of goat until it was tender in the tomatoey juices fragranced with berbere spice. The kind doctor tossing a hard red ball and teaching the children how to bowl, and them laughing triumphantly as another batted it away towards the melodious sound coming from another group as they sang their songs whilst weaving the mats that would lie on the dirt floors of their homes. Or they'd hang them as decorative pieces on their windows – windows that were simply a hole in the walls. The walls of a home that were made from earth, straw and sand, compacted and baked in the dead heat of the sun which, though relentless in its heat, made their homes strong. The mats were a little like the ladders these white people had, only brighter in colour and bore no resemblance to a ladder-like object that hung on the smooth grey walls of this white man's house.

Further along a group of men would sit around the elder, listening to his wise words, with a grunt of agreement coming from each of them every now and then. A couple of them carving an acacia wood cricket bat, copied from a sketch the doctor had drawn. Then there were the running feet of the children who'd chase the white van with a red cross on it as it trundled through the village, its tyres kicking up the dust from the ground, and the faces inside smiling and waving at the children as they chased it. The children's hotchpotch of bright clothes like a languid snake following it. And then the dancing and chattering about the kind doctor who'd come to live with them. His face always with a smile and in his hand a heavy leather bag.

But now, beneath this drop was nothing of what he could remember. Instead there was a sleek polished floor in a pale golden wood, joined together like a jigsaw with straight lines. Surrounding the shiny floor were smooth painted grey walls with three doors, one of them a deep charcoal grey with silver bolts and a spyhole. It was the door Tom had come in through when he had greeted them from the bottom of the stairs. Amanuel tentatively placed his feet step by step down onto each tread, tightly holding his sister's hand and clutching the matt silver banister as he went. The fever had now left his small body and his clothes were clean and carried a scent unfamiliar to him, yet as familiar as the ripe mango trees. This made him feel warm and needed, and for a moment he remembered his village and the warm embrace of his mother's arms, an embrace he missed. And the sweetness of her kindness that rushed into the depths of his lungs and made him inhale with a sound. Before he reached the last step, he turned his head and looked back up at the stairs he had come down. They seemed so high, and he had done it! Another moment in his life where he had achieved something important, even though unwittingly at the time.

Although this achievement had been easier than some.

The children followed Tom into the kitchen, where he pulled out two of the stools that were tucked under the counter and patted the mocha-coloured seats. They were almost as tall as Amanuel, and he struggled to climb up onto his. Tom walked around to him and gently eased him up onto the padded seat. He was almost weightless. Amanuel sat perfectly still whilst his legs dangled in mid-air; he'd never sat on such a tall seat. He'd never felt so high or important as he gazed about the room. The black screen of a television hung sleekly on the wall. Huge black and white photos of buildings that were odd-looking, with straight lines and sharp angles, adorned the walls in perfectly straight lines. There was no earth or sand or straw. His head moved to one side as he viewed each one, and his eyes widened with curiosity, his mouth gaping a little. He turned slightly in his seat and spied the desk where Tom had been working before they had woken up. It was a desk that was high like the chair he was sitting on, and a matt grey light shone onto the tilted glass top. He stared intently at the lamp; it looked peculiar to him, like an old man bent over. Tom caught his gaze on his work.

'I'm an architect.'

Amanuel, looked at him, unsure of the word he had used. It was long, like the words the kind doctor used, but it was a word he didn't know. His eyes grew bigger and he stared at Tom.

'I draw,' Tom said, realising that the word *architect* would have meant nothing to the two children who sat at his kitchen island. 'I draw pictures for clients,' he continued, 'houses, mainly.' The two children stared at him, simply watching his mouth move and a sound come out – a slow sound, but it wasn't melodious like the villagers' voices. Tom took up a piece of paper and drew a picture of a house. 'I draw,' he said again. 'Buildings – here, *you* draw.' He pushed the paper and pencil over to Amanuel. 'Draw,' he said once more, nodding his head and smiling, coaxing the small boy to enjoy the feeling of drawing.

Amanuel took up the pencil and gripped it in his hand. He held it in a clenched fist, pressed hard on the paper, and the lead snapped. 'Uh!' he said, frightened by what he had done.

'That's okay, we can fix it.' Tom went to his desk and returned with a pencil sharpener. The children watched mesmerised as he wound the pencil around inside the hole, making shavings in a triangular shape. A perfectly formed teepee shape. He placed it on the table. The intricately formed winding of wood shaving looked like the roof of their own house, not like the houses in the pictures that flanked the smooth grey walls of Tom's house. A rounded triangle of wood, like the reeds of the village rooftops, and for a moment it symbolised what they had left behind. A structure of their past where, from the top of the rounded triangular roof, the happiness and simplicity of their village could be spied. The unity and community spirit of the villagers that sang melodious chants as they worked, the children who played in the dust streets between the basic homes with an acacia wood bat and a red leather ball, the men who listened in huddled groups to the wise words of their elder. And the kind doctor who worked tirelessly with his Eritrean nurse. Those had been the happiest of times, and those should have been the memories etched in their minds.

But violence was the only memory for Amanuel and Abrihet now. A calm until the men from the mines and bad places had come – some not from Eritrea, their eyes different – and they came with an animalistic hunger to ruin, to dirty the women and young girls with crude, violent attacks, to murder in cold blood and to leave until the next time. And the next time would be soon.

Tom picked up the shaving, and its delicate triangular shape broke. It crumbled in front of the eyes of two children whose own home which had likewise crumbled, along with their young lives.

Brutally fractured at the seams.

Chapter Four

Eight years earlier – Adi Ada, Eritrea

The cries of a newborn baby could be heard from outside the medical hut. Cries that sounded like the bleats of a distressed lamb, where the noise seems to come from the deepest part of the throat and doesn't stop until the warmth of a breast is rested close to an infant's mouth and the soothing suckling begins – but this did not happen. A young mother paced the rickety veranda, her hands cupping her breasts tightly as she felt the milk seep through her lightweight top. Her own desire to feed her child and yet the uncontrollable feeling of nature taking over her body and succumbing and responding to the painful cries of her baby from inside the hut. Then she would stop pacing for a moment and stand and watch the moon as it threw a shimmering glow across the plains as she mumbled under her breath.

A velvet blackness was dotted with white stars, and a balmy night heat wrapped around the woman's words, carrying them up, trailing them higher and higher, with a need for them to be caught and heard.

The swaddling cloth she carried on the front of her body was empty. Normally cocooned inside it would be her baby, where his small face would nestle to her warmth and feed, but for days he hadn't fed. Instead a fever had raced through his tiny body. She had run with her infant to the medical hut, hammering frantically on the door until the nurse opened it. And now after days of not knowing why her son was dying in her arms, she had left his tiny body limp and unresponsive on the bed, and paced the wooden veranda of the simply made medical hut, waiting for her youngest child to respond. He lay on a bed fighting for his own small life, his small heart giving up and its rhythm slowing to a faint murmur. The dark arms of death standing and waiting in the corner, silently breathing for the life it would take.

Inside the hut the nurse, Elisabet, held a paraffin lamp as steadily as her hands would allow her to, as the baby lay in a foetal position. The light flickered while the ceiling fan hummed, easing away the humidity of the room. The sting of the needle was not the reason for the distressed cries of that child, but the fever that burned through his small body and which was stealing him of his life. The soles of his tiny feet curled in, and his naked body was covered in difficult-to-see rashes, his small fist clenched around Elisabet's little finger as she bent low above him. 'Shh, shh,' she said softly.

'Bring the light a little closer,' Doctor Sam said, as he traced his finger down the infant's spine. He inserted a thin sterile needle into the spinal cord and eased the fluid into the syringe, then took the captured fluid and spun it manually in a centrifuge. This would confirm his medical hunch. In the obscure light he dripped the fluid onto the slide and placed it under the lens of his simple yet adequate microscope. He had felt sure just from the rashes that were presenting on the surfaces of the infant's skin and the unstoppable hyperpyrexia that his patient's tiny body was compelled into that he was seeing the advanced stages of meningitis. Every minute of this fragile life was in the hands of a young mission doctor. He twizzled the knob on his microscope, bringing the fluid on the slide closer in.

'It's as I thought,' he said quietly. He adjusted the lens again, showing the fluid with the abnormalities he had suspected he would find.

'What is it, Doctor? Is it another case of malaria?'

He sighed, 'I wish it was – but no, he has meningitis.' He left his desk and took a small bottle out of the fridge and allowed the medicine to flow into another sterile needle before he pinched the upper arm of his tiny patient and pushed the needle deep into the muscle, tenderly rubbing where he had pricked, the baby faintly wailing with a heart-breaking warble.

'Are we too late, Doctor Samuel?'

'Time will tell. He's consumed by fever and he's weak, but the medicine will help. Is his mother still outside?'

'Yes, she's on the veranda,' Elisabet replied as she dabbed at the baby's small body with a cold, damp muslin cloth alleviating some of the discomfort of the fever. The cries of this tiny soul subsided momentarily as the doctor grazed his thumb along the babe's upper arm to soothe him where he had been jabbed. Doctor Sam glanced up at Elisabet and smiled briefly.

'Well done. Are you okay to stay with him while I go and speak with his mother?'

Elisabet nodded.

The mesh door closed behind him and a haze of warmth hit his face. Mosquitoes buzzed incessantly around a water pot, and the 'whoop whoop' from the hyenas prowling in the distance, scavenging for a carcass they could steal like unwanted beggars, echoed in the stillness of the night. He stood beside the infant's mother, who had waited anxiously, murmuring words of prayer up to the heavens with chants and begging to a greater being to allow her son to stay with her. Doctor Sam rested his hand on her arm. She turned and grasped his hand as she looked at him, waiting for that moment when he would shake his head and she would wail and crumble to the ground having lost another child, another child to add to the baked ground where she had already buried one. Her eyes swam with tears, and slowly she shook her head. Yet his eyes showed a glimmer of a smile and his mouth seemed to follow.

'Come,' he said, guiding her into the room where the nurse had now moved the baby so that he lay on his back and wore only a nappy. The penicillin was now running through his body and bringing down the fever that had once consumed him.

'He's still very sick,' he said, 'but I'm hopeful. When did he last feed properly?'

'Maybe three days ago,' she replied.

'Try now. He'll be hungry and is in need of hydrating.'

Elisabet let down the sides of the bed and carefully lifted the baby from it. His crying had now stopped. She cradled him in her arms as she beckoned to the young mother to sit in the wicker chair that rocked a little. With arms open the mother took her small baby, the swaddling of her carrier dropped, and there, as she held the most precious life close to her, he turned his head and rooted for the sweetness of her milk. Doctor Sam smiled and nodded his head at the sight, stroking the baby's head.

'This is a good sign,' he said.

She looked up and smiled at him as her hand gently caressed the softness of her baby's thigh and her other finger rubbed tiny circles around the sole of his foot, he curling his toes with her touch.

* * *

As the sun rose daily and baked the land, and the villagers went about their normal lives in their community, the young mother would leave the women weaving tapestry rugs for the market and would make her way to the medical hut where she would feed her baby, who would now cry only for his milk. At night when the calls of the wild cats to their young cubs broke the silence on the plains, she would come again and let her infant feed beneath the swaddling, cocooned against the nakedness of her breasts.

Two weeks had passed when Doctor Sam finally uttered the words she had longed to hear.

'I'll come and visit tomorrow and see how he is – but for now,' he paused, 'for now, I am happy with your son's recovery. He has a formidable strength and fight in that small body of his, and he's well enough to go home.' He sat at his desk and wrote up the notes of the youngest of the children he had seen and treated since his arrival in the village. He turned in his chair and tilted the desk light away from his eyes.

'Have you named him yet?' he asked as he scribbled the indecipherable words in black ink into a black book with gold edging. It was as thick as a bible and beginning to fill with name after name of patients seen mostly for vaccinations and beside each a date, the drugs administered and sometimes the last date of their life. He stifled a yawn as he added the notes. His own fatigue meant that a mother could walk away with a baby nestled against her heartbeat. Her baby hearing it, soothed by it – rhythmic yet dull.

She cradled him in the saffron swaddling that wrapped around her body.

'I have named him Amanuel,' she said. 'It means *God is with us*. And your name, Doctor?'

'Samuel.'

'The wise prophet bears that name. And it means *God has heard*.' She offered a smile of thanks. 'You're a kind man, Doctor Samuel. You've given me back my son.' The door closed behind her and the sound of her voice carried back into the room with the sweetness of her lullaby.

Doctor Samuel slumped back in his chair and ruffled his hands through his mop of brown hair. 'God is with us,' he muttered. He wasn't a religious man but that week the faith of the villagers, the faith and the resilience of a young mother's need for her child to stay with her was immeasurable. Medicine had played its part, but so too had the hope of this woman. And maybe for this medicine man God had heard. That day he learnt how his name had a meaning, a meaning that hit the very core of these people in a village. And from that day onwards he was known as Doctor Samuel, the kind doctor – because he was.

He stretched his arms up in the air and let out an audible groan.

'You did well, Doctor Samuel,' Elisabet said as she swilled the mop inside the metal bucket before swishing it across the floor one last time. 'You have made your presence in this village, you know that. It will be hard to ever leave.'

He shrugged. 'You're too kind, Elisabet. I was just doing my job, to save and preserve a life.'

'You did more than your job, Doctor Samuel – you gave a mother hope. Hope that was haemorrhaging from her.'

'Perhaps. Let me finish here. You go now, you look tired, go home and rest. Tomorrow, I believe, will be another long day.'

'If you're sure, Doctor Samuel.'

'I'm sure. Go and rest.' He touched her arm with a reassuring squeeze before going back to his notes.

Elisabet carried the bucket to the corner of the room and gathered her scarf. She draped the cloth over her head and wrapped it around her shoulders. It wasn't cold outside, but the air was filled with insects and mosquitoes. The door closed behind her and she walked the few yards back to her home.

The blades of the ceiling fan hummed, giving the faintest of coolness to the still air. Sam kicked off his trainers and threw his legs up onto the desk, the balls of his feet throbbing. He let his body slip further into the chair until he could push his head back and look up at the ceiling, his gaze caught on the whirring blades. The light on his desk buzzed whilst a moth attracted by its glow flickered about it, bashing its delicate wings against the warm orb. He cast his mind back to the day when Amanuel had been rushed into the medical hut, clinging to his own tiny life, his body limp and unresponsive, his eyes like huge black holes. Samuel looked around; each bed lay empty and clean, and the linoleum floor shone with the trail of a mop's swishes along it. He sighed loudly before kicking his legs down from his desk and pushing his body up from the chair. The beds now lay bare, but tomorrow and the next day and the next day would see them full again. Some lives he would save and some ... even he had run out of that medical power to help. And death, who lay lurking in the corner, would slide its black languid arms across the room and take them.

To the left of his desk was a cabinet. Samuel opened it and took out a bottle of bourbon. He poured a large glass and swirled the amber liquid; droplets of alcohol slid down the glass. He glanced over Amanuel's notes one more time and filled in an inventory form for the Red Cross for more supplies and antibiotics. Then the lid of his pen clicked shut and he switched out his desk light.

He sighed deeply as he breathed in the air, the wooden slats massaging some life back into his feet. The low-level hum of the generator and the noisy chattering of the grivet monkeys in the fruit trees broke the quiet of the night. He watched the curious creatures, aware that they were deciding whether they should scurry down from the trees and pull out the main plug to the generator.

If they did, that would throw the medical hut into darkness and close down the power to the fridges, instrumental in keeping the medicine and specimen pots chilled. 'Don't even think about it,' Samuel said through pursed lips, his eyes creased at the corners. He knew all too well their mischievous ways; they had done this so many times now, each one of them taking their own turn to dare to cause a little nightly mayhem for him.

A few weeks ago Doctor Samuel had sat tirelessly with a torch and screwdriver trying to ascertain why the generator had gone *kaput*. It was only when it happened far too frequently that he realised it had been because of the naughtiness of these monkeys and that there had been no mechanical failure.

The smallest and most daring threw down a mango from the tree where he sat jibber-jabbering. Samuel scooped the fruit up and laughed faintly at the creature's impishness. The glint of light caught on the blade of his Swiss army knife as he cut through the mango skin with skill and precision as if it was an incision. He turned the fruit as the sharp edge of the knife sliced through the ripe flesh, allowing the syrupy juice to trickle down his hand and along his wrist. He licked clean the stickiness of it before taking a sliver held on the knife to his mouth. It was perhaps the sweetest mango he had ever tasted. For this feeling of syrupy bliss, he would forgive the monkeys for their playful ways – this time. And to the young monkey who had thrown him a mango, he would smile with fondness. The monkey watched his human friend, leaned his head to one side and then scampered up the tree into the canopy of leaves.

A star fell through the sky and Samuel thought back to how Elisabet had sat on the veranda with baby Amanuel's mother, telling her to go home and eat. Consoling her when she had cried, a woman crying for her baby. He had never met a woman like Elisabet before. Every hour that he had been with the villagers she too had been there. And when the beds became empty, he'd watch on as she'd strip them and send the bundles of contaminated linen away to be laundered professionally. Weekly, she'd unpack the cellophane bags filled with starched white clean laundry, making each bed ready for the next patient and stowing away the unused sheets in a metal cupboard – the next patient would come soon. She would so tirelessly mop the floor that the odour of disinfectant hung heavy in the air. He'd never met a woman quite like her. He let the last piece of mango linger in his mouth a little longer.

'Life's good,' he said.

Elisabet had come from Asmara, the only daughter of a modest family. She had gone to school, where she had studied hard. There she had excelled in her small class and had gone on to train as a nurse. In the evenings she would work as a cleaner, and used the money she earnt to pay for English lessons.

Samuel had noticed her when she had visited the village with the Red Cross, bringing more medical supplies; her simple ways had caught his eye, along with the way she would talk with the villagers with a devotion to her job. She oozed an inner kindness and tenderness towards the people that she wanted to help. He'd watch as she'd clasp the hands of a grieving family member who'd lost yet another soul to malaria, tetanus or AIDS. He would crack a smile when she partook in the skipping games of the African children with their rope.

One day he stopped and asked in terrible Tigrinya why she did what she did. She looked at him with eyes that widened and a softness in her voice that left his heart unsure of its own beat, and replied in English, 'To be the best I can be with my people.' That day, Doctor Samuel had learnt that Elisabet would be assigned to his medical centre once her living quarters had been sorted out. She would have to leave the town where she had grown up and live in the village of Adi Ada. Samuel counted the days while a new hut was built by the Red Cross and the men of the village. It was simple but allowed the village's new nursing assistant to sleep well and live within the community, and be on hand for Doctor Samuel. The electricity she had was powered by the generator, and there was a basic water supply for a shower that hung on the outside wall behind a screen of reeds. Elisabet would now work alongside Doctor Samuel as his assistant and nurse.

A star-freckled sky wrapped around his heart, and he thought of Elisabet even more; her spirit had captured him, as had the land where he now worked. A country he did not want to return from, a country and village that would become his home.

Chapter Five

Samuel woke a few times through the night and lay in bed listening to the sounds that were more unusual than the low hum of planes that used to fly over his London maisonette.

Somewhere a disturbed cockerel started calling for the light, but it was still too early. The wistful mournful call from a hooting owl, and the haunting reply from its mate in the treetops, allowed Samuel to gently drift back to sleep again before his day would begin and his medical centre become full once more.

A rosy hue touched the tops of the mango and banana trees, and suddenly the glowing orb of the orange sun lifted into the sky. Samuel's sleep was again interrupted by the cacophony of squawking and wings beating in the fruit trees, the shrill chattering of the black-winged lovebirds as they petted their feathered mates. He straightened his arms upwards allowing his back to stretch further, and then he left his simple bed and went to the shower that ran with a sprinkling of water behind a screen made of reeds. The slow trickle fell against his body as he washed away the clamminess of the night's heat. Once dressed and ready for his day, he left his living quarters in order and made his way to his place of work, the monkeys watching his every move, babbling as they leapt through the treetop branches, following him.

A few of the women passed him by on their way to the well; this ran deep into the ground and the water was pumped up from it into a tank, then filtered. There they would stand

and pull at a lever to allow water to fill their pails for their families. Once their pails were full, they would walk along the dusty track back to the village. They smiled and wished him a good morning.

Opposite the medical centre sat another group of women their fingers working nimbly on the rugs and baskets they were making, their African melodies funnelling through the rising dead heat. Samuel walked up the two steps to the veranda of the medical centre. The mischievous monkey who'd thrown him the mango sat on the ledge of the railing, his beady eyes on Samuel, and cocked his head curiously at the doctor before skimming a ripe mango across the floor.

'Is that for me?' Samuel chuckled as he took up the fruit. The monkey chattered away before racing along the ledge and hurling himself up onto the generator and back into the trees.

Samuel pulled open the mesh door and then unlocked the main door and went in. He pulled the cord of the ceiling fan, expecting the familiar sound of the blades as they picked up speed before the mellifluous whirring from them sliced through the humidity in the room. He stood by his desk and pushed his fingers through the paperwork that lay neatly in a pile. A mosquito buzzed about him until it met an untimely end.

'Morning, Doctor Samuel.'

Samuel turned to see the smiling face of Elisabet as she swept across the floor.

'Ah, the sun's hot and it's going to get hotter,' she near-swooned as the back of her hand slid across her forehead, removing small beads of sweat that had begun to form. 'So, what have we today, Doctor?' she asked as she opened the cupboard and took from it two sets of white starched bed sheets. She carried them to the metal beds that were covered only in plastic and draped by a mosquito net.

'Another day of doing our best, Elisabet.' He watched as she held two corners of a sheet and threw it into the air, allowing the starched creases to drop from it before she laid its billowing form on the bed. A slight swoosh of air came from it, and felt pleasant as it caressed his skin. She smoothed her hands across the sheet, tucking it in with tight hospital-bed corners. She then covered the pillows in their cotton cases and left the nets to drape over the beds before going outside to pull out the makeshift benches and rickety fold-up chairs that had been tucked away the night before.

A steady flow of villagers began to congregate towards the steps of the veranda near to where the generator hummed, the elderly sitting back on the chairs, their legs outstretched, as if to pacify the pain or their own weariness. One woman, dressed in clothes as bright as the morning sun and as vibrant as the fruits that adorned the trees, rested her forearm on her cane; a cane that had been made by the men in the village from driftwood found in the shallows of the dried riverbed. Her eyes were sharp and black, her smile broad and toothless, her turban-style headscarf the rich colour of saffron. The soles of her feet were hardened by years of walking the dirt tracks, and her heart was as full of warmth as the baked ground beneath her. Her hope was as strong as the passion of the kind doctor who she knew would come to greet her.

Some of the villagers were aided by a family member, others were seeking a vaccination, and others were hoping to be healed, to be cared for; pregnant mothers, looking so young themselves, holding their swollen bellies. One mother was holding an infant who'd fought for his right to stay alive, and beside her was a daughter who waited patiently for her turn to be seen. An elder from the neighbouring village had walked many kilometres with a bicycle, a bicycle he had never ridden, but his hope in seeing Doctor Samuel was he would be able to ride his bicycle back home after his treatment. Patients arrived hopeful. The white people from a country where Manchester United were from and cricket was played gave them that hope. Doctor Samuel gave them that hope.

'Are you ready, Elisabet?' Samuel had already spied the queue of villagers. He took up his stethoscope from the desk and looped it around his neck. The hinges on the door squeaked slightly and the dry hot heat burnt down on his face. A bead of sweat formed immediately and trickled down the side of his face; he brushed it away. Squinting, he scanned the line of villagers in front of the medical hut's veranda. A myriad of coloured garments worn by his patients that day. A human rainbow of chatter and noise, not the dull quiet of an English waiting room, where nobody dared connect with eye contact, faces glum and unwelcoming. But this waiting room was full of life and colour. A few people took shelter beneath the mango trees. The older men were slumped in their seats, their sticks resting against their stomachs, their legs outstretched, some wearing a trilby-style hat protecting them from the sun. Doctor Samuel shifted his stethoscope a little and undid a button on his cotton shirt as the sweat from his neck gently slid down the front of his chest. He flapped the cotton against his wet skin. The air undulated along the track.

'Please,' he said, as he beckoned to the first of his patients, a young man, no older than eighteen. He held a stick carved by hand from the trees that stood with their green leaves overhanging like a living parasol, its handle intricately etched in the shape of a hammerkop head with its large, curved bill. There was the finest detail of a crest at the back, reminiscent of a hammer. The cane had been carved by someone who cared, who knew the value of it and the hand that held it.

The young man's stare looked straight ahead, his eyes a greyish colour glistened with a layer of deep wetness. He felt beside him, and there was no other person next to him. He was the first in the queue.

The old man opposite him, whose stick rested against his stomach, lifted it and jabbed it at the young man's stick. 'Boy, the doctor's calling you,' he said.

The dust from the track flew about a little as the young man pulled his stick in and stood aided by another villager, his gaze remaining ahead of him. He turned a little, and that was when Doctor Samuel realised – when he saw his eyes. Eyes that moved from side to side independently of each other. This patient was not lame, but blind. Doctor Samuel went straight down to him and took his arm.

'Please, come.' Gently, he led the man to the steps of the veranda. 'Two steps up,' Doctor Samuel said in Tigrinya as he guided his patient. The young man swished his stick in front of him, feeling for the height, and then moved his feet up the steps. Samuel remained at his side, his hand still holding the young man's arm while he opened the door. The blind man swayed his stick ahead, the whir of the fan swished overhead, every now and again letting out a rattle as if itself exhausted by the heat it was slicing through. The swish of its coolness hit their faces as they walked towards a bed in the corner. Elisabet pushed back the mosquito netting and helped the man to sit on the edge of the bed, before lifting his legs and swivelling him onto the mattress. She moved the pillow so that he could rest his back against it. She left him briefly. He gazed ahead, hearing the clickety-clack of the trolley's wheels as she manoeuvred it across the floor then stopped. He turned his head to the side where he could hear movements and her sighs every few seconds from the heat.

'The doctor will be with you soon.' She squeezed his forearm and left the trolley with its supply of packaged medical instruments. As the sun rose higher in the cloudless sky, and dust on the ground baked in the heat, the medical centre filled with villager after villager, until each bed was occupied, and a bicycle stood propped against a mango tree. Small children wailed as their arms were jabbed with an injection that would help protect them from disease. In another bed a man wheezed, his lungs full of unwanted liquid. He coughed up mucus as he held his chest. His breathing became more laboured and his discomfort was evident to the non-medical eye. Doctor Samuel, injecting children, looked over to the bed where the spluttering had come from.

'Wait a moment,' he said, his eyes creasing at the side with a gentle smile whilst he threw away the sharps and edged past the next parent and child in the queue. 'I'll be back. Stay right there, keep guard for me,' and he winked and poked the child's tummy.

'Hello, I'm Doctor Samuel,' he said to the old man as he took the stethoscope from around his neck. 'What's your name?'

A wizened faced peered up from under a felt trilby. 'Abel,' he spluttered through broken breaths.

Samuel eased his patient forward and lifted his top, then placed the diaphragm onto the gentleman's back and listened, moving it slightly each time. 'How long have you felt this way, Abel?'

'A few days, it's my chest.'

Doctor Samuel nodded.

'What is it, Doctor?'

'Pneumonia, I'd say,' he replied, removing the stethoscope from his ears and looping it around his neck again. 'I'm going to take a blood sample from you, but I'm pretty sure it's a fungal pneumonia. What have you eaten recently?'

'Rice, maize, goat stew, mango.'

'And the mango tree attracts the birds?'

Abel nodded. The side of his beady eyes creased as he leant back into the bed before coughing up another lot of phlegm into a paper cloth that Samuel had handed him.

'Bird droppings on the fruit, or from the dirt in the tracks, is the main contributor. The antibiotics should begin to help clear the infection, ease your breathing.'

Abel's eye lines told of laughter, warm smiles and affection and still an appetite for humour. 'A mango has done this to me?'

'Not a mango.' The doctor teased a smile. 'Just the bird droppings.' He squeezed Abel's shoulder. 'Now, clench your fist while I take your blood. And then, Abel, I want you to stay here for the night, just so that I can keep an eye on you. Sharp prick.' As Samuel drew away the needle and a test tube full of a deep red liquid, he pressed a gauze on the minuscule pinprick. Abel rested his hand on his; a man whose forehead was deeply engrained in lines that told of the decades he had lived in a village, which had seen good and bad times.

'You're a good man, Doctor.'

Samuel squeezed Abel's shoulder once more and then left him, still wearing his hat. He placed the blood sample in the fridge. The monkey which had gabbled earlier sat on the ledge of the open window and cocked his head mischievously, Samuel smiled at him.

'Leave the fridge alone! No tricks from you, my little friend.' The monkey leaned its head to one side and then watched as Doctor Samuel attended to the small boy who'd waited patiently for his jab.

A steady trail of patients came and went. Samuel tied a makeshift bandana around his head as the sun rose higher into the still cloudless sky, beating down on the arid ground and the village. The ceiling fan spun through the dead heat, and even though the medical centre mirrored the temperature of a sauna there was a calmness and restfulness that came with this space. Sweat from Samuel's brow seeped into the cotton bandana and his shirt clung to his back. He pushed up his already rolled sleeves. Elisabet wiped her brow and tied the knot in her long headscarf more tightly behind her head so that its ends hung like a vibrant twisted horse's tail down the nape of her neck and upper back. She then carried on working by Samuel's side, and when she wasn't by his side assisting him, she would bathe the head of a child who lay in a bed covered by a net, ravaged by a fever. Soothe another who'd cry from the jab in their arm. Rub the back of a pregnant mother whose domed-shaped belly squirmed with the pushing feet of an unborn baby, easing the discomfort of backache from a birth that neared.

Together they worked tirelessly until they bade farewell to their final walk-in patient and the sun began to drop. The spindly arms of a tree that bore no leaves stood like the silhouette of a stag's antlers, while the sky turned a liquid gold and crimson and shimmered a hue of red across it. The shadows of the undulating ground lengthened as the sun dropped lower and lower. A gazelle moved away from its herd and grazed on the flora that flourished in the baked terrain, its ears pulled back, listening for the unwanted sound of a predator.

Three beds remained occupied. A small child tossed and turned from a fever that had subsided a little. It was another case of malaria, but nets kept the ever-buzzing insects at bay and the paracetamol-based drugs allowed the child's high temperature to fall a little.

Abel rested in his bed in the far corner of the medical centre, his eyes closing every so often as his seventy-year-old body drifted into short naps in the humidity. And on the other side of the medical centre lay the young man who had been the first patient of the day, his eyes staring ahead, then moving independently of one another from side to side. His day had been filled with the noise of those around him, the cries from children, the clickety-clack of trolley wheels holding medical supplies, the whirring rattling of the ceiling fan. The coughing and heavy wheezing from Abel. The kind words of the doctor as he jabbed another arm and talked to his patients about cricket and Manchester United. Just a room of unrecognisable sounds and voices. The blind man's hands turned in themselves as he lay there, still. His stare seemed to be fixed ahead, but if you could see his eyes then you would realise that the stare was not fixed. All he could detect were shadows of light and dark. He'd never seen his own ageing, but his hands told him he was no longer a small boy who'd be led by his mother, or father, or friends, their hands always clasping his. Instead, now he felt his way with a cane that had been carved for him. A cane that he knew to be his because of the intricate detail of the hammerkop that would nestle in the centre of his palm.

Part of him wondered if the dreams he had were as real as what he had been described; whether the colours he oh so vaguely remembered were the colours that really existed, or whether one day his dreams would be as monochrome as the shadows in his waking hours. He heard the footsteps of a body nearing him. He could smell the manly sweat by his bedside. He turned his head. Doctor Samuel smiled. The young man didn't see that smile.

'I'm Doctor Samuel, and you?'

'Abraham.'

'Abraham, Elisabet's my nursing assistant; she's standing here too.'

J. V. Phaure

Abraham nodded and moved his hand out to the side of the bed to touch the two figures that stood beside him. Samuel bent down and allowed Abraham's hand to touch his and then Elisabet's. Elisabet took his hand, the bangles on her arm jangling as they bumped against each other. He could feel the softness of her skin and he grazed his thumb across it. Elisabet held his hand while Doctor Samuel shone a bright light into Abraham's eyes. Abraham's eyes flickered more as he detected the lightness and could sense the breathing of the doctor closer to his face.

'Cataracts,' Samuel said as he drew away from Abraham. 'Have you ever been able to see, Abraham?'

'Only when I was very young, and I can't remember. So only what people tell me – and then, doctor, and then I imagine.'

'It is not a difficult operation, and I can try to restore some of your vision. It may be a little blurry, but there is a chance it'll work.'

'I'll take that chance, Doctor.'

Samuel nodded, and his mouth lifted into a smile. He squeezed Abraham's arm. 'Of course; wait one moment.' He left the bedside and went to his desk where he swished through the pages of his calendar. Each page was full of clinics. He flicked the pages quickly, and then trailed his finger down the page, stopping at a blank space. He scribbled *Cataracts – Abraham*. He then returned to the bedside.

'A week on Sunday, Abraham. We can do it then.'

Elisabet interjected, 'Doctor Samuel, it'll have to be the Monday. Nobody works on Sunday, it's the Sabbath.'

'Right, of course, the Sabbath.' Doctor Samuel had met his first religious obstacle. 'So, the Monday, Abraham. Monday it is, then.'

54

A semblance of a smile slid across Abraham's face. 'I'll be here. What is today?'

'Monday, so we have a week,' Doctor Sam replied. 'Until then, you're free to go.' Elisabet took Abraham's arm, coaxing him to slide his body to the edge of the bed, and waited. She placed the handle of his cane in the palm of his hand. He shuffled his body forward and stood up. He could feel the presence of the figures in front of him. Samuel took his arm and led him toward the door.

'Godspeed,' came a voice from the bed in the corner. It was Abel, tipping his trilby-style hat. 'Godspeed, boy,' he said again. He knew Abraham was not going on a long journey but that his journey in life was changing. In a room where age and wisdom both sat, the voice of an old man to a boy could never have been truer.

With care, Samuel helped Abraham navigate the steps down from the veranda and walked him across to where he had been sitting that morning. The glow in the sky shimmered across the horizon.

'Which way is the well?' Abraham asked.

'To your right.'

'Thank you.' Abraham turned his body to his left and brushed his cane in an almost semi-circular movement along the ground. He never remembered seeing the well, nor the track that he would take back to his house, but he had been taught from childhood his left and his right, and the well was his unseen landmark. A landmark to head away from. Samuel watched on as his young patient walked away with only the sound of his stick tapping along the hardened, dusty track. Abraham could hear the monkeys in the trees and knew that they would continue along his path as if guiding him until he reached the huts of the community and the familiar voices of the people he knew.

As the tapping of Abraham's cane became less, Samuel turned. He stood quietly for a moment, his hands in his pockets. His skin cooled a little by the breeze, he took in the beauty of the sky, a setting sun that became a heaven of fire, a battle-cry to the black starlit ether. He stood for a moment in time and allowed the quintessentially African landscape to seep into the pores of his skin, to stay in his mind forever. An image he could stand and look at for a long time and lose himself in. He breathed it in, his mouth moving to form a smile of inner calm and a horizon that encapsulated him like a welcoming skyward hearth. A sight Abraham might soon see himself.

The sound of the door swinging shut interrupted his moment of silence and simple awe. Elisabet came down the steps to put away the chairs; she was another sight that made him stop awhile too. He took his hands from his pockets and pulled his shirt away from his chest, fanning himself. He watched her while she tucked one chair away before he went over to help her.

Together they folded the chairs and leant them against the side of the generator, and Samuel carried the bench to the same place. He turned once more to watch the silhouettes of feeding gazelle, whose legs appeared to undulate as the sun fell and a sheet of midnight blue began to cover the sky.

As the starlit blanket covered the village in Eritrea, Elisabet placed the mop and bucket in the corner. She tucked in the bedding around the small child who lay at the far side of the room, and took her shawl from the chair. 'I'll leave now, Doctor Samuel.'

Samuel turned from his notes and looked up at her. 'Thank you, Elisabet. I'll see you in the morning.'

She inched the door open and Samuel's gaze remained on her until the door swished shut behind her. The young monkey jibber-jabbered along the veranda and Sam smiled when he heard her bidding the furry creature a good evening, the sweetness of her African song reaching his ears like a gentle melodic lament as she idled her way home. He listened until the honeyed tones disappeared between the slight sway from the mango and banana trees, and the night seeped in over the village like a warm cloak, enveloping it in its darkness. And there in the medical centre, Samuel rocked in his wicker chair, the fan still rattling, the paraffin lamp glowing while Abel slept, and the small child whimpering while her small body fought against whatever it was that seemed to be attacking her. It wasn't malaria, though.

The small girl, no older than maybe six, had stood in line patiently. Her mother's hand gently caressed the beads in her braids and her other hand smoothed a baby swaddled against her. Her daughter's body swayed from side to side each time her mother's arms brought her in closer and cupped the side of her face with the palm of her hand. A motherly embrace holding her steady, the heat of the sun unabating on the roof of the medical hut. The fan rattled uncontrollably, shifting warm air throughout the room. A line of patients fanned themselves with handkerchiefs and pieces of card. The child's forehead was beaded in sweat. The unrelenting heat became too much, and her body could no longer tolerate it. That was when her own mother's figure could not steady her. That was when her legs crumpled beneath her, her eyes rolled up to the back of her head and her small frame lay on the ground.

Her eyes flickered open and closed, open and closed. Her small body trembled frenziedly. The blurred face of a man close to her.

Samuel shifted his arms beneath her and scooped her up, her body limp and the trembling diminishing. An arm fell by her side and dangled in mid-air. He gesticulated with his head in the direction of the bed in the far corner by the open window. Elisabet moved urgently but calmly, pulling back the cotton sheet and giving space for Doctor Sam to gently lay the girl down, her eyes still flickering, his face still blurry in front of her. Her petite frame was now a still kind of motionless. Beads of sweat trickled uncontrollably down her face, her neck glistening and clammy. That was when he had realised it wasn't malaria.

The day's business of the medical centre had subsided. The need to be with one small patient was apparent. The blistering heat of the day had now moved on and the mating calls of owls and howls from the wilderness, became the distant soundtrack. Samuel allowed his eyes to rest briefly. The silvery moon lit the village below as the young doctor tended his patients through the night, observing their every change. The small monkey sat on the ledge of the open window and peered in. He twitched his head and called to Samuel.

'Hey, little fella,' Samuel said with a smile. The monkey's eyes twinkled in the dim light. 'You're back then,' he said. 'Wotcha up to?' And with that, the curious little monkey sloped his head and disappeared into the branches of the mango tree. Sam laughed gently and as the chair rocked intermittently its slow movement eased Sam into a slumber.

Chapter Six

Elisabet knelt by the side of the rocking chair and shook Sam gently. He murmured in between sleeping breaths.

'Doctor, Doctor,' said Elisabet.

Samuel peeled open one eye and then the other. He blinked a few times before focusing on the figure that was close to him. He drew in a breath. 'I must have dozed off,' he said, looking around the room and seeing his three patients still sleeping. The trolley that contained all the instruments for triage and nightly observations was next to him. The clipboards for the patients hung at the end of their beds. He drew up his wrist to look at the time. It was 6 a.m. He pushed himself up from the chair and took up his bandana from the armrest.

'Elisabet, why are you here so early?'

'Because you've been here all night and you need to change, and the sun's already in the sky. It makes no difference to me, I was awake.'

'It's still early.'

'And you need to go refresh yourself, Doctor.'

'Freshen up,' he said with a smile. 'Okay, you're right. Who am I to question my nursing assistant? But first, before I do, I need to hand over.'

'Exactly!' Elisabet pulled a comical face.

'Last obs were done at 5 a.m. and another set will need to be done at 7 a.m. I need to run tests on the young girl. It's more than malaria, I'm pretty sure of that. The mother …' He paused for a moment. 'D'you know her?'

'Yes, it's Johanna. You remember?' she replied. When she said the name, she pronounced the J as a Y and with a softness to it, and it had a ring to it, not a hard sound. 'She's the mother of Amanuel.' Her eyes searched Samuel's face for some kind of indication. She could tell just from his body language that he was worried about his young patient.

'Amanuel? The young baby I treated for meningitis?' Samuel sighed and creased his eyes. His forehead crinkled in a perplexed frown. 'Damn it,' he said under his breath. He pressed his thumb and middle finger across his forehead massaging his temples. He sighed again, this time more heavily. *'Damn* it,' he said, more vehemently.

'How bad is it, Doctor?'

'I can't be sure.' He breathed heavily through his nose so that it was audible. 'I need to run tests. 'But I don't think it's good news.' He pursed his lips. 'Yep,' he exhaled, 'I need to run tests,' he repeated, giving himself time to think and weigh up the prognosis. 'But in the meantime we need to get a screen around her. And wash everything down. I want to err on the side of caution here. And wear a mask, Elisabet, always.' Pulling the mask back over his face he went to the side of the room, where against the wall was a blue concertina curtained screen. He wheeled it over to the bed in the far corner. He opened up its leaves and wrapped it around the perimeter of the bed. The window remained open by the child's bedside, allowing a slight breeze to waft into the hut, along with the dulcet tones of the women singing as they wove together. The blue curtains swayed a little as they caught in the air being circulated by the ceiling fan. Samuel then filled an iron bowl full of water. He soaked a white flannel with red stitching and wrung it out, and then dabbed her forehead with it. Then moving it gently across her cheeks and slowly down to her small neck that glowed with beads of sweat. She murmured between each movement of the flannel.

'Here,' he said to Elisabet handing her the wet flannel. 'Keep her comfortable until I get back.'

Beads of sweat formed immediately and trickled down the girl's forehead. If her hair had been similar to that of a Caucasian child's it would have been drenched and clinging to her head and forehead. But instead the small colourful beads in her hair caught the droplets of sweat and they shone a little brighter. The sweat from the fever fell into her tightly braided strands and glistened like particles of sand that caught the light. The vibrant colours from her beads seemed to snatch away the seriousness of what was consuming this small girl's body and dispel it, as if to appease the frantic worry that would swallow her mother whole. Disguising the sickness momentarily, but only disguising it until that disguise surrendered.

And instead a man would stand at the bedside with a book in his hand – a holy book – and the water that he'd sprinkle would bless the small body that lay shielded behind a blue curtain that billowed gently under the overworked ceiling fan. And there in the baked ground a mother would lay to rest her firstborn, her daughter, who'd now lie with her younger brother. Together again, keeping him company, no longer alone beneath the arid sun-hardened ground. Would that be the only happiness that might console the breaking heart of a mother? A heart that had already been broken and would needlessly be broken again.

Doctor Samuel pulled the curtain along its rail and cast a warm smile to Elisabet who sat by the bedside with only her eyes now showing. A smile that telegraphed his thoughts – *I won't be long.* He collected his leather satchel from his desk and left the medical centre. The door swung shut behind him. On the veranda's ledge, the small monkey who'd grown accustomed to seeing the doctor gave a look of curiosity and darted away, lobbing himself with ease and agility onto the top of the generator and into the branches of the mango trees.

The sky held a warm glow shimmering like a rose-pink chiffon scarf across it, and a small creature followed in the branches above the dusty track. The doctor's home was only a short distance from the medical centre, no more than a couple of hundred yards. Outside it, parked to one side, was a beaten-up cream Land Rover jeep with an open top. Doctor Samuel pushed open the wooden door to his hut and shut it behind him. He brushed to one side the beaded curtain that hung as an inner door, its strands rattling faintly as they fell against each other. The floor had been laid with a hessian-style matting throughout. The wooden bed was hidden behind a floor-to-ceiling screen made of reed, and was still as he had left it the day before, with the sheet drawn up to the pillow and a mosquito net hanging around it. His black journal sat on an upturned small barrel that was decorated with the tiniest of mosaic tiles and stones by his bedside, and a battery-powered lamp stood on its surface. Next to the lamp was a photo frame with a picture of a sailing boat and a medley of smiling faces and a golden dog, a retriever. Next to the photo was a bundle of opened blue handwritten airmail letters.

He sat on the edge of the bed whilst he inched off his trainers with his feet. He rubbed his bare soles on the roughness of the floor; it seemed to give an oddly comforting feeling, similar to that of an all-over pumice stone pedicure. Still clawing his feet on the hessian floor, he stood up and undid the khaki chinos he had dressed in the day before and let them fall to the ground. His cotton shirt that had clung to the sweat on his back smelt of the day and night. He threw both his trousers and shirt onto the wooden chair by the screen, and they landed in a crumpled heap over it. He took his bandana from the bed and, dressed only in his boxer shorts, walked to his shower. While the water had got warm enough to allow the suds to foam from his shampoo yet still cool enough to refresh his body, he stood naked under the trickle from the shower head. It was no bigger than a watering can rose and resembled just that, too. The water ran over his torso, trickling over the taut muscles of his shoulder blades. He washed the bandana in the soapy suds, rinsing away the sweat from it. He wrung it out and let it hang from a small part of the reed that worked as a hook for something as light as a bandana. It would dry in no time in the sweltering African heat.

He pushed his fingers through his hair, allowing the coolness of the water to run down his face. He closed his eyes and let the water wash over his five o'clock shadow, a shadow that would remain on his face. The coolness of the water allowed for some kind of revitalisation. Closing the water tap lever, he wrapped a lightweight linen towel around his waist and padded back to his bedroom, where he took clean clothes from a wooden cupboard and dressed.

The living quarters of his hut were as simple as the sleeping area. A table, where he could eat, sat nestled in the corner with two chairs. A small wooden sofa that had a simple foam padding covered in a tapestry woven by the women in the village, rested alongside the reed screen. A small fridge, powered by the generator and big enough to store some essential dairy products and, if luxury allowed, a bar of milk chocolate that would stay protected from the heat of the day, and a couple of bottles of chilled Asmara beer. Next to the fridge a small hob with a gas unit below it sat on what appeared to be an old wooden bookshelf, and on the shelf below, instead of books there were a couple of pans, some crockery and a tin full of utensils and cutlery, some dried food in a glass jar and an array of herbs and spices. Stacked next to the shelf was a pile of medical books and journal-style magazines from the British Medical Association. It was a far cry from his modern state-of-the-art London kitchen.

He opened the fridge. It buzzed noisily, and the internal light illuminated. The bottles of lager clinked as they rolled against the side of it. He took out two eggs and cracked them open straight into a bowl and whisked them vigorously before spilling them into a small frying pan. Once he had scrambled them he decanted them onto a plate with a sprinkling of ground black pepper. He made a strong black coffee with his one-cup Italian percolator and the coffee beans he'd purchased from Jeremiah. He scooped the beans into his hand and admired them as others might admire a superyacht. Their hue captured him as he tumbled them into the grinder. It was the only item from his London kitchen that he had brought with him; in fact, his instructions, when accepting the position that had been given to him via the main missionary hospital, had said he should travel lightly and bring few personal effects. Home comforts would be virtually non-existent in the village he would be living in. And although he would be part of the community his living quarters as a British citizen working overseas would offer him a little more than basic, although basic really was how he was living.

Now he sat in the silence of his simple accommodation. The sofa was as comfortable as you might imagine, and he tossed his feet up onto the cane coffee table in front of it. The aroma of his black coffee drifted in the warm air and he took a mouthful, allowing the rich toasted flavours to burst in his mouth. He was in good company when it came to coffee, with the undeniable freshness of the beans and rich flavours that the Eritreans prided themselves on.

An upturned book still rested on the table – *Out of Africa*, a parting gift from Kate – and next to it sat another framed photo. He smiled fondly at the faces that seemed to smile straight back at him while he shifted the scrambled egg about his plate with a fork. Once he had finished he left the plate in the washing bowl and retrieved his trainers.

He took up his satchel from the coffee table and threw the strap over his arm. He bent down and picked up the framed photograph of the smiling faces. They posed in an almost semi-circular formation, their arms linked around each other's shoulders and waists. A girl with blonde hair stood in the middle of the group. With a pretty face that held a beam that stretched from ear to ear, she was flanked either side by a guy in a puffa jacket and Sam. He smiled fondly at the memory of the day when the picture had been taken.

They had spent the weekend in Deal with a raucous evening at the Zetland Arms, a rustic-style beachfront pub. The following morning their walk along the beach had been littered with runners, walkers, lovers grasping at their final hours of a weekend away. The picture was of them all together on the seashore with the sun casting a glowing shimmer of crystals on the sea, and the Pier Diner on stilts hovering above the water, which would be their final destination. A diner where they'd had breakfast, Sam's last breakfast with the gang before he had flown away to Nairobi, where he'd met Tim, who worked full time for an independent humanitarian organisation, then had travelled on to Asmara, in Eritrea.

There he'd been given the keys to his car, a clapped-out old open-top cream Land Rover Defender, along with a map of the towns and villages, with a circle scrawled in red around Adi Ada.

'Miss you guys,' he said under his breath, and placed the photo back down onto the table. He left his hut to return back to the medical centre, leaving behind the smiling faces of his younger brother and best friend.

Chapter Seven

London, seven months earlier

The light sliced in through the upper-floor sash windows of a Victorian terraced house. It was the end of a string of five pretty double-fronted façades, all with the obligatory sash windows and white satin-painted shutters. The in-look of London's interior design. The brickwork of number 5 Kildare Mews had been painted in cream, and a pale pink rose trailed up along the wall and over the four-panelled dove-grey front door. A frosted glass window above the door had the number 5 etched into it in oversized white lettering. Outside the front of the house were two black planters, each with a miniature box tree clipped to perfection, a herbaceous lollipop to the eyes of any passer-by. A wrought-iron railing ran along the row of houses with a black gate that opened into each of the immaculately kept front gardens. A run of stone steps led up to the front door of number 5 with a stone balustrade tying them in. To the side of those steps a another run of steps led down to basement front door, and on it the number 5A in silver gleamed under the large polished silver knocker.

Kildare Mews was tucked away from the prying eyes and passers-by of Kensington Olympia. The area had always been a more affordable part of West London to buy in, due to it being at the end of a branch of the District Line. The line, although frequently used, wasn't quite as readily available as the District Line to Ealing Broadway or Wimbledon.

As London prices rose, areas such as these became the whispers of the rich behind their hands as they gossiped over iced flat lattes with soya milk: *Hold the chocolate sprinkles; they can't quite afford Kensington, Notting Hill or Brook Green.* Kensington Olympia began to rocket. Ever since the Westfield Centre was built in Shepherd's Bush, it became perhaps one of the most desirable spots in London to buy in. And it was now firmly on the map and a young buyer's paradise.

In the early noughties a modest four hundred and fifty thousand pounds had sealed the purchase on a two-bedroom maisonette in the quiet mews. It was the wannabe place to buy, sandwiched between the uber-busy and trendy High Street Kensington and the now up-and-coming Shepherd's Bush, with the salubrious Brook Green a stone's throw away, and the even higher price tags of Holland Park, where the celebs hung out. The maisonette offered a quieter side of an otherwise busy West London postcode. A few hundred yards away was Sam's favourite drinking hole, the Havelock Tavern, a gastropub which offered the most amazing lamb shank Sam had ever eaten, and a spicy Bloody Mary that even as a doctor he found was his go-to medicinal tonic after a night out on the tiles.

The only noise that could be heard inside the mews house was the intermittent rumbling of the overland fast train to Watford.

Daily, he took the District Line service where he'd change at Earls Court for the Circle Line until he'd reach Farringdon with a brisk six-minute walk to St Bartholomew's Hospital, where he worked as a consultant respirologist with three other consultants.

This morning, he turned the crisp white envelope in his hand. It was postmarked Turkana, Kenya. Slowly he eased his finger along the edge of the envelope, prising it open. He took out the letter and unfolded it. In blue letters running along the top of the sheet were the words TURKANA MISSION HOSPITAL, TURKANA, KENYA. He took a slurp of his freshly made coffee and savoured the flavour briefly before allowing his eyes to scan over the printed lines.

Dear Dr Samuel Edwards,

We would like to thank you for applying for the position of Lead Medical Practitioner at the Turkana Mission Hospital. Unfortunately, the Mission Hospital is led with a strong Christian ethos and as much as your medical credentials are exactly what we would desire, it is with regret and with much deliberation that due to the intricacies of religion, this would be an inappropriate appointment at this time.

He went to push the letter away, slightly deflated that being non-religious, an atheist in fact, should even matter. Never before had he been turned down on a religious preference. He was a doctor – wasn't that what was important? A man who'd trained to save and prolong lives. Worked long hours, had been at every patient's bedside with a natural and compassionate bedside manner. He could feel his hackles rise. He paused and went back to read the obligatory *'however, thank you for taking the time'* kind of crap that is added to all rejection letters to appease the blow. He shook the page a little, removing the crease. It continued:

However, we value your passion and desire to work within our communities …

He stopped. 'Not enough to offer me the job,' he muttered.

… and we would like to offer you a position that has become available in one of the communities outside the village of Adi Ada, Eritrea. Our mission hospital works closely with the Red Cross and within the small village medical centre, we are looking to appoint a medical practitioner of your calibre and experience. This we feel would be better suited to a physician of your beliefs and indeed

your impeccable experience. The management and running of the medical centre will be led by you, and you will be assisted by a nurse who has worked with the Red Cross and is a native Eritrean. The references that we have received from Professor Henderson of the Tropical Diseases and Respiratory Faculties and Mr Fairchild, the leading chest surgeon at St Bartholomew's Hospital, London, were outstanding. It would be a failure on our part to neglect to extend this position to you.

We trust you understand our reasons and hope that this will be acceptable to you. The role of the physician to run this village medical centre will start with immediate effect and its term will run indefinitely.

With very best wishes,

Professor Zaneebar

Turkana Mission Hospital, Respiratory Medicine Department

Samuel thumbed the letter, reading each line over and over again, and exhaled heavily. *I'm good enough for your village – my beliefs don't matter there,* he thought, and snorted with cynicism while taking another slurp of his coffee. It was cold. He gazed out of the window and watched as a plane climbed until it became a dot, and its vapour trail was the only trace of it ever having been in the sky. He watched the trail until it began to fracture and disappear. *An indefinite term,* he thought. That would mean changing his life significantly, disappearing like the vapour trail and leaving the comfort of his bachelor pad, handing in his resignation and moving a million miles from his friends and family and – Kate.

He grazed his teeth on his bottom lip and mulled it over. The news he'd received was something he hadn't considered before. He had spoken at length to both his superiors, Professor Henderson, one of the most recognised figures in the medical world of tropical diseases and respiratory medicine, and Mr Fairchild. Clearly, both had sung Sam's praises in the references they had submitted to Turkana. But that post would have been for a two-year sabbatical, and his post in the team of four consultants at Bart's would have been kept warm by a locum.

The NHS would have still paid his salary in full, and he would also have received a tidy allowance whilst he was overseas. In return he'd learn more about the African communities, and be able to write his papers on the medicines and advanced stages of the respiratory diseases that were affecting these rural villages, and the still widespread issues of AIDS and how to contain it. And more importantly, gain considerable knowledge and experience by working in an underdeveloped country. But after two years he would return to his much-loved position at Bart's; that was his plan, and he hadn't ever considered anything different. But now he was having to do that, and with immediate effect.

Not only that, but also his considerations were now based on the religious ethos of a hospital. Should that be the reason for his change in life? After all, his beliefs, or rather lack of them, had derailed the straightforward plan of a simple two-year sabbatical.

It had started by being a golden opportunity for him, one that he'd sat discussing over a couple of India Pale Ales with Professor Henderson at the Hand and Shears. This was the local haunt for the students, lecturers and doctors from the teaching hospital that they fondly referred to as Bart's. He'd first made the pub's acquaintance years ago, on his walk back to his lodgings from Charterhouse College with a bunch of like-minded students, all of them just starting out on their journey to become brilliant physicians. It was the place where one of his first ales was poured to be drunk through a yard stick, with the booming chants from his fellow students *'Down it, down it, down it!'* And the roar of applause as yet another student was initiated.

And now, some twenty years later, he was a consultant respirologist, with the same old background sounds of those initiations taking place while he sat with Henderson, the head of his game, and deliberated a two-year sabbatical at the Turkana Mission Hospital.

'It would be a great opportunity for you, Sam,' Prof Henderson had said. 'You've no commitments, ties, family constraints. It's a-once-in-a-lifetime chance, and seldom does the NHS fund this sort of thing. Take it! You'd be a fool not to.'

With the amber nectar of the IPA finished, the two men had left the raucous noise of the students behind them. A wry smile had crossed their faces, both knowing that feeling of setting out on a new journey in life.

And now for Dr Samuel Edwards, reading the bombshell letter, that journey had just got a hell of a lot bigger. The opportunity wasn't the same any more. It was a life change. A whole new start. A whole new picture. A different landscape. An *African* landscape.

He exhaled loudly and glanced out of his window, tilting the shutter slats a little to view further along the street. Kate would be arriving soon. They'd arranged to go for a walk along the river before seeing friends for lunch at the Sun Inn, nestled in the sleepier suburbs of London's Barnes village.

Sam had met Kate in his first year at medical school. She was reading general medicine. She'd caught his eye at the Freshers Ball and after a few conversations caught here and there, they began seeing each other. It was nothing too serious at first, and in the years of medical school they'd split up and got back together countless times. But it never quite worked out; there was a lust with no love. And now they seemed to be just good friends with the occasional benefits. Post graduating, Kate had had a string of failed relationships, and when each of them ended she would wallow in her glass of red wine with Sam and confess that she was doomed, and would be nothing but a sad old singleton, and probably turn into some mad cat hoarding woman. Over one drunken night of self-pitying they'd made a pact that should they still be single by the age of thirty they would marry each other.

Sam smiled gently to himself at that thought, as he pushed the letter around the table. Kate was an amazing woman, the life and soul of every party, but she didn't stop him in his tracks. She didn't make his stomach somersault uncontrollably when he saw her. She didn't fill him with that intoxicating desire that he expected would come from a woman he wanted to spend his life with. But living in Africa indefinitely would mean never seeing her, her smile, her ridiculous ways, her drunken silliness, her friendship. His Kate. And telling her that was going to be the hardest thing he would ever have to do. Perhaps harder than the decision he'd already made in his head. He was going to accept the position at the village medical centre.

The intercom buzzed. *That'll be Kate,* he thought. He got up, leaving the letter on the table, and padded through to the hallway.

'Hello.'

'Hey, you, it's me,' came the cheery voice from Kate through the small silver speaker on the wall.

The door clicked open and she stood in the hall, beaming. 'Ready for our walk and the pub?' she said through her smile.

'Sure. I'll just grab my coat.'

As Kate stood in the kitchen doorway the tilt of the sunlight through the shutters caught her hair. She looked different this morning; there was a freshness in her face, and the tip of her nose glowed from the crisp air outside. Sam felt a pang of unease. He knew he had to break the news to her, but seeing her looking the way she did, it felt wrong. There was never going to be a right time. But this morning, why did she have to look so lovely and fresh and ready for a day out with him? He was about to ruin it all.

'Sam, I need to talk to you,' she said as she leant against the door.

He stopped stuffing his wallet into his pocket.

'Something's come up,' she continued. 'I've been meaning to tell you but I wasn't sure how to.'

For a brief moment, Sam's unease subsided. He'd been given a lifeline to work out how he was actually going to tell her that he was leaving. 'What is it? Have you decided you don't want to marry me anymore?' he laughed.

'Well, hmm ...'

'You have, haven't you? Come on, you know me, sock it to me. I can take it.'

'It's not that I don't want to marry you, I mean I would if I could, it's just that–'

'Seriously, Kate, is it that bad? What's up?'

She sighed. 'It's just that I've been offered a job.'

'Right, and ... That's good ... Isn't it?' he asked, his brow furrowed.

'Yeah it is, but...Well, it's not in London.'

'Where is it?'

'Deal, in Kent. It's just perfect. It's a small practice, and I applied for the position a while ago. I didn't think I'd get it and I hadn't heard anything, so I figured it wasn't for me. So I kind of didn't say anything to you. But I got a letter yesterday, offering me the position. It's not a big practice – there's two other GPs and a nurse practitioner – but they wanted a female doctor ... and ...' She seemed to gallop on with it all, not allowing herself time to take a breath.

'They want *you*,' Sam said, smiling.

'Yeah. And I want to go.'

'Take it, Kate. That's amazing. And you know my little bro, Tom, he's in Deal. He can show you around.'

'I know, but you're in *London*.' For a split second Sam wondered whether he should actually be believing in some other deity. He'd been given the perfect opportunity to tell Kate his news. She was leaving London, and so him accepting the position in Eritrea wouldn't seem quite as bad.

He seized the opportunity. 'Not for much longer,' he replied as he swung his coat over him and handed her the letter.

'What's this?' she said as she took it from him.

'Read it.'

The room fell silent as she read. He watched her. She blinked several times until she finally spoke. 'Africa?' Her eyes lifted from the page she was reading and searched his face, waiting for him to tell her it wasn't what she'd read.

He didn't, though. Those words never came.

He nodded. 'Looks like we've both been offered a new job.' He searched her face for some kind of response. A crack of excitement, maybe. A joyous smile, perhaps. She bit her lip and a frown creased across her forehead. Her glance went back to the page. She tried to stop the tremble in her hand, hoped he hadn't noticed. She read the word again. It seemed bigger and bolder, maybe a little blurred. She tried to look up at him.

'Are you going to take it?' Her voice was quiet. The word *Africa* still blurred. The tremble in her hand still present. Her stomach churned.

He nodded, unsure of her response.

'Right.' The word caught in her breath. Her glance dropped.

'You don't think I should?'

'No.' She shook her head. 'I think you should.' She nodded her head quickly. 'It's just ... it's just.' She paused. She could feel her head shaking from side to side in disbelief of what she'd just read. 'It's *Africa*.' The word stuck in her throat, choking her silently.

'I know.'

'And there's no return date.' The knot in her stomach tightened. Her throat seemed to close as if she needed to run from the room and gasp for air. Her eyes caught his for the first time; she kept her gaze on his eyes, on his face, every inch of him. Waiting for him to flinch, waiting for him to tell her he had arranged a return date, and that it would just be the sabbatical that they had chatted about. She waited in the silence, a dead silence. She could hear her own words echoing in her head, *there's no return date.* And then his words came.

'I know.'

She felt the sting in her eyes. 'And ...' she tried to swallow the lump that jarred in her throat. 'I'll miss you.' She placed the letter on the side. Her words said as silently as the sound that comes from feeling helpless.

'Hey,' he said realising that the girl in front of him was falling uncontrollably into a mire of uncertainty. While she was going to Kent, he had slammed her with an ace card with his own destination of Africa. He shifted the chair out of his way and stood closer to her, lifting her chin with the crook of his finger. 'There are planes, I can fly back. It's not that far, Kate. Kate? Hey.'

'Yep.' She nodded, and a tear fell down her cheek.

He'd never really seen that look on her face before: her eyes full of tears, tears for him. He brushed her cheek, his thumb catching the teardrop that trickled down her cheek and onto the top of her lip.

'Hey, come here.' He wrapped his arms around her. He could feel her warmth, and her hands grappled at the back of his jacket. She clung onto him. She hadn't been expecting to feel as lost as she did. She hadn't been expecting to feel as helpless as she did. She wanted to whisper into his chest, *don't go*. Yet she didn't. She just let him hold her.

And her heart broke silently.

Chapter Eight

Adi Ada, Eritrea

The walk back to the medical centre was short, although the day would be long and unforgiving in the sweltering heat. The women of the village had made their daily visit to the well, carrying fresh water as they meandered back to their homes. Their voices rung out in melodic tones as they chattered to each other, with one hand holding their pails in place, as if carrying water in such a way was simple. It *was* simple to them, as simple as a child standing on one leg to balance in a game of hopscotch. Life was simple here in the village of Adi Ada; there was a calmness that fell upon the community. A warmth in the air that carried on from the soles of their feet and deep into their own souls, as if each and every one of them had been sun-kissed at birth with a kindness that ran through their veins and effervesced into the colourfulness of their lives.

There was no hustle and bustle of stressed pedestrians on pavements, no noise of frustrated drivers, no outbursts of unnecessary road rage, no one-fingered gesticulations from cyclists thinking they owned the road. The only time a klaxon hooted was on the arrival of the Red Cross van or Jeremiah's rusty open-back wagon. And then the village of Adi Ada was filled with a noise of familiarity and a welcoming excitement from the children chasing their weekly visitors. A little like the ice cream van in England that would bring the smiles of summer to the doorsteps. Always random but always giving the same rush of smiles and excitement.

Weekly, Jeremiah arrived in his wagon, with his arm hanging out of the wound-down window, his straw trilby hat shielding the sun from the short fuzz of his head, his broad grin that gave way to two large dimples and a few gold teeth at the side of his open smile. He would swagger around the van and let down its tailgate, high-fiving any hand that came up to his own. His truck would be brimming with crates holding bananas, yams, sacks of chillies, a crate full of live birds, the vibrant colours of yellow and green from the maize that the women had laboured over in the fields and the strong aroma of coffee beans that punctured the dry heat. The chickens pecked through the open sides of their crates, squawking for freedom and the need to scratch the earth near the mud huts, laying eggs for the villagers who'd buy them with the coins and odd *nafka* they had in their leather hide pouches.

Hessian sacks brimming with crimson, as if the sun that rose and fell in the sky seeped its glowing arms over the berbere spice that spilled over onto the base of the wagon's buck. In the treetops a cacophony of shrill calls from the birds and their mates. And higher above the trees, the fullness of branches bubbling with the incessant chattering of the monkeys waiting for a banana to fall carelessly to the ground.

Sam cast his eye up and caught sight of the curious little monkey who had become more daring than the others. He followed him in his own pathway of treetop pavements, the leaves casting dappled shadows as they swooped and swayed from the agile leaping. The sun, already high in the sky, drenched the ground below. In the haze of the heat Sam could already feel his loose shirt cling to his back.

'You're a funny little thing, aren't you?' The monkey stopped and waited for Sam to catch him up. 'I think I need to give you a name. Yeah, I definitely think you need a name.' The monkey, as if understanding, leapt up and down and somersaulted before whizzing off, his monkey chattering carrying in the dull heat.

The line of chairs was already outside the medical centre, and a trickle of villagers began to congregate there, the elders taking a seat, each one dabbing their brows from the rays of sun that hit them, nodding and smiling as Samuel passed them.

'Morning,' he said.

Just ahead of him he could see the Red Cross van, and to the side of that Jeremiah with his truck surrounded by a mass of women all needing to buy their supplies. Their headscarves and clothes were a myriad of colour as they bustled about the produce, waggling their bowls and bags ready to fill with food that would nourish them all.

Sam inhaled the aroma of fresh coffee as he neared the truck. 'Jeremiah,' he hollered holding one hand to the side of his mouth. 'Put some coffee aside for me, and some berbere.' Jeremiah gave him a golden grin and saluted.

Then Sam veered off towards Tim at the medical van. He wanted to make sure the supplies he got would suit the ailments and diseases that were presenting themselves daily. He also needed to make sure that a delivery of surgical instruments was on the vehicle for the cataract operation he would be performing on Abraham. He could see Elisabet talking with the aid workers at the side of the van, and to the side of her three children stood, one of them holding her hand, the other stroking her skirt as if she was a divine goddess, and the third child simply standing by her. Sam watched her as she cupped her hand about his head. And every so often she smoothed her hand on the back of his head. And when she did that, the small boy would turn and look up at her and smile. And she would return the smile whilst she carried on her conversation with the aid worker. Sam strolled over with his hand outstretched to welcome them.

'Morning, Sam,' Tim, one of the aid workers said, as he shook Sam's hand. 'Elisabet was just saying that you're looking at performing surgery on one of the villagers. A cataract procedure.'

'Yup,' Sam replied, clasping his hand with a firm shake. 'He's an eighteen-year-old with virtually no sight at the moment. A simple cataract op would give him the sight he should have. It seems crazy that he's lived like this nearly all his life, when in actual fact an operation at a young age would have rectified everything. Just mad.'

'Sam, this is Africa, and you know as well I do that the simplicities of first world medical interventions are just not here. You're right, it's mad – but hopefully it'll change now, with you here to make that difference.' He moved to the back of the vehicle and unlatched its double doors, taking from it two boxes full of everyday potions and lotions and medical equipment, and plonking them down onto the dusty track. 'I've got these two boxes, and then ...' he pulled forward another two smaller boxes which had the surgical instruments that would aid the cataract surgery. 'This should do it,' he said, patting the boxes. 'You know, if this is a success you'll have a queue of patients with the very same problem lining up at your door, and not just from this village.' He laughed and slung the boxes on top of the other medical supplies.

'If I have a queue of villagers with cataracts and can give them the ability to see once again, then it can only make their world brighter. Quite literally,' Sam said, pulling up the smaller and lighter box and handing it to Elisabet. 'And I have a beautiful nurse to assist me, too.' He cast a look towards Elisabet and smiled tenderly. Her skin took on a hue of colour and she felt it tingle and prickle down her spine. She brushed her cheek with the back of her hand. She took the smaller box and gave it to one of the children by her side then, open-armed, took another box for the medical centre.

'Come,' she said to the children, tucking the box under one arm and scooping her other arm around them. Two of the children skipped along whilst the third child, carrying the box of supplies, walked by her side.

Elisabet turned back and looked at Sam. The sleeves of his white cotton shirt were rolled up and his collar open. As he shared a joke with Tim and laughed, she smiled. His laugh was a sound she liked to hear, and she noticed faint lines forming at the side of his eyes. She watched him as he patted Tim on the back and disappeared around the side of the Red Cross van. As she approached the veranda of the hut she stopped at the top step and twisted the back of her saffron headscarf so that it fell across her shoulder. This time when she looked back in the direction of the van, Sam's eyes caught hers. *He's seen me watching him*, she thought. She wrapped the tail of the scarf around her again, and hurried the children back to their mothers who, still nattering, were buying produce from Jeremiah. Then she went back to the hut.

The door closed behind her and Sam stood watching it. *The first thing Abraham will see is going to be an image of intoxicating beauty*, he thought.

'That's it, Sam, that's your lot until next time.' Tim slammed shut the van's back door. 'She's beautiful, isn't she?' he continued, making his way towards the driver's door. 'Unspoken for as well.' He threw Sam a wink. 'But be careful. Women are different here. Africa's different.'

'What d'you mean?'

'You know as well as I do, my friend. I saw the look.'

Tim shut the door and rolled down the window. 'See you Thursday, Sam.'

'Yep, Thursday. Take care,' Sam replied, taking his hand from his pocket and slapping the bonnet of the van. A swirl of red dust kicked up from the rear wheels and its klaxon honked as Tim drove away. Sam inhaled before placing the boxes one on top of the other in a small tower, and then carried them back to the medical centre.

Inside, Elisabet had begun to unpack the supplies and put them in an orderly arrangement in the meds cupboard. The only patients occupying the beds were the young girl, still shielded by the curtain rail and, in the far corner Abel, whose cough had lessened, and his breathing was less raspy.

'Where shall I put these ones, Doctor Samuel?' Elisabet asked, holding the packaged instruments and medicine for the cataract operation.

'I'll take them,' he said as went to his desk, his hand briefly touching the softness of her skin as he took the medical equipment from her.

The ceiling fan rattled above them.

She stood below it, her hands now empty but with the touch of a man still left on them. She tucked her scarf back and hastily made her way to the white sink in the corner filling a bowl from the tap. Droplets of water splashed onto the back of her hand, and she wiped it across her forehead. Then she took a white cotton flannel from the linen cupboard, donned a mask, and made her way to the girl's bedside, drawing the curtain behind her. She sat for a moment and let her breath slow down as if allowing the momentary feeling of whatever was consuming her to filter away. Her heart raced beneath her blouse. Did it race so fast that the sounds of its beats could be heard? Did the flush in her cheek show? Was his touch deliberate, or was it merely just a doctor taking the supplies from her? Yet it had seemed like a prolonged space of time. Her eyes rested momentarily on the open window where the vivid colours of a butterfly's wings flitted about before resting on the sill. The light catching on its wings was like an iridescent rainbow. She watched it, allowing her senses to rise inside her.

The world carried on outside the walls of the medical centre, simply turning, and the brilliance of the sun's light beamed through into a room that was swathed in sanitisation. Yet it was now filled with a realised love. She felt weightless in her own thoughts, but her heart beat faster and harder and deeper than that of the small girl who lay beside her. *Did my own mother's heart beat in this way when she met her father?* she wondered. *Why am I thinking this way? Does every woman think this way? Feel this way? Should I feel like this when my job is to tend and care? I am an African woman. An independent African woman.* The girl who lay beside her in the bed whimpered in her sleep.

'There, there.' Elisabet swabbed her forehead gently. 'There, there,' she said again. As she wrung out the flannel her own thoughts went back to the moments before. The moments before when she had hurriedly filled the bowl with clean water and taken the cotton towel from the cupboard. The moment when she had handed him the supplies. The moment when she'd stood at the veranda's step and caught his gaze on her.

The sliding of curtain rings jolted her thoughts.

'How's the patient?'

Elisabet pulled her mask closer to her face, casting her eyes down to the water bowl, the cotton cloth unravelling from its folds as it swirled beneath the cool water. Wringing out the flannel, she hoped he hadn't noticed her momentary lapse of concentration. She rested the cloth on the edge of the bowl.

'She's still so hot.' She didn't turn to look at him. *Will you walk away and allow the curtain to fall back down?* she urged silently. He didn't. Instead he pushed the curtain across a little more and entered the enclosed space. Elisabet swallowed before she went to get up.

'I'll leave you. Abel is—'

'Why?' He took up the clipboard that hung at the end of the bed. 'Stay here. I can see to Abel.' The slight pressure in his hold on her shoulder eased her back down into the chair.

'But the villagers outside will want to come in and be looked after and—'

'And the villagers will be.' He moved around the side of the bed and placed a thermometer under the young girl's arm and waited. With a gentle touch he lifted the beaded hair that clung to her skin. He then took the blood pressure band and wrapped it around her arm, allowing it to fill with air before releasing it. He scribbled the numbers on his hand. Lifting her arm gently, he removed the thermometer. She felt clammy to the touch. 'It's still very high. Keep her as cool as possible and administer another 500 mg of paracetamol. Have you ever inserted a cannula before?' Elisabet shook her head. 'In the supplies cupboard you'll find the sterile packets. Could you bring me one, some gauze, some sterile solution and a saline pouch?'

She left the bedside, closing the curtain behind her. Sam wheeled the stand to the side of the bed. Noting the observations on the clipboard, he looked up at his young patient.

When Elisabet came back in she asked: 'How sick is she, Doctor Samuel?'

'I need to get her hydrated.' Elisabet watched as Samuel felt the top of the girl's hand then pierced the skin and allowed the cannula to run into the vein. 'The pouch, please.' With a line running up to the saline pouch and into the girl's hand, a shot of red backwashed into the line. 'Once that's finished it'll need to be changed.' He rested his hand on Elisabet's shoulder as he passed her. 'Keep her cool,' he smiled, and left. The curtain's loops rattled and clinked as they brushed back along the rail, hiding away the sickest child in the medical centre. Elisabet remained behind it. Had the feelings in her only been felt by her? He had been assertive, precise, a doctor. She dabbed the girl's head. How foolish she felt.

On the veranda the naughtiest and most daring of monkeys sat on the ledge, his lips wrapped around a fresh mango. He scampered up the column and leapt to the other side.

'So, what have we today, my little friend?' The monkey somersaulted with delight as the human in front of him engaged in chatter with him. 'You're a funny little thing. You know that, right?' The monkey cocked his head. 'D'you understand me?' The monkey made a high-pitched sound and scuttled up the column again, this time hanging upside down. Sam shook his head. 'I've no time to play, little fella. See all those villagers over there?' – he glanced over to the villagers congregating on the rickety chairs and make-do benches – 'They need me more, my little friend.' With that the monkey darted away, swinging up onto the generator, and disappeared into the branches of the mango tree. Sam's broad smile stayed on his face as he greeted the villagers, who had formed a steady line along the track and past the open mud hut that had no sides, just half a wall around it. A little like a simple pergola or a bandstand. A bandstand it wasn't, but a pergola in this sweltering heat it could have been, although it sat empty, the coolest of spots, yet the emptiest at least.

The stream of villagers outside the medical centre lessened as the sun reached its peak and then began to fall. The chickens bought that morning clucked and scratched about the area pecking at any spilt maize and grain, their claws turning up the hardened ground with each scrape. Jeremiah was finishing tying up the hessian sacks of grain and maize, and threw the empty crates that had housed the live birds onto the wagon when he saw Sam approaching him.

'Ah, Doctor.' Jeremiah's grin was broad and the glint of gold flashed from his open lips. 'Your coffee beans and berbere. The coffee's good, my friend. See you again.'

Sam paid with the loose coins in his pocket: 'See you, Jeremiah.' The wagon spluttered whilst a puff of smoke billowed out of its exhaust and the chickens fluffed their feathers indignantly, turning their fluffy bottoms on it. The children ran alongside until running would have been too far. Jeremiah sounded the klaxon and his arm waved one final salute to the throng of gleeful young faces. And then all that could be seen was the dust that threw itself up like a smoke screen, obscuring the track. Jeremiah, with his huge golden grin, was gone until next time.

Sam idled his way back to the chairs. There were just two women waiting to be jabbed in the arm, and an older woman, Abel's wife, come to help him. Abel had been given the all clear to go home to recuperate, with an assortment of antibiotics – and strict instructions to wipe down mangoes, and all other fruit and veg, before eating them.

'Please,' Sam smiled, ushering the women into the medical centre, carrying his coffee beans and spices, and leaving behind just a row of empty chairs outside it.

Chapter Nine

As the days blended into each other and the medical hut filled and emptied like the silent ebb and flow of the sea brushing onto a sandy beach. Sam swung in his hammock. He'd bought it when he'd first set foot on African soil. Now as he rocked beneath the canopy of the fruit trees, he contemplated the life he'd chosen, and the words that Tim had spoken so seriously: *African women are different.* An African woman's face had never remained etched in his mind so deeply that even now, when his time was his own, he could still see her. The way she brushed her hand on the back of the child's head whilst she stood chatting with Tim, as if that child were her own. When she stopped at the veranda, she too had looked back. He hadn't imagined that. But then there was her wish to leave Abrihet's side, the sickest child, the one who needed constant bedside care. Why had she wanted to leave so hastily? Was her reason to leave hidden behind the mask that shielded her face? Yes, her eyes had told the story. He had seen it: she couldn't get away from him any faster, and his feelings were not reciprocated.

How are African women different? he wondered, as the hammock gently swayed. Cradling a chilled beer in his hand, he raised the neck of the bottle to his lips. He had visited Johanna after Saturday's clinic, and now she sat by the bedside of her eldest child, Abrihet. A child who lay in a bed with a saline drip to hydrate her. It wasn't malaria but tuberculosis. It was an impossible task for the professionals to stay with her daily, hourly, and so now it was Johanna staying with her daughter, giving some respite to Samuel and Elisabet. *Is that what Tim had meant? The determination of a woman to sacrifice all to save her child. Could that possibly be how the women were different here?*

Amanuel, Johanna's weeks-old baby boy, had been one of the doctor's first patients when he had newly arrived in the village. A baby clinging to life and a mother who wasn't ready to let her God take her child. She'd previously given him one of her children through malaria, and she'd not give another. He recalled his image of her pacing the veranda, chanting prayers to the God she believed in. A woman of Christian faith who now sat with her only daughter, not wanting her to die and lie in the baked ground which had already claimed one of her children. Wanting to take her home, where Amanuel was now stronger and crawling and growing day by day, in the care of her mother and aunties. Was that what Tim had meant when he'd said that? Where normally the values placed on a female child should have been different. Was it because this community, this small village called Adi Ada, was not Muslim, but was where the women were respected by their men, where a woman was a woman and not anything else? Where their values were from a bible. But in the towns and lowlands there was wealth, and the people were predominantly non-Christian; the women were nothing more than an object of exchange from birth to marriage. He mulled over the day's events, and took another swig from his bottle.

The warmth of the evening fell around him, the coolness of the beer sliding down his throat like sweet nectar. Above, a scurrying noise on the roof of his hut caused him to look up, and he chuckled under his breath and took another swig. The monkey perched himself on the edge before shimmying down the curtain beads and throwing himself onto the end of the hammock.

'Hey, little fella.'

The monkey cocked his head.

'Wanna a beer?'

He tilted his head to the other side and scratched his ear.

'Hungry?'

He somersaulted, made a loud shriek-like laugh, and then hurled himself up the trunk of the tree and onto the highest branch. Then from amid the deep rich green leaves he lobbed a mango at Sam, walloping him straight in the stomach. Sam bent up his leg in a kneejerk reaction.

'Hey, little chap. Steady on!' The monkey somersaulted madly and shrieked in his own hysterical language.

'D'you think it's funny?' The monkey's hysteria and excitement increased until he stopped and bear-hug shimmied back down the trunk before he rested once more at the end of the hammock with his own mango.

'You *were* hungry, then,' Sam chuckled, taking his Swiss army knife and slicing into the mango's sun-blushed skin. The monkey sat contentedly, his lips chomping around his fruit, his sharp beady eyes watching.

'It's good,' Sam's eyes diverted to the watchful gaze, his tongue removing every last drop of the syrupy liquid.

'So, my little friend. I'm Sam – and you?'

The monkey blinked several times, his lips still smothered around the mango.

'Katumba,' Sam whispered. 'I'm going to call you Katumba.'

From the treetop the noise from the troop of monkeys echoed through the leaves, calling out for their youngster.

'You'll attract the *siafu* ants.' Elisabet bent down to pick up the mango stone on the ground.

'It was Katumba's.' Sam hadn't noticed her coming up to his hut, and he hastily tried to assert himself in a hammock that wouldn't stay steady.

'Katumba's?' She crouched on the ground and glanced sideways at Sam, her eyebrows knitted.

'The monkey.' He swivelled his eyes into the treetops where a canopy of lush green leaves hung with mangoes hanging ripe and ready. Even in his own head he knew what he had said sounded utterly ridiculous – and there was no sight of any monkeys.

'The Eritrean beer is good, isn't it?' A glint of a smile crossed her face.

Holding the bottle up in the air so that the light shone through the glass, he tipped it a little to gauge the contents. 'Okay, agreed it sounds crazy. Umm, who'd have thought? But yeah, it was the monkey's. And … Katumba – yep – that furry little thing, who switches the generator off and on, he's a monkey. And yeah, it *is* good, you're right. D'you drink?'

She cast him a smile. 'Well, make sure he cleans up after himself. The *siafu* ants aren't so nice. Do I drink? … sometimes for occasions, and maybe today is an occasion. I just passed by the medical centre to see Johanna. Abrihet seems a little better.'

'That's good; the drugs are finally working, then. But she's not out of the woods yet.'

'Out of the woods?' She looked about. 'What woods?'

He sighed into a smile with the innocence of Elisabet's literal thinking. The loveliness of her misunderstanding of English expressions. 'Not real woods. I mean that time will tell, and she's still very sick. TB can be fatal. I should be—'

She shook her head and hushed him. 'It's the Sabbath. We respect these days.'

'And I'm not religious, I'm a doctor. The only doctor here, and there's a child who's sick.'

'Johanna's with her. And you too need your rest. The people here have grown to become very fond of you, but they will not think fondly of you if you break the Sabbath, religion or no religion. Tomorrow's a big day, for you'll change Abraham's world. A world where he will see again.' She turned to leave, still holding the mango stone.

'Elisabet ...' he stopped and rolled himself out of the hammock and moved towards her. She turned, the tail of her scarf lying across the open neck of her blouse falling against her collarbone and resting softly on her breastbone, the silhouette of her frame catching in the light as the sun began to drop in the west. The huge disc-like earrings swinging on the golden hooks from her ears. They were as vivid an orange as the scarf on her head, as sun-blushed as the mangoes that hung from the trees.

She stopped and looked back at him. Her eyes, as dark and deep as velvety chocolate, stared back at him, waiting for the next words that he would utter, her hand falling back to her scarf as if tucking her hair behind her ear, her eyes still searching and waiting.

'Have you eaten?' His voice offered a sound that in his head meant *don't go*. In the moments before where he had stood and allowed every part of her face, her features, the silhouette beneath the thinness of her top, to be traced into his mind. A beauty that struck him, that stopped him from breathing. He stepped forward, holding the neck of his almost-finished beer bottle hooked between his fingers. 'I mean ... will you stay?'

raising the beer in front of him and shaking it gently. 'I could do with the company. Katumba doesn't say much. Makes a fair amount of noise, though.'

He smiled a smile that seemed to flutter as freely as the butterfly she'd watched on the window sill earlier. Fluttering until the smile caught up with her own and rested. Offering her a happiness inside that effervesced like a warm heartbeat, in time with her own, in unison and where she wanted to be. Her eyes reached his, and her head moved in a way that could only mean the word *yes*. A stirring of feelings, a pang of anxiety, as if love was the titanic wave, and she fell in head first.

Her shoulder rested against the opening of the beaded curtain falling about her like a waterfall frame. Her eyes scanned the room before resting on the picture of the smiling faces that sat on the cane coffee table. *His life back home, where he'd return to one day* she thought.

'Beer?' he asked, taking two bottles from the fridge. She nodded. 'I have some sour pancake bread, spiced chickpeas and yoghurt. I learnt to cook it when I first arrived. Can I tempt you? Although I think I might have overdone it with the berbere; the chickpeas are a bit, umm, how can I put it ...'

'Hot?' A smile inched along her face and her head tilted to one side, a shaft of light catching the vividness of her earrings. 'I'd like that.' She took the beer bottle and shook her head to the offering of a glass. 'Who taught you to cook this? It smells good.'

'Tim, after he'd met me at Nairobi airport. He kinda took me under his wing. Wears many hats, that one. My safari guide with a medical head and compassion that seeps through his veins.' Sam inched his way past her and back outside, expertly holding the dishes and his bottle. 'I spent a week on safari with him, met his parents and stayed at their reserve, then we travelled through Ethiopia before coming here. We took tracks across lands that just made me hold my breath – you know that feeling when you just can't quite take it all in? The vastness, the heat, the wonderment of wild animals. It's like David Attenborough in real time.'

'David Attenborough?' Her brow furrowed.

'One of our TV presenters, just the main man in the wildlife world, brings all this to our sitting room. Then we made our way across in the clapped-out Defender I was given to get me around in. Got us through, though,' he chortled. 'I've never seen stars like it at night, when you lie next to a huge canvas tent and the calls of the wild surround you, lying on a mat by a burning fire and the sky is black like a sparkling dot-to-dot, where you could make a million pictures. Or a blood-orange sunset that blows your mind.' He took a swig from his bottle. The beer stayed in his mouth for a while.

'You've never been to Africa before?' she said, as she twisted the end of her scarf.

'Never.'

'I've never been to England.'

Sam balanced the dishes on the hammock while he pulled up two hand-decorated barrels and patted on one for her to sit on.

'I can show you where the sun sets by the water. Have you seen it yet?' she said, taking a small plate from him and some *injera*.

'No. Until you came on board I've been swamped. I've learnt how to cook a few meals but that's about it.'

She offered a smile. 'Would you like to see it?' She took a tiny bit of spiced chickpea from her lip with her finger.

'Yeah,' – he took another swig, his gaze firmly on her – 'yeah, I would.'

'So come on,' she brushed off the crumbs from the pancake-like bread. 'Let's go!'

'What – *now*?'

She shrugged. A beam stretched across her face. 'It's the Sabbath, Doctor Samuel, so yes, *now*. We can eat this when we get back.'

'Wait.' He got up to leave her for a moment. 'The *siafu* ants, right?'

The beads of the curtain rattled softly behind him as he took the food inside.

The track meandered behind the run of huts where the children danced and ran, the mountain range looming high in the sky. The women chattered as if words became vibrant explosions of colour, and a bubbling of African music funnelled its way through the village. Sam kneeled low to the ground and took a close-up shot of three children dancing. Around them the drummers of the community played in a rich and musical art form. Never did the drums play without people dancing. The reverberating beat of rhythm was the glue that held this community together, the elders sitting close by, amused by the larking about of the generation that they hoped would become as wise and giving as themselves. An aroma of coffee from the slow-brewed jug was always a pleasure that filtered through the air, where grass had been laid on the ground awaiting the coffee ceremony.

In his own hut he would relish the quick café espresso shot. But these men sat, their faces creased with lines of laughter and happiness, their eyes beady yet alive, and coffee in small cups, colourful cups, as colourful as life itself.

Further along as the tracks widened and the huts became more dispersed. A different sound permeated through a village that was transforming with night falling. Young adolescents moved about the mango trees, a ghetto blaster booming music from the radio station in the nearby town, a polyrhythmic nature of moves and a beat transcending through their bodies. If a place could give birth to rhythm and dance, Africa was that place.

Sam stopped and let the joyful sounds of the older kids move him. There was a lack of dancing with partners but their enjoyment was in a group, their bodies in separate isolation in their moves. His foot tapped on the ground – the urge to join them was overpowering. An almost out-of-body movement; he had never felt this urge before. And then without a care in the world he felt the beating ground beneath him, and there he was with them. That joyful moment, and there *she* was too, not by his side, not in his arms, but in a gathering of rhythmic, pulsating bodies – dancing in Africa.

She slipped through the dancing youths until she reached the edging where the mango trees loomed around her, their fruit hanging like nightlife lanterns. A spit turned on a fire, roasting the haunches of a goat. Sam's own need to follow her took over his body as he pushed forward, following her. The music a faint beat in the sultry heat. Fireflies darted about them and two dragonflies hovered nearby, together yet apart. Their wings a shimmering transparency of silver. Turquoise blue bodies poised in the air until flitting to where they knew they'd find fresh water.

And there it was ahead of him, a lake of liquid red gold. A fish darted up as if for air and then dived back down. The lacelike wings of the dragonflies wavered above the still water, the simple circles of water rippling from the centre where the fish had been and gone, until they too disappeared.

'This is it,' she looked out to the crimson mirror ahead of her. 'Where the sun disappears into the water.' Her own words floating down into the motionless pool. 'Swim fishing—'

And there she felt the touch of his hand against hers, the prickle in her spine, the somersault in her stomach. The tender and intricate sense of a human cat's cradle between their fingers.

And her feelings for him swallowing her whole.

Chapter Ten

The line of chairs and rickety benches sat waiting to be filled. Each morning, a trickle of villagers would arrive. Today was no different, except that for one villager it was. The screeching calls from the troop of monkeys swinging through the branches echoed through the leafy canopies, the youngest of them moving out from his elders. The door of the medical hut swung on its hinges. The sweetest song from a blue breasted bee-eater trilled on an overhanging branch, its lightness on its perch adding a pop of electric blue to the lush green leaves. its song a calming lament to a morning that would unfold and bring about a new world for one of Doctor Samuel's patients. Sam stood listening to the bird, its feathers bluer than the ocean, deeper in colour than the sky. He rolled up his sleeves, ready for his day.

The swishing of a stick on the ground neared the row of chairs. The monkeys' banter became louder and more penetrating. An excitement that even they couldn't control. The call of the monkeys guiding him. The smallest and youngest of the monkeys leapt onto the generator and over onto the rail of the veranda and rattled along it, as he sat and gazed up at Sam.

'Katumba. How ya doin', little fella?' Katumba twitched his head from side to side. From his pocket Sam took a handful of nuts and tentatively held out his hand, shaking his hand gently, so that their shells knocked together in his palm. Katumba edged his way forward slightly. And then with a curiosity that even this little monkey couldn't withhold, his slender fingers inched their way into Sam's palm. Sam gently shook his hand again and allowed the nuts to roll forward, resting in the crook of his fingers.

Katumba's spindly fingers reached into Sam's hand, while his beady amber eyes remained on the prize of the nuts. A smile stretched across Sam's face as man and monkey shared a handful of nuts on the veranda of a medical hut in Africa.

As Abraham took his seat at the front of the row, Sam watched. When he had finished filling the nut holder and made his way down to the chairs, the blue-breasted bee-eater flew down and latched its claws onto the wire of the feeder, and there it feasted.

'Abraham, good morning.'

Abraham stared ahead, his cane held in his palm. One of the villagers threw him a reassuring smile. A smile he couldn't see. Abel moseyed past: 'Godspeed, boy.' Abraham stopped and waved his stick in the air. A smile moved across his face. A smile that Abel saw.

Doctor Samuel extended his arm. 'Are you ready, Abraham?'

'I think so, Doctor.'

'Come, there's no need to worry.' Doctor Samuel led Abraham up the steps of the veranda and through the open door. The bird trilled as it perched on the windowsill. Sam spied it and Abraham heard it.

'The birdsong,' Abraham said. 'My father says it's the voice of the blue-breasted bee-eater, and it's blue like the deepest seas. I can't remember what this colour is or even what the sea really looks like. Will I see it, doctor?'

'I hope so, Abraham. Here, take Elisabet's hand.' Holding his arm out, Abraham waited in anticipation for the touch of Elisabet's. Linking her arm into his, with her hand cupping his, she guided him to the bed in the corner of the room. A screen had been put around it, enclosing the small area where Doctor Samuel would carry out the procedure. A trolley sat tidily by the side of the bed with a number of packaged items and a bowl. On the far side of the room, Abrihet still lay in her bed. The fever had now subsided and Johanna was still by her side. She smiled gently as she watched Abraham disappear behind the curtains; just the tapping of his stick on the ground could be heard.

Elisabet, holding Abraham's hand, took the cane from him and rested it against the wall. With his hand still in hers she turned to him, taking his other hand and holding it tightly, her thumb grazing his skin, let the fear that trembled through him wash into the palms of her hands. Then she let go briefly to lift his legs and twizzle him onto the bed, and adjusted the pillow behind him. She took his hand again. It felt clammy in hers, and every time she let her grip go the trembling returned.

'Doctor Samuel will be here soon.'

The curtain swished open and Doctor Samuel stood ready in scrubs. 'Are you ready, Abraham?' he said, pulling up his mask across his face.

Abraham nodded.

'This won't take long at all, maybe twenty minutes. The recovery is longer.'

'And then, Doctor?'

'And then, Abraham, I hope you'll see how blue the sea is, how red the sky is at sunset and see the vivid colours behind the birdsong you hear.'

Abraham stared ahead, a greyish-brown film covering his eyes. They moved from side to side.

'You'll feel a slight prick, it's just the anaesthetic. But you'll be awake, Elisabet's here by your side. When I'm done, I'll cover your eyes with a plastic eye shield. Now, lie back and try to relax. Here ...' he clasped Abraham's hand and steadied him as he lay further back. Sam pulled the overhead light down, its brightness shining straight into Abraham's eyes. A light that would cause anyone else to raise their hands as protection from the dazzle.

Abraham allowed his body to relax, and lay back into the pillow. Not seeing the needle, he flinched at the sharp scratch, then he felt nothing. He saw neither the beautiful woman by his side nor the doctor who performed the surgery. As the clock on the wall ticked, its hand moved around its face, a gateway to time. A time that would seem as long as being in the depth of a black hole. Each tick of the second hand whilst the light still shone brightly into his eyes. The shuffling of feet, the noise of instruments, the silence of breath. The light then became black, a black void ahead of him, not even a shimmer of light or dark or shadows that moved. Just a dead black.

'It's all done now, Abraham. The patches are in place.'

The curtain loops rattled along the pole and Sam peeled off his surgical gloves. Elisabet closed the curtain behind them. She followed him out onto the veranda, where Abraham's parents were waiting anxiously.

'Doctor? Did it work? Can my boy see?' his mother asked.

Samuel removed his face mask. 'I don't know yet. Time will tell.'

'Can I see him?'

'Of course, but not for long. He needs to rest for a few hours. It was more difficult than I'd envisaged. It took longer than antici—'

Abraham's father extended his hand. 'My son has not seen since he was eighteen months old. You're a miracle man if he can see me. If my son can see me, his mother, his grandmother, his grandfather. Your name, Doctor Samuel, means *God has heard*. And if my son cannot see, you did your best, my friend.' He walked inside with his wife.

Samuel leant both hands on the rail and sighed inaudibly. 'My name,' he closed his eyes and let the sun beat down on his face, a line of sweat forming on his brow, his bandana already marked by perspiration. The door opened, and Abraham's parents left. They had kept their visit brief, knowing that their boy needed to rest. But they would return in a few hours.

To Abraham's family the walk back to their humble home seemed as though a lifetime of steps had been paced. Between the footprints they saw in the dusty track were the swishing swoop-like shapes made by the hammerkop-headed cane, the only evidence now that their son had made it to the doctor that morning. Every marking was a stark reminder that his sight had now been left in the hands of the kind doctor. The kind doctor who came from a country where Manchester United played in shirts whose colours their son had never known. What was a 'colour' in his head? For over sixteen years they had raised him in a sea of darkness, and now the only tangible sign of that darkness was the swoop on the ground from the cane that rested by his bedside in the medical hut. A bed where he still lay in darkness with a shield protecting his eyes. *Will he see our faces?* Bamidele, his mother, thought. *What will he think when he sees our faces? Will he like what he sees?*

At home, she beat the rug from her floor with the broom, the dust spilling into the warm air, her beating becoming more vigorous.

'Bamidele ...' Anbessa took her hand and steadied her. 'Bamidele,' he whispered, his hand still holding hers. He knew her feelings, he knew why the rug was being hammered by the force of a woman who knew only gentleness. She turned into him, her hands in his chest, her face burrowed into him, and there she wept. And as he stood and held her, the feelings inside her were in him too. A teardrop fell down his cheek.

They stood around Abraham's bed; the curtain screen had been removed. The shield protector was still covering his eyes. His hand went up to it, feeling it, tapping it gently with his fingers. 'I might finally see,' he said faintly.

'Your eyes will be sensitive, the light will feel bright,' said Doctor Samuel. 'Are you ready, Abraham?'

'I'm ready.'

Samuel slowly edged away the shield, letting the faintest of light flood in. He tenderly peeled away the mask holding his hand by Abraham's eyes as if to protect them from the glare of light.

Abraham blinked several times, and a watery liquid washed over his eyes.

'Are you okay?' Samuel moved the mask away completely.

Slowly, the face of his mother became clearer to Abraham. She smiled as his eyes met hers. His eyes still, they didn't move independently of themselves. 'I can see,' he said quietly. He stretched his hand out to his mother and mapped out the lines of her face. 'I can see. You're more beautiful than I could ever have imagined.' She clasped his face with her hands, the tears falling uncontrollably down her cheeks.

Samuel moved to one side and took from the surgical trolley a mirror. He took Abraham's hand and placed it on the handle lifting it towards his own face – his young man's face he had never seen.

'And this is you,' Samuel said.

'That's me.' The tears streamed down his cheeks. 'That's what I look like, that's my face. That's my face,' he said again and again, touching it, making sure it was real.

'That's your face, my boy.' His father stepped forward and held his son's head against his chest and kissed the top of his head and said in his breath. 'God has heard.' His eyes rested on Doctor Samuel. 'God has heard,' he said again, his voice broke and his own tears fell.

Chapter Eleven

Deal, Kent

A few weeks had passed since Tom had found Abrihet and her younger brother, Amanuel. The forlorn and broken bodies of those two young children swept up on the beach, clinging to life, attacked from above as living prey by the hungry gulls with their sharp claws and beaks. The two had been found cold, hungry and scared, and their survival was still unknown to anybody in the town.

Daily, Tom had avidly watched the news, hoping that some clue of where they had come from might arise. Had their parents been on the boat? But there was nothing. It was as if the search for bodies had no place in the news; once gone, there was no point in finding the souls that needed to be saved. As if the treacherous journey of travelling across countries and oceans bore no human worth of sea-searching for missing bodies. Kate had been able to buy clothes from the local supermarkets without causing any suspicion from her neighbours, her own sister had children of similar sizes. But at some point the two children would need to venture outside the house. They couldn't remain locked away in it forever, imprisoned by kindness. The need was greater now for Tom and Kate to come up with a plan and have every possible answer ready for the barrage of questions that would come their way, with no let-up.

Deal had a predominantly white demographic, so two Eritrean children who spoke English haltingly staying with Tom would require a sturdy back-up story. The ethnic diversity at the local primary school was non-existent, and the secondary school was a short bus ride away. Kate knew from her surgery's database that in the area families from an ethnic minority were in the minority, and even then they leant towards the Asian ethnicity. People would talk, and before Tom and Kate knew it, questions would be asked, and visits by unwanted officials would be made. How would they explain the children? How could they *ever* explain the children?

Amanuel lay on the sheepskin rug with a sketch pad and colouring pencils. Tom had spent his time teaching him how to hold a pencil and lightly shade the page without breaking the lead. And when the lead did still break, Amanuel no longer grunted in displeasure or fear, but instead would take the pencil sharpener and make another finely formed teepee shape. He'd spy the pencil's point and smile with contentment. And sometimes he'd prod his skin with its sharpness leaving a pin-head-size indentation, then circle it with his finger until the flesh had popped back and the prodding had never happened. It was as if breaking the lead was part of a ritual, piecing together a life that once was. Tom would watch him as he'd take each miniature teepee between his thumb and finger without letting them collapse and carefully place them on a sheet of perfectly shaded paper. A shaded paper that was a bird's eye view of a landscape of colour. A boy's eye view from a grass-reed rooftop, with his father mending the reeds. A small boy's eyes already mapping out the community that was home. Where his heart would beat to the sound of the drum, where his body moved in a polyrhythmic nature, where his sometimes-bare feet skipped the rope that turned, and where he'd run as fast as Jeremiah's truck before being hi-fived and sent back. And now here it lay on a sheepskin rug, his precisely mapped-out village. After weeks, his sheet of paper began to form a miniature model village of wooden shavings woven between the colours of their seasons. Tom would watch curiously from his drawing desk and piece together the previous existence of this small child. But colouring on the floor, imagining the world he'd left behind, left him quiet. Sometimes he'd look up to Tom as he coloured, his eyes as wide and open as the sea that had almost swallowed them whole. Yet it hadn't. It hadn't even spat them out. Instead it had pushed their boat to a shore where a man would find them. A kind man. *Is the sea a friend of God's? Did God hear and the sea listen?* Amanuel wondered in his small mind.

And when the sun dipped in the sky and the children had eaten their supper, Tom would carry Amanuel to his bed. Creating a miniature community of wooden teepee homes would leave one small boy exhausted.

Kate arrived later that evening, and she waited on the sofa whilst Tom settled the children before coming back downstairs and pouring them both a glass of Merlot.

'So, what's with the saved pencil shavings?' Kate asked taking a generous sip from her glass.

'A budding architect,' he mused. 'Wherever he's from, he's got a keen eye. But if you look closely, every shaving forms a home. If you look hard enough you can see the community he's building. It's like a model village, but instead of me – a qualified drawer who makes some model scale development that will be sold off for millions – this kid has made his own village out of shavings. Clever, right, or just the bare truth?'

Kate glanced at him. 'So, what's this huge splodge of red?'

'Dunno,' he paused. His finger traced between the tiniest of buildings. 'He's telling his story with art.'

'You think that's where he's from, where they're from?'

'Pretty sure. Until they open up and tell us, though, it's just guesswork.'

'But until then, what's our story?' Kate said, tucking her feet under a cushion.

'I don't know yet – but whatever happens they're not going back. Or being carted off to Alcatraz.'

'Alcatraz,' she laughed. 'By that you mean the detention centre.'

'Yeah, a building with no soul. What architect could design such a thing?'

'Not you, not you, Tom.' She rubbed her hand across his and clasped it. 'Hey, listen. I grabbed these today in the supermarket.' She took some books from a bag. 'I wasn't sure really where to go with this, but I figured some Usborne books would be good for showing them their sensory words. It might bring out how they feel. I don't know, just like touching and feeling, could evoke something. I stood for ages poring through the children's books but as these two aren't from here, seeing white characters in strange costumes won't make much sense to them. And then I thought, *Kate, for goodness sake you need a real bookshop. Where the shelves breathe words.* I found these, in that quirky little bookshop just off the High Street. You know the one just by Le Pinardier wine shop.' She pulled from her bag a small book. The cover was illustrated with a black woman cradling a small baby. She brushed her hands across the title, *Lullaby*, by Langston Hughes, then opened it and allowed the pages to fan through her fingers like a deck of cards toppling one after the other. 'I thought this and these others would be good for Amanuel; simple language, tender illustrations. Something familiar, but with new words, a new language. Abrihet would like them too. She's kind of like his mother now.'

'They're amazing, Kate. I'll show it to the children tomorrow.' He sighed heavily. 'Shit, is this too big? Are we mad doing this? Will we ever get away with it?'

'I don't know whether we'll get away with it,' Kate replied, 'but they need to learn English, and at some point we'll need to make them legal. If they're ill I can't just help myself to antibiotics. The last batch will never be noticed, it was too small. But Tom, I could be struck off.'

'Make them legal? That'll never happen, not in a million years. We'll be fobbed off with a huge amount of paperwork and then wait for it to filter through a system. In the meantime, they'll be sent to Alcatraz then deported. Put on the next boat back like human livestock in freight.'

'Will it be that bad, Tom?' Her forehead furrowed.

'It's not going to be a bed of roses. I mean, look at the building – it sends shivers down my spine when I see it. Rolled barbed wire that would shred you alive if you tried to scale it. Windows so far up from the ground that to even try and reach them your fall would kill you. And then that deep ditch surrounding it, not even filled with water. Just another white man's obstacle to keep unwanted people imprisoned. That's why our children can't get caught, and can't go back.'

Kate swirled the wine around her glass and watched as the caught droplets slid down the curved edge. 'You're like him,' with her stare fixed on the trickling drops. She tilted her glass, allowing the wine to catch it. Tom watched her face. Her gaze was mesmerised and her thoughts were falling like the drop of wine.

Tom lifted her chin with the crook of her finger and smoothed his thumb on her cheek. And smiled.

Tom rinsed out the empty glasses and placed them in the dishwasher. Before turning out the light, he went back over to the model village. *What's the red part of it?* he wondered. *How deeply is this little boy thinking? What has he seen to draw so much red?* His index finger snaked around the houses and rested by a cluster of them under them a drawing of a red cross. The pool of red was further away past some trees and out beyond the village. *What does any of it symbolise?*

He double-locked the front door, turned out the light and went upstairs.

The harsh buzzing of his watch woke Tom at 5.30 a.m. He peeled one eye open before reaching his arm out from under the duvet and turning off the alarm. Leaving his bedroom door ajar he crossed the landing; the children were still asleep. They were oblivious to the movements from outside their room, the sound of the shower drenching his body and the buzzing of the electric toothbrush. Nor did the cacophony of morning birdsong seem to stir them.

It was the voice from the top of the stairs that stopped Tom from opening the front door fully and leaving the house for an early morning run.

'Please.'

Tom stood with his face to the door, sighing into it, wishing he had imagined the voice. All the talk last night with Kate and how they would manage the whole nightmare of a situation was now playing in real time. *Only it isn't real*, he kept telling himself. *It really is just that I'm imagining it.*

'I come you?'

He pressed his head into the door. The voice *was* real. With the words he knew would come at some point, but he wasn't ready to deal with them, to even know how to deal with them.

He turned around. Amanuel stood at the top of the stairs in his shorts and t-shirt.

'You don't have running shoes,' Tom replied, knowing that wasn't the only reason why taking him for a run was impossible.

Amanuel looked down to his bare feet. 'I have running feet,' he said.

Tom's face broke a smile. He had no answer to that. He exhaled, tipping his wrist, glancing briefly at the small black screen, it was 5.52 a.m. He pursed his lips as if thinking over the question, then: 'You're too small. You won't keep up.'

'My feet run.' And there he stood, his head held high, his shoulders back, arms folded, his stare on Tom. His eyes did not leave Tom's face, drilling to the back of his skull, and he didn't flinch.

'Wait,' Tom replied. He pushed the door to and slipped up the stairs, and crept past Amanuel. He poked his head around the bedroom door, Abrihet lay in a foetal position under the covers; a slight murmur came from her. Tom turned back and put his finger to his lips.

'Shhh, quietly then, while she sleeps.' He went to walk down the stairs and that's when he felt the heat of the small boy's hand in his, and a static warmth snaked down his spine.

The lock clicked behind them and together they walked down to the beach, Amanuel's hand still in Tom's. Tom in running shoes, Amanuel with bare feet.

The saltiness of the sea breeze caught in Amanuel's throat and pushed its way down into the depth of his lungs. His eyes watered as the wind whipped about him, and he lifted his arm up to show Tom the goose bumps that prickled his skin.

'Here,' Tom crouched down and rubbed his arm, 'you're cold.' Amanuel stared out into the sea, listening to the sound of the shells and pebbles as they scuttled up and down the beach, taken by the waves. Waves he had crossed, a grey expanse of coldness, bashing against the boat he had sailed in. Huddled together with others from places he didn't know, some of them not even speaking the same language as him. He stared out to the sky that fell into the sea, without chaos, without screams, without fear. It just slipped into the sea and a grey mass became one. His hand dropped from Tom's and then it happened.

With no warning his body turned, and he ran. His legs ran faster, his feet barely touching the ground, his t-shirt rippling around his tiny frame. All Tom could see of him were the soles of his feet as he ran faster into the wind, passing a line of rickety beach huts, an upturned sailing boat, a scrawl of fishing nets. Tom speeded after him, but Amanuel had gone, just a flash of his shirt in the distance. Then he stopped, his heart racing in his small fragile body, beating against his rib cage, pounding like the drums in his village. Drums in his village that would only be played when his people danced. Yet now, the drum in his own young body beat. Beat in time, and then he turned back on himself, his own melodic internal drum, pushing him back towards Tom. Tom crouched down, his own breathing out of time, and took Amanuel's arms either side with a gentle grip. 'You can't—'.

'I have running feet,' said Amanuel. And once more the warmth of his hand nestled into Tom's.

'Right, but you can't just run *off* like that, d'you understand?'

'I have running feet,' Amanuel said again.

Tom shook his head and shrugged, and together they walked back to the house. Not a word was spoken between them. But an understanding had formed that a small boy could run. Needed to run. Had run. The beat of a village drum existing in him.

Chapter Twelve

The front door clicked shut behind them. Amanuel followed Tom into the kitchen.

'Frosties?' Tom spun around, shaking the box of sugary cereal. A beam stretched across Amanuel's face.

'They were my favourite,' said Tom, 'when I was your age. They're *grrreat!*'

Amanuel's face lit up, and a chuckle that only ever comes from a child came from this small being. That infectious gorgeousness of a child's laugh. His arms clutched around his waist as he doubled over at Tom's goofiness. He didn't know what *grrreat* meant, but when Tom said it, he pulled the silliest of faces and sounded nothing like he normally did. Shaking the box and shifting his head from behind it, Tom said it again.

The tears streamed down Amanuel's face as his body fell from side to side until his tummy ached. He held his sides, shaking his head to stop. Tom shifted to the other side on the counter and swung Amanuel up in his arms, and the small boy laughed like he used to when he had chased alongside Jeremiah in his truck. High in the air with his knees scrunched up until Tom slowed down, tweaked his nose and plonked him onto the stool, then left him to delve into his bowl of sugary golden flakes drenched in cold creamy milk, his small face stained by streaks of happiness. The spoon he could now use expertly, and orange juice replaced the water he'd first drunk. He'd still pick up the bowl by cupping his hands as if to drink from the pool, and he'd guzzle the sweetened milk, leaving a huge milky smile that his tongue would lick up.

Tom pulled a stool up close to him and perched on it. 'Your picture, I like it. I like it a lot.'

Amanuel's eyes widened. 'My village.'

Tom smiled. 'Your village.'

Amanuel pushed the bowl away from him and clambered down from the stool. 'Abrihet, I go,' he said. Tom watched as Amanuel left the room and went to wake his sister, his stomach now full of sugary goodness.

With the silliness of him at breakfast cleared away, Tom went back upstairs and moved quietly past the bedroom. From the bathroom door he could see Amanuel at the window, transfixed by the seascape. The gentle sound of the waves lapping up onto the beach left him mesmerised, and he inched closer and let the tips of his toes balance on the softness of the carpet. When a seagull swooped down from the greyness and perched itself on the window ledge, he gasped and fell back. It strutted along the ledge, its wing bashing against the window. The lightness of his fingers pressed against the pane of glass and the bird's beady eyes stared at him while it swiftly jabbed its long beak at his fingers. Amanuel snatched them back. In the distance a fishing boat sailed across the waves – visible, invisible, visible, invisible – as it powered itself across the water. The darkness of the clouds parted, and a glint of light caught on the window. The seabird soared off, screaming as it wheeled through the sky.

The lock on the bathroom door turned and the gentle running of water could be heard. Moments later, Tom crossed the landing with a towel wrapped around his waist. Amanuel turned towards Tom. 'I see bird who hurt people,' he said, 'he came again.'

'Hmmm, those pesky gulls. You're safe inside, they can't get in. Right, I have to get dressed and do some work. Are you okay with Abrihet?'

Amanuel nodded, 'I okay.'

Outside, the postman's whistling broke the otherwise quiet road as he strode up Tom's driveway and dumped a load of letters in his post box. Tom tilted the slats of his shutter, closing away the nosiness of the passers-by.

'Hello, Tom.' Abrihet stood at the door.

Tom looked up from his work. 'Hi there, Abrihet, you hungry?' She nodded. 'Your brother's already eaten. What d'you fancy, cereal or toast?

'Toast,' she said as she sat at the kitchen counter and waited. Next to her sat the small pile of books that Kate had brought over the night before, and Abrihet ran her hands along them.

'Have a look,' Tom said, pushing them closer to her. 'They're for you and Amanuel. Kate thought you might like them to help you learn some more English.'

They gleamed under the halogen lights, causing a reflection on their shininess. She tentatively opened the cover and gasped. A lion with a fluffy mane smiled back at her; she'd never seen a lion smile before. Her fingers stroked the softness of its mane and glided across the page to the tip of its tail. Her finger moved over to the words. 'Tuh huh ats not my li–on.' Tom stopped for a moment and moved around to where she sat, he put her finger under the letters again and placed his tongue between his teeth. The sound he made sounded like the snake when it shot out his tongue and the villagers would beat their sticks on the ground and watch it slither away.

She put her tongue between her teeth and made that sound too. 'Th-at's not my lion, his tail is too furry.'

'That's right, you see his tail, it's furry,' Tom smiled.

'Furry,' Abrihet repeated. 'Furry. Th, th, th.' She turned the page and saw the same picture, but this time the lion's nose was shiny. She smoothed her fingers across its nose: 'Shiny'.

'That's right, shiny.'

As she munched on a piece of toast with lashings of crunchy peanut butter, she turned each page. 'I like.' She slipped down from her stool and took her plate to the sink. She pushed the lever down and let the water run over the plate, her hand smudging around it, then shook it dry and left it on the side.

That morning, whilst Amanuel shaded in his paper, Tom helped Abrihet read from the books.

By the time Kate arrived the children had gone to bed.

'How was today?' she probed, hoisting herself onto the stool.

'Good! I became a teacher and Tony Tiger as well as an architect. Well, I kinda taught Abrihet some new words and sounds. I think she knows them, just doesn't recognise them. But she liked the furry lion book,' he laughed. 'Drink?'

'Yeah, I'd kill for a cuppa. Any more clues on who they are and why they're here? You know they'll want to go out at some point. They'll need to, for their own well-being.'

'That's kind of already happened.'

Kate tilted her head and her eyes creased at the sides. She moved the mug away from her mouth. 'Kind of?'

'Yeah, this morning I was about to go for an early run. They were both asleep, at least I thought they were. But Amanuel appeared at the top of the stairs and asked to come.

'But you said no, right?'

'I tried.'

'Tell me you didn't take him.'

He shrugged. 'I couldn't not. I said he was too small, he had no running shoes. But—'

'But ...?' Kate shook her head in disbelief.

'Okay, so what d'you say to a kid who eyeballs you, and I mean *proper* eyeballs you, and says, "I have running feet"? I couldn't argue that, so he came with me. It was early, and there was no one about.'

'And then what?' She pulled the mug nearer to her and cupped her hands around its warmth.

'He stood by the sea and watched the waves, he just stared out like he was in a trance and then ...'

'And then ...' Kate pushed.

'He turned, and he belted it, like a flipping Olympic runner, faster than me. He was gone like a rocket, his bare feet hardly touching the ground. He stopped right up past old Bert's boat shed, and then he turned and sprinted back to me. Not even with an inch of breathlessness. And then he slipped his hand into mine, looked at me, and that was it.'

'Did anyone see you?'

'No.'

'Okay, good – but seriously, Tom, we need a cover. I'll lose my job if I'm caught, and your name'll be mud.'

'I know. But his look, Kate – it hit me *here*,' he thumped his hand his on chest.

'I get it, I do.'

'What if we just carry on as normal, take them out? If anyone asks, I'll say they're a university friend's children, they're staying with me for a while as their parents are relocating. Just make it normal.'

'Relocating from where?

'I don't know, Kenya. Everyone likes Kenya.'

'So you're choosing a country based on everyone liking it?'

'Why not? Who doesn't like Kenya? Your old lot will think *Born Free,* Virginia McKenna, and your younger lot will just think the obvious safari, elephants, lions, David Attenborough. Where to go for a honeymoon.'

'Are you serious, Tom?'

'Deadly. They're not going to think, refugees, asylum seekers, migrants. Would you? I mean if I said *Kenya* to you, what comes into your head?'

Kate exhaled. 'Safaris, reserves, bucket list holidays.'

'So that's it, they're from Kenya and they're staying a while.'

'Okay so that works, but what about after that? They'll come a point when they need to be reunited with their parents. What about that part?'

'Man, I don't know! Let's just get through this part.'

Kate took a slurp from her tea. 'It's some part, Tom.'

'I know, but we can't do everything. The children will get scared and confused, and they need to just play normal.'

'Normal? None of this is normal – and what about their parents?'

'They weren't on the boat.'

'How d'you know that?'

'Because when I found her, she said it was her and her brother.'

'Listen, I've got a full surgery tomorrow, but I'll see what I can find on their parents, but with a whole load of nothing it's like looking for a needle in a haystack. I'll call you tomorrow – and, Tom ...'

'Yep.'

'Be careful on your runs. Seriously. I mean it.' Kate grabbed her keys and kissed Tom on the cheek, 'I mean it, see you tomorrow, gorgeous.'

Tom opened his laptop and googled "immigrant boat found on Deal beach".

No results found.

He scrunched his lips together and googled "bodies found drowned on Deal coastline".

He tapped his fingers on the edge of his laptop, the page filled with article headlines. He scanned them all, looking at the dates, scrolling down the page – 'Bingo!'

Migrants feared drowned in a major search and rescue operation off the Kent coastline. Search aborted.

'Found you,' he murmured, and closed his laptop and turned out the light.

The following morning after breakfast had been tidied away, both children stood haphazardly in the sitting room. Tom beckoned them to sit on the sofa. Abrihet sat first, perched on the edge, and Amanuel sidled up close to her, his eyes widening as Tom paced the floor trying to work out how he would explain any of it to them. And once he had explained it, would they even understand?

He sat on the leather pouffe and leant forward. 'Okay, listen up, guys.'

Amanuel tilted his head and reached for his sister's hand.

'Abrihet, both of you being here is illegal.'

Abrihet listened, her brow furrowed. 'I don't know your words.'

Tom scratched his head and his foot tapped repeatedly on the floor. 'Umm, sure, right, oh God. The boat, the boat you came on is not allowed.' He gestured with his hands, *not allowed*. He stretched his arm out angrily, 'Go home! D'you see, to come like that is not good with our government. Does it make sense?'

She nodded.

'Eritrea, where you are from, No! Go home!' waggling his arm with a *No* signal. He paced around the floor as if playing charades. 'Country with problems,' he gesticulated both thumbs down. 'Understand?'

She nodded.

'Okay great. My country,' he stopped. 'Well, they like Kenya. You know like the furry lion.' Even saying those words sounded crass to him.

She squinted. 'But not like my people,' she said.

He rubbed his fingers across his forehead and then dragged them through his hair. He had just told two children who had run from something so treacherous that they were not liked. God knows how many months, years, it had taken them to get here – and he'd just told them they weren't wanted. That the country they had escaped to for safety wouldn't help them, didn't want to help, didn't care to help them – but did like lions and zebras and honeymoons under canvas.

He pulled up the pouffe and leant forward, his legs astride. 'It's difficult. If you stay with me, your only hope is to pretend. To pretend you're Kenyan, that your parents are from Kenya and great friends of mine. Otherwise they'll take you. The government, police, border control. They'll *take* you,' he blurted.

'Why?'

'Because politics, laws, ignorance.'

'But why?' she asked again. Her eyes fixed on his.

'Why—'

'Why save us, if you do not like us?' Abrihet asked.

'Not me! *I* like you. But I'm not everyone.'

'White people, kind people. Tiger safe.'

Tom diverted his look to Amanuel and the words he had just spoken. Six words that meant everything to this small boy; every truth he knew came from his lips. A child full of innocence, uncomplicated, a simple existence, who saw the simplicity of humans and the colour of another person's skin that gave them the hope they had been craving. Tom felt his eyes sting with tears.

'The kind doctor, he called Doctor Sam.' Amanuel folded his small legs and arms, and his full lips pouted and his eyes widened. 'White people, kind people, they like cricket and Manchester United.'

Tom grazed his teeth along his bottom lip. His hands turned in on each other and he nodded his head up and down slowly, then inhaled and exhaled audibly. His nostrils flared a little as he tried to force the tears back and attack the sentence he needed to say.

'I know, little fella.' He bit the inside of his cheek. 'I know,' he said again, his eyes fixed on both of the children who sat in front of him. His own eyes mirrored the eyes of the people on the boat. The children had seen that look before, when death stares you straight in the face, snatches from you the most loved and treasured beings in your world and leaves your heart dull and aching. A breaking that can never be fixed. Where every part of your body wants to scream a howling noise with that feeling of hope shot to pieces and a grief that swallows you whole. The children knew the face they were staring at; they had seen it before. Together they sat in the room for what seemed a lifetime. All holding onto the same feeling. Loss.

The only sound was the faint swishing from the dishwasher as the water washed around inside it.

'Kenya is nice,' Abrihet finally said. Then she turned to her younger brother and explained in Tigrinya that from now on they would say they were Kenyan, should anyone ask. And Tom was a great family friend. He was like the kind doctor, and now they would stay with him in safety in the country where Manchester United were from and cricket was played.

And all would be well. All *would* be well.

Chapter Thirteen

Adi Ada, Eritrea

Sam walked through the village towards Anbessa and Bamidele's home. The months were rolling past and he'd been there almost a year. The enjoyment of the Sabbath couldn't come any quicker for him. His six days at the medical centre were long, although long days spent with Elisabet made them go fast, and when Tim arrived with his supplies he timed it at a better hour of the day, when they could chill for a while on the veranda with a cold beer. But when the cockerel crowed from villager's rooftop on a Sunday, Tom would roll back over and let it crow until even a goat would bleat loudly to hush it. He embraced every Sunday like a warm hug, a day when he could venture out and see more of the country he had made his home.

He would often drive to the once-Italian city of Asmara, about an hour away, and wander the streets that were littered with cafés, bars and Italian restaurants. He'd meander through the small back streets that had names like Via Bologna, Via Trieste and Via Venezia, where the houses were built in Italian colonial style. Where culture and the arts were plentiful, satisfying the appetites of the upper classes and businessmen back then. A city which Italians saw as their *seconda Roma*, the local people as their Holy City, and Sam as a romantic dream metropolis. He would while away the day in a city steeped in history, where once the opera house would have been visited by the privileged few, and the Asmara Cinema; then there was the Romanesque cathedral that stood majestically, resounding loudly in its dominance of the religious faith.

From his favourite restaurant, La Dolce Vita, he'd sit and snatch a phone conversation back home while demolishing his bruschetta and carbonara, and delight in an affogato to finish. It was the only time he could have a decent conversation or Facetime his brother or Kate, where the wifi was on another level; he'd plan when his next visit home might be, although it was hard, as he was the only doctor in the village and he couldn't leave without any cover. Sometimes his calls were ended abruptly, as he needed to dash to the cinema where they screened the English football matches and Manchester United were playing, and he'd dodge the classic yellow Fiat 500 taxis that tootled about and the old VW beetles hurtling along.

This Sunday, though, he'd have to visit Asmara another time, as he had accepted the warm invitation to Anbessa's and Bamidele's.

He knocked on the wall of their home.

'Ah, Doctor Sam, you made it! I believe Bamidele's inside,' Anbessa said as he came from behind and patted Sam hard on the back and shook his hand, 'I've been feeding the goats. Let me call her. Bamidele, Bamidele, we have company.'

Rubbing her hands on a cloth and swishing it over her shoulder Bamidele hurried to the door, her smile huge and the bangles on her wrists jangling.

'Doctor Sam, please, please come through.'

The house was split into three, two bedrooms behind walls of reed and a kitchen that homed their family space. Colourful woven rugs hung from the walls like a tapestry of wallpaper, clay urns rested along the wall of the kitchen for the water that Bamidele would collect daily, joining the other women.

An opening led to their simple shower and washing area. Cinnamon infused the air, and the warm aroma of coffee tingled Sam's nose.

'I have made some cinnamon breads,' she said, patting the chair, 'so please take a seat.' She left and busied herself in the kitchen area before returning with a delightful spread of sweet cake-style breads. Sam took one, 'Bamidele, these are delicious!' He licked the sugary cinnamon coating from his fingers.

She smiled, 'Thank you. I have something else.'

'Wow! You do? I'm not sure I have room for any more,' he chortled.

'Doctor Sam, please, this is for you.' Bamidele handed him a colourful string of beads joined with a clasp. 'Let me.'

Sam lowered his head and let her place the handmade jewellery around his neck. 'These are the colours, that my boy, my only boy, has imagined for so many years, and now you have realised his imagination, to you we owe everything. You are a good man. You are truly a good man.'

Tom took Bamidele's hands in his and clasped them. 'Thank you.' As the three of them enjoyed fresh coffee with the sound of the drums beating outside, Abraham fell into the hut excitedly with his friends, 'Doctor,' he grinned.

'Abraham, how are you feeling?'

'I'm feeling good, Doctor. Mum, Dad, I'm going to the mango grove, the ghetto blaster's being played – d'you hear it, man? Good evening, Doctor. Good evening.' His face was beaming from ear to ear and his body was already moving with the beat that reverberated around the village. He raced away into the night, filled with music, and leaving at the side of the door his hammerkop-headed cane. It had been left against the wall for weeks now, but its handle still held within it a genuine care and warmth and feeling of a young man who had once been blind.

'You see how happy my son is. This is because of you, Doctor,' Bamidele said. 'This community is a good one. The people, they're good people, they're kind, they're deserving. And that's what my boy, my only child, can now see. Not only hear it and feel it, but *live* it now with the vision you've given him.' She stopped. She looked towards her husband, who stood with an assured pride for the woman who had guided their son from birth to adolescence. 'But there are times,' she continued, 'when I would wish for my son to be as before. He was protected from the brutality that has been here. The sights hidden from him.'

'Bamidele, not now,' her husband lay his hand on hers. 'Tonight is a good night.'

She nodded, and smiled gently at her husband. 'You're right, Anbessa.'

'Right, I have to leave and prepare for tomorrow's clinic,' Sam laughed. 'The day has run away with us. My, I got here when the sun was out – and now, well it's not.'

Anbessa extended his hand and placed it on Sam's shoulder with a firm grip. 'God has heard.'

Sam smiled, 'And I have learnt something too, Anbessa. Anbessa means *lion*. You're that too, the protector of your family. And Bamidele, I'll hold this necklace very closely to my heart. Thank you.'

He walked back through the village and past the children who danced and laughed and played joyously. He gazed over at the huddle of men who sat about with their coffee and clapped intermittently as the drum played and the children moved in rhythm. He wandered past the mango grove, where he saw Abraham congregating with his friends, his hands cupping their faces, and smiling broadly. The faces he had once not seen, the laughter he had not witnessed with his eyes, and the moves of their bodies as they danced to the local radio station booming out on the ghetto blaster. Sam smiled inwardly, seeing how a procedure seen as simple in the first world had given a young man his life back. He moved away from the noise and down towards the pool, in the trees above. Katumba came down from the mango trees and followed him.

Sam sat on the bank and kicked off his shoes, letting the water run between his toes, its coolness tickling his feet. He picked up a loose stone from the dusty ground and turned it in his hand; its smoothness emulated the softness of Elisabet's skin, a momentary touch he could not remove from his mind. He grazed his thumb along the rounded edge and then flicked his wrist back and watched as the pebble glided with two hits of the water before it disappeared, leaving only a ripple in its wake.

The quiet calm engulfed him, the silence drowning out the noise of the village. The rustle of the mango tree leaves whispered in the breeze. Two dragonflies hovered and danced above the pool, together yet apart. A snake slithered through the rocks until it submersed itself in the coolness of the water and then slid onto a rock where it basked in the dead heat. The sun dropped in the west, bidding a farewell and casting a red warmth across the still water, turning it into a liquid gold.

Sam's thoughts meandered from the moment he had given the letter to Kate to read, to now – a world so different to where he'd come from. The serenity of an African paradise, simple and wanted, had drawn him in. Pulled him into its heart where an indefinite timeframe had seemed impossible, and yet now leaving it was unimaginable. His hand touched the beads around his neck. He exhaled; the village was home.

He cast his memory back to his first night there, where he had been met by the frantic fear of the young mother Johanna and her baby Amanuel, who had clung so hard to his own precious life. He had met Abel, an elder whose wisdom of life had remained with him. Then Abraham, who had settled for a life of no sight, who now danced with his friends, with faces he could see now. Johanna's daughter, Abrihet, who lay recovering from tuberculosis. Jeremiah, whose golden grin remained throughout the day as he sold his produce from the open back of his wagon. And Elisabet, a woman who gave him that feeling that he'd never quite managed to feel. That feeling when your stomach somersaults and your mind is swamped with a beautiful intoxication.

Life *had* changed. Life had become richer than he could ever have anticipated, and yet Bamidele had left him with a feeling of something unknown. He wondered, why did she sometimes yearn for blindness? What secrets lay hidden in this village?

He hadn't noticed the company that had joined him until he turned slightly. 'Katumba, can you skim a stone?' He drew up another stone from the ground. The monkey sidled up closer to Sam. Perched upright on his haunches, his face with a mischievous look, his small amber eyes twinkled. Sam's pebble plopped along the water, Katumba cocked his head, then somersaulted frantically, shrieking and clapping his spindly black leathery hands.

'You like that, right? Here.' Sam smiled broadly as he eased a pebble towards the monkey, nudging it across the earth. *Will he skim it? And if Katumba does, will anyone believe such a fantastical story? Of course they won't.* The smooth-edged pebble skimmed the surface of the water, leaving in its track three ripples that spread out from their centre. Katumba leapt in the air, shrieking with excitement. He puckered his lips and scratched the back of his ear. Sam sat open-mouthed. 'You *did* it, Katumba, you understood me! You just skimmed a stone, little dude.' The monkey tilted his head and twitched his black nose, then somersaulted madly – one, two, three times. Sam threw back his head and roared with laughter. The monkey somersaulted again, shrieking loudly as he did so.

The impatient babbling in the treetops from the troop of monkeys beckoned their young one back into their fold. A herd of elephants moved softly in the last of the light towards the water's edge, the smallest staying close to its mother, glances from their eyes speaking of a steady love for their family. In a mass of grey, they came and drank before they stood and swayed slowly.

The sun cast its final glow over the water, leaving only the silhouettes of a monkey and man side by side in the silence, as if the golden orb had fallen beneath the water to swim with the fish and cast an underwater light onto what lay beneath. A cloak of black crept in, appearing like magic at each sunset. The mating call of an owl echoed as it swooped low overhead, and Sam lay back and watched the night sky as the galaxies tumbled and darted in the sheet of black. Pushing himself back up, he brushed the dust from his feet and wriggled his feet back into his trainers, leaving the quiet of the night to the wild night creatures.

Over the coming days, sitting by the pool and watching the sky envelop the wild, Sam would skim stones, and beside him Katumba would sit too. Whilst Sam sliced through a mango, Katumba would wrap his lips around the fruit, leaving just the stone in the middle. Sam taught the monkey how to perfect the art of skimming. And when the troop of monkeys in the trees would shriek out, the furry creature would dart off, shimmying up the trunk to join them. There was a tranquil calm that Sam would find by the pool, a place where he could let go of the hot, sticky days at the medical centre and allow the quiet to coat him.

He hadn't noticed the figure behind him.

'May I join you?' she said, crouching down beside him.

He patted the ground beside him, 'Sure.'

'You've been quiet over the last few days.' She spoke almost in a whisper.

'Just thinking about stuff.' He took up a stone and smoothed his finger over its edge.

'Stuff?'

'Something Bamidele said the other evening.'

'Are you going to tell me?' She pushed her body forward and tilted her head towards his face.

He sighed heavily. 'She said she wished she could have been blind, to not have been able to see what had happened. Or something like that. Anbessa stopped her from saying any more. Why did he stop her?'

'This is Africa,' Elisabet cast her eyes out to the water. A crane flew above and landed, its long beak diving down and capturing a fish. 'An unease of people, faiths, greed, sadness.'

'But every country, city, town, village has that.'

'Not like here. The women and children can be raped by the men who know nothing but corruption, the people are stolen, the men here are slaughtered. Families brutally attacked, children orphaned, witnesses to the torturous trauma. The girls are sexually abused in a way that nobody can forget. And why? … greed, illegal greed? You haven't seen what Bamidele has seen, what any villager has witnessed. It will happen. That is the sadness, and that is why she would think her son was once protected from it.'

'And you, Elisabet? Have you seen it?'

She nodded, her eyes filled with the tears that she'd shed for many. 'Yes, I've seen it. In the mission hospital, where I worked in my training, a young girl came in and when she couldn't take a seat and quietly touched behind her, then I knew it was an unspeakable kind of suffering. I don't know if they realised she was pregnant. I don't know if they even realised she was a person.' She took her hand and placed it on the stone that Sam held in his hand. She offered him a smile. 'Teach me.'

His eyes rested on the touch of her hand, her skin as smooth as the pebble he held. He moved his body toward her and searched the depth of her eyes, the soft contour of her cheeks and the fullness of her lips. Her eyes stayed fixed on his. Taking both her hands he pulled her up to her feet.

'So, crouch down like this.'

She copied him.

'Keep your eye on the water, take your wrist back, now flick it.' He held her as she did this. 'See, three skims. You did it. Katumba got three, too.'

She furrowed her brow. 'Katumba? As in Katumba the monkey skimmed a stone?'

A broad smile stretched across Sam's face. 'He sure did; he's pretty damn good.'

'You and this monkey. I've never seen this before. You skim stones and eat mangoes together like he's become your friend. How did you do it? Nobody has come close to the monkeys here. I mean they're naughty and loud, but they've never come down from the trees.'

'Search me, I just get on with him. I'll teach him cricket too,' he laughed. 'Come on, let's get back. I'm starving.'

'Do they say in England a man's best friend is his dog?'

'They do.'

'And you have a monkey.'

His smile was one of happiness that extended to his eyes. 'And I have a monkey.' A glint of mischief sparkled in his eyes. He tossed his head, beckoning her to walk with him.

And there she watched him just a step ahead of her with a smile captured in her own head.

Chapter Fourteen

Kent, England

His face pressed up against the bars, his small hands gripping the cold iron railings, his eyes widening as he stared into the enclosure.

'Don't put your fingers inside.' Kate knelt low down by Amanuel's side and jerked him back slightly. He pulled his fingers away and tightly held onto the soft cuddly bear Kate had bought him to comfort him when they had first arrived.

'Why you keep like this?' he asked, peering through the railings at the tiger as it padded the stretch of its terrain, sideways glancing at the other faces peering in at it before slumping down at the fallen trunk of an old tree, its body thumping to the ground, its face watching the crowds as they ooh-ed and ahh-ed at its size and ferocity. It curled its upper lip and snarled at the audience it had.

'To keep it safe.'

'Who want him, why safe?' His button nose protruded between the bars. 'Like elephants?' His brow furrowed. He peered more closely at his teeth. 'He eat me?'

'He'd eat all of us,' she laughed. 'Gobble us all up for breakfast.' She tickled his tummy. 'But he's safe in there and we're safe out here.'

'He's *grrreat*,' he whispered under his breath.

He held her hand tightly and looked back at the tiger. Its eyes creased, and it snarled again, showing the sharpness of its teeth. He dared not look too long and pushed closer to Kate's side.

Tom and Abrihet had already reached the monkey enclosure by the time Amanuel and Kate joined them. Three monkeys sat on an overhung branch where the fronds of leaves tickled the lagoon below. A smaller monkey chased about the low-hanging branches before dangling upside down and shrieking noisily. Amanuel giggled at the monkey's playfulness – it was more daring than the others and was showing off. It somersaulted on its branch before snatching a banana from a bunch that lay close by. Its lips smacked about the banana as it sat, its eyes soulful amid the brown fur of its face. It stared at Amanuel in sudden quiet contemplation and curiosity.

'Katumba,' Amanuel whispered through the high bars. The monkey shrieked and hurled himself up the branch and swung playfully from the trees. 'Katumba,' he said again. Kate brushed the back of his head and smiled down at him. She had no idea what he'd meant and didn't ask.

'Hot dog! Who wants a hot dog for lunch?' Tom asked. The two children looked at him quizzically, unsure why he'd ask such a question; the day was pleasant, but to them it felt pleasantly cool – the sun was not beating down, and the ground was not baked hard. *So, why would a dog be hot? And why would we want to eat a hot dog?* The sweet aromas of the caramelised onions sizzling at the hot dog stand wafted through the air. Tom grabbed the children's hands and marched them towards the stand where an orderly queue was forming. A cheery man stood behind the stand, his skin white and pasty, his smile broad. But from the queue there was no sound, there was no banter or cheerful melodic voices, no vibrant colours or baskets to fill. There was no chatter between the people as they waited. Just faces behind faces, all looking ahead, solemn and dull. The men took out their wallets and paid, and the women stayed close by. There were no herbs or spices, sacks of coffee or animals. Amanuel and Abrihet watched as notes with the Queen's head were exchanged for very little. They shuffled forward, Amanuel's eyes firmly fixed on the vendor's mouth, waiting for the golden grin to come, like Jeremiah's. It never came.

Two figures cast a shadow over the four as they approached the front of the queue. A radio buzzed from behind: 'Charlie, Oscar, Romeo, proceed.' The volume dropped. Helmets sat on short-back-and-sides haircuts, and shoes were sturdy with a polished gleam to them. One of the men twizzled his radio volume, then his hand reached out and held the small shoulder in front of him. Tom froze, while Kate held Amanuel's hand more tightly and threw a sideways glance at Tom. The hair on the back of Tom's neck stood up, the palm of his hands began to sweat, his heart thumped against his ribcage. He pulled Abrihet in closer to him.

'Think you lost something,' the officer said. Amanuel turned around and stared up at him. His eyes widened as the two men towered above him.

'Found on the floor by the monkeys,' the officer said holding out Amanuel's bear.

The second policeman looked the children up and down.

'Thank you,' Kate said, breathing deeply as she took the bear and crouched down to Amanuel. 'Here you are, darling,' she said as she nuzzled the cuddly toy into his chest, 'we can't lose Bruno, can we?' She looked up at the police officer. 'Thank you,' she said again. 'That would have been a tearful car journey … you know how …' She fell silent.

The policeman looked into her eyes for a long time and then back at Amanuel, and flicked his glance to Abrihet.

'You're welcome. Don't want to report him missing, do we?' he said, twiddling with his knobs again.

Kate murmured a nervous laugh. 'Gosh no.' The police officer looked the two children over again and then back at Tom and Kate. His radio crackled: 'Charlie, Oscar, Romeo, sighting at the east exit.' Kate stared at the radio.

'Enjoy your day,' the man said, winking at Amanuel, 'and look after Bruno.' The officers turned and headed off. Amanuel continued to watch them as they walked away, their hands by their sides.

Kate exhaled and turned to Tom, 'I don't know about hot dogs, but I could murder a gin!'

Amanuel's legs swung on the bench. He contentedly clutched a soft bun, oozing with ketchup and American mustard smothered over a frankfurter. He'd had no idea that the men had the power to take him. That they were dressed like the people in the detention centre, and that he could have been like the tiger, trapped behind bars, slumped on a concrete floor with a metal bed and a toilet in the corner, hemmed in by whitewashed walls and a small barred window to allow a chink of light into the room. He'd had no idea that this was what Tom had meant when he'd said the children weren't wanted. So Amanuel just sat with his bear, so quickly named Bruno by Kate, eating a hot dog while the ketchup dribbled down his chin.

Abrihet gazed ahead, her stare transfixed by the moving bodies in front of her, all idling their way to some place. She hadn't realised how tightly she'd been holding her hot dog until she caught the ketchup with her finger before it fell onto her front.

'Those are not our friends?' She stared into the distance. 'Those men, we must be careful, not drop bear again,' and she took a bite from her bun.

Tom's gaze too remained fixed ahead. 'Yes,' he said.

The zoo had been their first outing out since they'd arrived, and although nobody had queried the colour of the children's skin compared to Tom's and Kate's, the fear that escalated in their bodies was immeasurable and the same. A lost bear could have changed everything. A lost bear could have made them become as one with the tiger. Yet whereas the tiger's capture had made it safe, their capture would return them to a place they had run from, where two parallels were infinitely different, and they would not be different.

Her eyes flicked rapidly as she stared out of the window trying to focus on at least one building before it disappeared as Tom sped past the string of terraced houses before veering onto the slip road for the motorway. The grey skies hung low, a fork of lightning split the sky and darkness dropped. The mellifluous sound of the windscreen wipers eased one small boy into sleep, his head drooping with heaviness. Abrihet shuffled a little closer, allowing him to rest against her. A line of dribble ran from the side of his mouth and he snuffled in his sleep.

The indicators on the car flashed and bleeped, and the near-silent purr of the engine stopped. Tom eased the passenger door open, Abrihet climbed out and Amanuel's head dropped further, hanging to one side. Tom gently cradled his head and undid his seat belt before scooping him up as he brought himself out with Bruno. The car's locking system flashed, they walked a few steps to the house and Kate closed the front door behind them, shutting out the outside world from seeing.

But the outside world had already seen.

Tom threw his keys down on the ledge in the hall and climbed the stairs with Amanuel in his arms. His head still resting on Tom's shoulder, with the dribble now dried, leaving a crusty white trail on his chin.

'I'll be down in a minute. I'll just get this little chap into bed.' Tom eased the bedroom door open with his foot. Amanuel still slept as Tom pulled back the covers and lay one exhausted little boy in the bed. He teased off his blue pumps and snuggled the cover over him. Amanuel snuffled in his sleep and turned his body in, snuggling deep below the duvet, and there he slept with his bear.

Kate had already made a beeline for the kitchen, her stomach reminding her that they'd had only munched on a hot dog since leaving the zoo.

'Are you hungry, Abrihet?' she called out.

'Yes.'

'Me too, I'm ravenous.' She flung open the cupboard doors and scanned the shelves. 'How about, hmm what have we got? … beans on toast. How does that sound?

Abrihet nodded.

'Well, that little man's out for the count,' Tom said.

'Fancy beans on toast, Tom?'

'Sure, why not. D'you want that gin now?'

'Love one. Just a small one, though.'

Abrihet pushed the beans around her plate before scooping them up with her toast. They were soft and sweet, and the sauce tasted not dissimilar to the hot dog sauce, just thicker and sweeter.

'His name Amanuel,' she said as she skilfully moved the beans and doubled over the toast as if it were a chapati or flatbread.

Kate looked up from her plate. 'Yes,' her brow furrowed.

'Not Darling – you say Darling. His name, Amanuel. Now they know, you say the wrong name.'

Kate took her hand, but Abrihet pulled hers away. Kate shot a nervous glance at Tom, 'Aww, Abrihet, *darling* is a word, umm, it's a kind word, that's what we call people here. People we like and love. Maybe you have a word in Eritrea like this. A good word.'

'So, the men in hats know this word?'

'Yes, they know this word, they will use this word too.'

'Oh,' she said. 'And they think we Kenya people?'

'I don't know.'

'So, they take us anyway?'

'No, they won't take you.' Kate shook her head vehemently and cast a look towards Tom. 'Tom and I won't let them take you. D'you understand?' She bent herself down to the stool and clasped Abrihet's hands. 'We won't ever let them take you. I promise. Ever.'

'The kind doctor, he always say that word.' Her eyes stared into Kate's, watching the blackness of Kate's pupils dilate. Abrihet's own eyes filled with tears, and she stared hard enough so the tears wouldn't fall. Her teeth clenched, holding back the emotions that would gush if she allowed them. But she wouldn't. She was an African girl, different to the white girls.

'What word?' Kate asked tenderly.

'*Promise*, he say this word to my people. Abraham, Abel, Jeremiah, my mother, me.'

'And did he keep it?'

'If *promise* is a word for seeing, saving, caring for my people. Then yes, he did. The kind doctor made a promise.'

'Then you believe me and Tom when we promise to keep you.'

She nodded. 'I hope.'

'Abrihet, I have something to ask you too.'

Abrihet looked at her, happier that Amanuel was safe and that *darling* was a good word. And the word *promise* meant they would be okay.

'When we were at the monkey enclosure today at the zoo, there was a small monkey. It seemed to connect with Amanuel. She stopped and tucked Abrihet's beaded hair behind her ear. He said *Katumba*. What does it mean?'

Abrihet stared at Kate and then at Tom and then back at Kate.

'Are you okay, Abrihet?' Tom said, leaning across the counter.

She sat silently, the beans on her plate displaced from the toast.

'Katumba is a monkey.'

'You mean it's the word for monkey?' Kate smiled. 'That's nice, I'll remember that.'

'No.' Her eyes glazed over and her lower lip dropped. 'No, Katumba is a monkey.'

'Right,' Kate's voice was just a whisper. She didn't ask any more.

'I go sleep, thank you.'

'Okay. Goodnight, Abrihet, sweet dreams.'

After Abrihet had gone upstairs, Kate cleared away the plates. 'What d'you think she meant, Tom? That Katumba's a monkey? D'you think she's getting confused with the books I gave her?'

Tom's eyes creased at the sides. 'Dunno.'

Kate fell into the sofa, leaving Tom to finish making her gin and tonic and grab a beer from the fridge for himself. The bottles clinked together as he teased out a Peroni – a little like Jenga, making sure nothing toppled. The light in the fridge beeped a reminder that the door had been open for longer than expected. He pressed the red ignition button for the chill bottle compartment. *Promises made by a kind doctor. Katumba was really the name of the monkey. So, it's true, after all – this little dude was part of Sam's life.* He closed the door of the fridge, eased the lid off his beer, and joined Kate on the sofa along with her gin and tonic. Closing down the memories of his brother flooding his mind.

'Want to stay the night, sink a few gins? The other spare room's made up.'

'Why not?' She snuggled further down into the sofa with a mound of cushions around.

The beaded braids fell onto Abrihet's cheeks as her head sank into the pillow. She tried to close her eyes, but the things she'd seen flashed pictures into her head. Her eyes filled with tears, and one by one they trickled down her cheeks silently. In a house where she could have everything she felt alone. Where every step outside the door was filled with fear; fear that she didn't think would have existed in a place where Manchester United were from and cricket was played. A land of hope that had suddenly become as dangerous as where she had run from. The faces she'd see in her mind, battering it like an uncontrollable kaleidoscope swirling and tumbling out of time. Uniformed men frightened her. Tigers in cages frightened her. Cages frightened her. And Katumba reminded her, the tears fell hard. *Katumba* – she said the word over and over again until the room fell silent and the only sound that came from her lips was *Ka*. The dark sky fell around her and the warmth of her bed cocooned her like the arms of her mother. Her memories were stolen by the night, allowing her to sleep. Allowing her mind to rest.

Chapter Fifteen

Six months had passed since the children had been found on the beach. The life they had left behind in Eritrea was almost a distant memory. Kate would buy them books and clothes from a supermarket just out of town. Tom would listen to them read and teach them to draw. The only problem that remained was that their own existence was still hidden from the outside world. Amanuel would build his community from pencil shavings each day, adding – more to the picture that was once their life. Only now it became like the true model development with the transparent glue Tom had bought and shown him how to use. Nothing would change; it would all stay fixed, just like his memory.

Each morning, Tom would run the same stretch of beach at 5.30 a.m., and with him Amanuel would run faster, like a gazelle, his feet still running feet. Every morning had been the same until one.

Amanuel stopped at the beach huts near the Zetland Arms, his faced creased as he winced.

'You okay, Amanuel?' Tom stopped, his body bent over double, his hands resting on his knees as he took deep breaths in and out.

'My side, it hurt,' Amanuel replied his hand rubbing the side of his stomach just below his ribcage.

'Stitch. We'll rest for five.'

'Stitch?' Amanuel asked, not knowing what Tom meant.

'The pain in your side, it's called a stitch. It will go, I promise.'

They slumped down on a craggy rock that bisected the lapping waves from the eroding banks of the shore. The sun, rising steadily, cast a reddish glow in the sky. The gulls wheeled ahead, snatching at fronds of seaweed that lay straggled on the beach.

'Tom?'

'Yep.'

'When it be all right?'

'When will what be all right?'

'When it be all right to be real again?'

'I don't know. Soon, I hope.'

'I counted the days.'

'Right.'

'It is one and eight and zero days.'

'That long – a hundred and eighty days?'

'Yes, a hundred eighty days in your house.'

'And you're happy, Amanuel? You and Abrihet are happy?'

Amanuel didn't answer. He simply gazed out to the sea and watched as the waves brushed up onto the shore taking the pebbles with them with a soft clattering sound.

'Are you okay, little chap?'

'You see that sea?'

'Yep.'

'It didn't eat us. It ate my people. How can I be happy? Where I am from the water did not eat people.'

Tom placed his arm around Amanuel and pulled him into him. Holding him tightly. Cupping his head against him while he nuzzled his lips against the short fuzz of his hair and sighed into him. His other arm squeezed away the pain of the stitch and the pain of the people eaten by the sea, his hand gently brushing along Amanuel's arm.

'And your water, is it like the sea, grey when the sky is grey, and blue—'

'When sky is blue?' Amanuel looked up at him. 'Blue? When, sky is red, water is too. Doctor Sam say sun had fallen into it and was lighting it below for all the fishes to see.' His voice lifted as he said *the fishes* as if it thrilled him inside and the fish really did see in the warm glow of the red light.

Tom swallowed. He hadn't heard either of the children say *Doctor Sam*, but today his name had been said. He swallowed harder, pushing down the lump that caught in his throat.

'Tell me about the red water.' He paused. 'And Doctor Sam.'

'The red water was where elephants drank from – mother, family, grandmother, baby. They drank there every day – and their trunks would hold so many leaves.' He laughed joyously. 'The mango trees fed them.'

'Sounds amazing. Mangoes – lucky elephants.' Tom picked up a pebble and turned it in his hand.

'You know, elephant is like my people,' Amanuel continued.

Tom looked at him curiously.

'My people are kind people. We are all together. We don't go. We stay, we love, we build our families together. We never leave. And when the wise and old elephant leaves our world, its family cries, like us. They love like us. You know this, Tom?'

'I didn't, no. And what else makes the elephants like us?'

'The wise grandparents look after the young. And when danger is there, the elders protect. And the elders of my people look after the young. No matter who you belong to. Every child is their child. And when elephants come to the red water to drink, they know they are protected by my people. Until they move away. But this time they stayed because bad men came ... Doctor Sam did that.'

'Did what, protect you?'

'He always protect us and Elisabet. But now, he did what you do now.' Amanuel opened Tom's fingers where the pebble rested in the palm of his hand. 'That. He do that – and then you know what he do?'

'No, what did he do?' Tom's voice caught in his own breath, as faint as a whisper.

Amanuel took the stone from him. He steadily scrambled the rocks where they sat and bent his body low on the pebbles, he threw his arm back and flicked his wrist and watched as the pebble skimmed across the waves as they brushed up onto the shore, every small crest pushing the silence of a life it had taken.

Tom's lips puckered and his eyes followed the stone as it glided across the water and then fell beneath the depths of the waves. He smiled and let out a soft sound of air from his nose. 'Three skims,' he murmured.

Amanuel turned and beamed. 'You see that, Tom, three times,' he said as he strode back to where he had been sitting, still holding the beam that lit up his face.

'He did that? He taught you something special,' Tom exuded an air of calmness, yet inside his heart cried out.

As small boys they had sat with their father skimming stones into the river that ran behind their house in Salisbury. They threw sticks off a tired rickety wooden bridge into the water, and would run to the other side to see whose would appear first. The memories of a childhood with his older brother were now memories being awoken in a small boy from Africa no older than him when he had first skimmed his stones and played Poohsticks. Was it fate that had brought these children to the beach, battered by the winds and sea? Was it fate that the sea had not eaten them, had let them be, to find what they were searching for? Happiness and hope. Two children from a village that Sam had spoken about to Tom. Elisabet, the name he would mention with an intimate tenderness in every conversation he'd have in snatched moments of respite on a mobile line that crackled and buzzed and lost connection. And Katumba, a monkey who Sam had joked could skim a stone as well as him – Katumba was real, and the elephants who drank by the sun-soaked pool were true too. The protection of a village by the elders; all stories that Sam had recounted. The two children he'd found on the beach had been part of Sam's life, the kind doctor who those children knew well. His big brother. And as yet they did not know that Tom knew him too, and loved him as much.

'You okay, Tom?'

'Sure.' He swallowed hard and slapped his hands on his legs. 'You ready to go? Stitch gone?' He pushed his shoulder into him, nudging him with fondness.

'Stitch gone, you promised.'

They ran past the rickety-looking beach huts, past the Crab Shack where the sign read CLOSED. Past the boat shed where Bert the old mariner worked, which lay still and quiet, and past a tired unseaworthy boat with the words *True Princess* inscribed along her side, resting on a wooden cradle, waiting patiently to be sanded down and painted, to then carve the waves once more.

As they neared the string of houses that overlooked the beach, the RNLI station's light ignited. A red Ford Cortina drew up and parked outside. The driver, one of the crew, looked up as Tom and Amanuel slowed their pace to turn into their driveway. Neither of them noticed the red car or even the figure opening up the station. But the figure had noticed them.

'I take shower, Tom and then we have Frosties, yes. They're G-R-REAT.'

Tom could still hear the laughter that came from the depth of Amanuel's belly as the bathroom door closed behind him. He could still hear the ringing of his words from behind the locked door, *They're G-R-REAT.*

It was whilst Amanuel was in the shower and Abrihet was still sleeping that conversations were being had. Conversations in the RNLI station, where two crew members sat over piping hot tea waiting for the rest of the team to arrive for a practice run on the stretch of sea that lapped around the breakfast diner at the end of the pier.

'That immigrant boat on the beach, d'you remember it, Steve?'

'The African one you mean, Rob? The orange dinghy?'

'Yeah, you sure there were no survivors?'

'Well the search was called off after twenty-four hours by the coastguard, just drowned bodies. Why? You think we should have looked for longer, mate?'

'Dunno. You know any black families on the seafront?'

'Can't say I do. Why?'

'Just saw a small black kid with a white man, running on the beach.'

'Right ... And?'

'Bit odd, innit?'

'Is it, mate?' Steve plonked another sugar lump into his already sweetened tea. The spoon clanged heavily against the mug. Rob watched as the tea slopped over the side. His eyes creased at the side.

'Bit odd,' he said again under his breath.

Amanuel poured lashings of cold milk over his cereal; the bowl was almost as big as his small face. His run on the beach with Tom would leave no flake left uneaten, right down to the very last mouthful, where the golden colour had turned into a pale yellow floppy and soggy flake. He picked up his bowl and drank the sweetened leftover milk, just as he had done the very first time he had been given cereal for breakfast, the bowl cupped in his hands as if drinking water from the pool.

He wriggled down from the stool and went to his drawing of his village that lay on the side, still with an array of teepee shavings over it. He carefully took it down from the side and lay it on the floor, the soft rug beneath him cushioning his full tummy. He held a grey lead pencil between his fingers, and began to draw what appeared to be clumps of large greyness by the red pool. Tom sat at his drawing desk and watched on. A red pool that he had thought signified something bad, something horrifically awful, was beginning to change. Amanuel smudged the shades of grey until what stood by the pool of red was in fact a small herd of elephants. Every stroke of his pencil smoothed across the page until the elephants' eyes stared back at the small artist. Eyes that could see into

149

the inner soul. Eyes that knew love and pain and grief. Eyes that simply knew. The trunk of another almost hugging the smallest, and the edge of the pool of red now had a splattering of grey where their feet had made their way to what Amanuel had spoken about at the beach.

The red pool bore no torturous significance. It was the water where the sun fell into it and lit beneath the surface for the fish to swim and see. And then the sky became littered with the whitest of twinkling dots and the moon shone in its ebony frame. The pool on a child's picture of his life was where his sister Abrihet would swim freely, swimming for fish. The pool of red was where Doctor Sam had skimmed stones and taught Amanuel to do the same, and had taught the smallest of monkeys to skim, too. The pool had brought happiness, love and protection, where the elephants swayed as they drank in the sun-scorched days.

Chapter Sixteen

Adi Ada, Eritrea

As the months turned into years, Sam became part of the community. He was still Doctor Sam, the kind doctor, but now he was the villagers' friend; he was one of them. Elijah and Johanna's children, Abrihet and Amanuel, were now older, ten and six. Amanuel was now just about old enough to help his father with the couple of goats they had, and the chickens, and Abrihet would help her mother and the other women fetch the water for the day from the well and harvest the fields of the farmers nearby. Abraham had realised his own dream to study and attended the college in Asmara, where he would learn to become an engineer.

Elisabet grew more beautiful each time Sam looked at her and yet he had always remembered what Tim had said: *African women are different.* But if *different* meant that he would let her go, then that was something he couldn't do. He had fallen in love with an African woman. His heart had fallen in love with Africa.

Katumba sat above in the treetop, watching as Sam swept out his house. He had done this at least four times that day. He rearranged the simple furniture outside and placed a water jug and glasses on the table. The sun belted down its heat, and he sighed from the sweltering warmth of its unrelenting power. He took up the broom again to sweep underneath the hammock. Katumba watched intently and lobbed a mango at Sam.

'Hey, Katumba!' The monkey threw himself about in somersaults, shrieking with each turn. He'd watched Sam all day busying himself. Katumba hurled another mango at Sam.

'Oi!'

Katumba ran the length of the branch and swung from it before hurtling himself into the hammock. He tilted his head and watched Sam sweep the ground yet again. Then he shrieked out loudly as if to say *why do you keep sweeping the ground and not eat mangoes with me?*

'Katumba, seriously I don't have time for your monkeying about. You know how important this to me. Isn't there a monkey in the trees who you quite like?' Katumba tilted his head and scratched his ear, then took the fallen mango and smacked his mouth around it, devouring the syrupy goodness and discarding the stone on the newly swept ground. 'Seriously, Katumba, I've just swept there. You'll attract the ants. Are you trying to sabotage my evening? Go to your family!' Katumba's amber eyes stared back at Sam, he cocked his head and a wave of sadness filled this little monkey. The tone of Sam's voice had changed. It wasn't a cheerful voice that came back at him, and he realised that he wasn't wanted in Sam's life, or at least not that day. He blinked and the twinkle of curiosity and mischief that had always been present in his eyes diminished. Instead they glossed over with a watery liquid, the sign of an emotional manifestation. He blinked several times and turned his shoulder away. If he had been human, he might have looked back over it one more time to question whether he really wasn't welcome. His small leathery black hands grabbed the smooth bark of the tree's trunk. The hammock swung gently as his nimble feet left it. He didn't shimmy with his usual speed and agility, but steadily climbed up high to the very top, where the canopy of green hid his existence from below. The only sound of his disappearance was the rustle of the leaves as he moved through them and the sway of the branches as he leapt away from Sam's house.

Sam picked up the broom and swept the ground again. The beaten earth was as clear as it had been before and there was no sign of the ants that would have descended like an army on a discarded mango stone. Like the absence of Katumba the stone too had not been left.

In a small village in Africa, a monkey had understood the words of a human and moved away. But a human had not understood that the tone of his voice had pushed away a creature, a creature who had feelings and emotions too.

Gently the hammock swung. A slight breeze moved around the village, snaking between the walls of each home and above, through the canopy of leaves of the fruit trees, like the whisper from the breath of a cold wind that would never share its harshness on this African earth, but only beckon a cry to relieve the community of the sultry heat that fell like a fire from the sky.

The beaded curtain of Sam's door rattled a little and there came a soft rapping on the edge of the wall.

'Sam, this is my father, Yonas, and my mother, Haben.' Sam turned and saw the figure of a woman in a vivid orange dress that cascaded like a waterfall of hot lava over her strong, womanly frame. He billowed his shirt a little from his chest, his heart pulsing against his ribcage. If he hadn't been a doctor, he would have been sure his heart had skipped a few beats. He moved towards them, his arms extended to welcome them both to his home.

'It's wonderful to finally meet you, Haben, Yonas.' He held Yonas's hand in a firm grip.

Haben, his wife, watched on as her daughter gazed at the man who had come from England and worked tirelessly as the community's doctor. The man whom Elisabet would speak of most evenings before she had finally left the family home and moved into the small village of Adi Ada, where her new life had begun. She watched her daughter's eyes as they lit up; she could see how much this man had inspired her only child, and she could see from the way Elisabet looked at him that her daughter's heart was filled with a feeling that made it beat ever faster. She had felt that way once, too, about her own husband. She recognised that fire in her own belly that came from an intoxication of love, desire and yearning.

But Sam was not Eritrean, and she knew that Yonas would not be easily charmed. Sam came from a country that was so different to their life in Africa. She too had hoped for her daughter to find and fall in love with one of their people. And now the once small girl, a girl who had transformed like a caterpillar becoming the most beautiful butterfly, desired something unfamiliar to them. Haben could see it clearly, and she smiled gently as she watched on.

'My daughter has told me much about you.' Yonas's hand dropped from their grip. 'You are from England, is that right?'

'Yes, London.'

'And you come here, why?'

'To better my knowledge of tropical diseases and write my medical papers.'

'You do not stay long then, for this?'

'Originally I had applied for a place at the Turkana Mission Hospital. But—'

'So why *here*?'

'Yonas, please. Your manner is not presentable. Let him finish.'

Yonas shot Haben a dismissive look. Haben took a small step back.

Sam allowed a smile to form across his face and his eyes confirmed a sense of well-being to Haben. 'It's fine,' he continued. 'I'm not a Christian, and the job at the hospital required someone of faith.

'And your faith is ...?' Yonas asked.

Haben shook her head slowly as if to slow her husband from his incessant tirade of questions.

'Does it matter, Father?'

'It matters.' His voice was gruff.

Sam took a deep breath and clenched his hands, rubbing his fingers between the clamminess of his palms. 'I don't have a faith. I don't believe in a God. It hasn't made me any less of a doctor. And as for staying in Adi Ada, my post is an indefinite one. I have come to love being here, and leaving is not something that I have even considered. I can't consider it.' He turned a little and his glance caught Elisabet's. 'Your daughter's a wonderful nurse, for one.'

Elisabet smiled back at him and a rush of heat brushed into her cheeks. Her mother smiled at her, and her head moved with a gentle nod of reassurance.

'Please forgive my manners,' said Sam. 'Would you like a drink? I have some cold beers in the fridge and fresh mango juice.' His hands trembled a little from the directness of Yonas's questions and his own assertiveness. 'Haben, please, what can I get you?'

'A little juice would be lovely, thank you.'

'Here, I'll help you, Sam. Father, you'll have a beer, I know that.'

Yonas nodded.

'Please take a seat by the hammock and I'll bring them out to you. The sunsets here are quite spectacular, although I'm sure you already know that. But for me it's another reason why leaving here would be difficult.'

'A *sunset* is keeping you?' His mouth turned down and his brow creased with lines.

'Yonas, please.' Haben shooed her husband outside.

'I'm sorry,' Elisabet said, taking the mango juice from the fridge. 'My father's a proud man and you're not from here. Give him time. He'll come around. It's just different. He's of another generation. Set in his ways. And, well ...'

Sam touched the edge of Elisabet's hand. He took the bottle opener and cracked open three bottles of beer and took an empty glass for Yonas. 'It's all good, I get it,' he said, and gently ushered Elisabet to join her parents at the table.

Sam tossed the bottle tops into the bin, and that was when he remembered the words Tim had said when he had first arrived: *African women are different.* Elisabet was different, but this was a difference he wanted, a difference he needed, a difference he loved. He loved Yonas's daughter, and he would love her all his life. He simply needed Yonas to see that. He wanted Yonas to respect him as a man of a different colour of a different faith, of no faith, who believed in evolution and knew that the idea of a man having one less rib because it had been used, according to the bible, to make Adam, was scientifically incorrect. The science outweighed the fable. But the colour of his blood ran through his veins the same as Yonas's beneath the different colours of their skin. And like Yonas he too loved Elisabet with every inch of his body.

The night sky began to drift lower upon the village, and a warm hue of light flickered throughout the village from flame-lit torches. They danced in a vulnerable way, the way fire does, pushed by the summer's evening breeze. Outside

Sam's hut, the lit torches attracted the night insects and a moth fluttered nearby, teased by the light but scorched by the heat.

Elisabet softly nudged her mother. The two women got up, to leave Sam and Yonas alone with their beers and the distant call of mating owls and the rustling sway of the branches as a troop of monkeys traversed their pavement in the sky.

'Please excuse us; I believe I'm needed in the kitchen.'

'Haben, no, it's fine, I can sort it,' Sam went to get up.

'Not at all – it'll be good for me to prepare your meal. It's been a while since I've had the opportunity to be with Elisabet, since she's moved to the village.' She cast a look over to her husband. 'And I suggest, Yonas, you listen with your ears and not speak with your mouth.'

Inside Sam's hut mother and daughter prepared the meal.

'You love this man, don't you?' Haben said, taking the spoon and stirring the thick stew that had gently braised for several hours.

'Yes. You know when your heart sings and your thoughts burst, and you can't wait to see his face, to hear his voice. When you will the night to speed along,' Elisabet said as she prepared the first *injera* in the skillet and skilfully cooked it until the batter formed a perfect disc, a little like a pancake. She scooped it out of the pan and placed it on the base of the large shallow plate. She poured another ladle of batter-like mix into the pan. 'I knew from the moment I first saw him,' she continued. 'Is that what love is? When even their slightest touch sends your body into spasm. When they catch you watching them, and you feel the heat in your cheeks burn. Since the first day—'

Haben turned to her daughter and her mouth gently moved into a smile and her eyes saw. 'Do you want to be with him?' She poured the stew over the unleavened bread, then she filled a small basin of warm water to take out with them. 'Elisabet?'

'It won't ever be possible, will it? Sam doesn't talk about his parents, so his own father will never give his permission. And Father would never agree! He's already said as much. Sam's not African, he doesn't believe in God. That's it.'

Haben held the water basin. 'Agree?' She rested the food on the side and cupped her daughter's face, 'We've just come to *meet* Sam, Elisabet. Do you want to marry him?'

'I was just thinking about his family; he has a brother who he phones almost weekly.' Elisabet let out a soft sound as she smiled.

Haben smoothed her daughter's face. 'I'll talk to your father. He can be a stubborn old fool sometimes, but he too knows the feeling of love and I will remind him of that. Come, the men will be hungry and one of them probably needs rescuing.'

Outside in the fading light, the two men sat. Sam still with a full bottle of beer, in his head turning over the words he wanted to say.

'Yonas,' he finally blurted out. 'I know I'm not from here and I'm not Eritrean and I never will be …' He could feel Yonas' sharp eyes on him. 'And obviously one of my reasons for coming out here was to be the community's doctor.'

'And you are that, are you not?'

'Yes I am, but I'm also part of this village. My stay here was never going to be short; my terms were indefinite. And you're right; originally, I was looking at a sabbatical at the Mission Hospital to write my papers and work on the advancement of medicines for tropical diseases. But I didn't get that post because, well … because I'm an atheist and it went against the values and ethos of the hospital. To live here with an indefinite contract wasn't a decision I took lightly. I understood what I was taking on. Can you not see that? I've been here for six years now; I've taught the children how to play cricket, and the men in the village now carve bats from the acacia trees. I'm their doctor, but I'm their friend as well. Does that not mean anything?' He stopped.

The corner of Yonas's mouth dropped to his chin. 'Six years doesn't mean you won't go away. It shows commitment for now – but that's all it shows.'

Sam closed his eyes, and with his head in hands he said, 'But I love Elisabet. I would you like you to give me your blessing.'

He waited.

His wait was long and unanswered.

That night Yonas and Haben lay in their bed in Asmara, about twenty kilometres away from Adi Ada. The lights from the street cast a dim glow through their window. Yonas turned restlessly under the covers and with each movement he huffed heavily.

'For pity's sake, Yonas, what is it? You've not lain still since you got into bed.'

'He wants to marry Elisabet. He asked for my blessing, woman. What d'you expect?'

'I assume you're talking of Sam here. And I hope you put him out of his misery and gave it.'

'I did nothing of the sort,' he huffed.

Haben sat bolt upright in bed. 'Are you telling me you said *no*, Yonas? What's wrong with you, man?'

'I will *not* allow it.'

'And what *do* you allow, Yonas? What is it you want for our daughter? That she runs away, that she elopes? That we never see her again. She loves him, do you not see that with your own stubborn eyes? Does he need the colour of his skin to be the same as ours, to care for and love our daughter, Yonas? Our daughter, d'you hear? She is not just yours. She's mine, too. I carried her for nine months, laboured with her, gave birth to her, kept her alive. You, you just *put* her there! And her happiness is what is important, not your pig-headed way. You know how it is to love.'

'He does not believe in God.'

'And … ?'

'It'll never work.'

'In *your* eyes – but you haven't even let it have a chance. I will *not* allow that.' She threw the covers off her.

'Where are you going?'

'I won't sleep in the same bed with you until you give your blessing. And I won't cook, either.'

'So, you'll starve me into submission.'

'Not at all, Yonas. You'll make yourself hungry and your nights will be lonely. You forget I too can be stubborn. Good night, Yonas.'

Chapter Seventeen

Kent, England

'Police Emergency.'

'Connecting mobile 07787 554364,' the operator said.

'Thank you. Go ahead, Caller. You're through to the police. What is the address or location of your emergency?'

The line went silent, just the heavy breathing of the caller.

'Go ahead, Caller, this is the police. Are you in any danger? I have your location as Seaview Parade, mobile ending in three, six, four. Do you need urgent assistance?'

'No.'

The line buzzed intermittently, just the sound of the heavy rasp.

At the other end of the line, steam from the caller's tea funnelled into the air. He stirred it with a slow repetitive motion, the spoon scraping against the bottom of the mug, grating it across the bottom like sharp nails on a blackboard. He clanged the spoon against the side, leaving a swirling ripple in the hot drink. A small bubble popped.

'Caller, do you need urgent assistance?'

The caller licked the spoon dry and placed it on the table. 'I've seen something. Something wrong.' The voice was low, gravelly, his breathing shallow. It carried a heavy Kent accent.

'Something wrong? Could I take a few details first? Are you in any danger?'

'Danger, me? No.'

'I have your mobile number ending in three, six, four. Is this correct?'

'Yeah, that's right.'

'And your name?'

'My name, you need it?'

'It'll be added to the details given. Are you in any danger? Are you alone?'

'I'm not in any danger. And yeah, I'm alone. But I wanna stay anonymous.'

'In order to help you I'll need to take some more details. Where exactly are you located?'

'My address is 9 Seaview Parade.'

'And the postcode, Caller?'

'CT10 5BY. But that's confidential, right?'

'The address you have given me is the RNLI station. Is this your correct location?'

'I need this to be off the record.'

'Caller, none of this can be off the record. You say you want to report a suspicious sighting, is this correct?'

'Yeah. A kid.'

'A child? And where's the child now? Are you with the child?'

'No! I'm alone.' The hands on the clock above the concertina door moved slowly around its face, the second hand edging its way towards the twelve. The caller's leg shook uncomfortably under the table. He bit the inside of his cheek, his eyes firmly fixed on the hands of the clock. 'The kid, he's with a bloke in one of them new houses along the beach front. The modern ones, you know the ones, the designer ones.'

'Do you have a description of the male?'

'Yeah, about six foot, brown hair, wavy, not short hair, you know what I mean? Like a surfer. Wearing running gear.'

'And the child?'

'Ain't one of us.'

'What d'you mean? Do you have a description of the child?'

'Red t-shirt, blue shorts, bare feet, coloured.'

'Caller, are you saying the child is black?'

'Yeah.'

'Can you give me a full description.'

'I *told* you! Red top, blue shorts, bare feet, coloured!'

'How old is the child?'

'Dunno, maybe seven or eight.'

'And the male? Could it be his parent?'

'He ain't one of us.'

'Caller, I have to advise you on your responses. Please refrain from using derogatory terms.'

'He ain't his dad. Wrong colour.' He stirred his tea again and licked the spoon, then put it down and played with the handle as it rested on the table, pushing it like a lever from side to side.

'The male is white, is this correct?'

'Yeah.'

'Do you have an address of the house?'

'Do you need the address? Can't I just report something that seemed sus?'

'Is the child in any danger? We'd need an address.'

'The immigrant boat that came in, the one a few months ago, you know the one.'

'There have been many. Can you be more precise?'

'The one they found by them designer houses, it was empty.'

'And you say a child you want to report as suspicious?'

'Yeah, ain't none around like their type.'

'Their type?'

'Yeah, coloureds.'

'Caller, do you have an issue with non-white people? I have to remind you again of the negative approach of referring to what you have seen as *their type* and *coloured*. This is inappropriate and racially aggravating. Is this address correct for us to send a unit down and assist, and take down any further details from you at the scene?'

'Yeah it's right, I want my name left out, though—'

The main door of the building where the caller sat clicked shut. The small hand on the clock rested at seven.

'Rob, you got the kettle on?' One of the RNLI crew walked into the room.

Rob cut off the call.

'Everything all right, Rob? You're sweating heaps, man.'

'Yeah, Steve. Kettle's just boiled.' He scratched his nails across his five o'clock shadow.

At the police call centre in Kent, the operator said, 'Hello, hello, Caller, can you hear me?' then stared at his screen, the cursor still hovering on the last word.

'Everything all right, Pete?'

'Not sure, Colin. Unusual report.' He pushed his chair back. 'How would you describe someone's ethnicity if they weren't white?

'Dunno, Asian, Black, South American, Indian ... depends, mate. Why?'

'Just had a report of a suspicious sighting, describing a kid as *coloured* and *not our type.*'

'Sounds like the caller has a few racial issues. Have you sent a unit down?'

'No, not yet. It just seems to be a black kid with a man near the beachfront houses.'

'Casing a job?'

Pete shrugged and let out a sigh. 'Dunno, mate. Do I send a unit in?'

'You can't not. The call's logged.'

Pete stared at the screen. The tone in the caller's voice hadn't been one of concern, neither had it been one of urgency, and the noise he'd detected in the background had sounded like a spoon stirring a drink. As if the caller had had time to think his call through. Making tea or coffee seemed an odd task to do whilst phoning through on a 999 call.

He pressed return, and the cursor shifted from the notes he'd made. He typed in the box below: *There is concern that the caller may have had a xenophobic manner.*

He put a call out: 'Oscar, Radio 8, have a non-urgent report. Anyone in the vicinity available to take a look? Location, the RNLI station, Deal.'

Uniform came back immediately with their unavailability due to a blue light incident on the M20.

But then he heard: 'Oscar, Radio 5, we'll take it. Over.'

'Bravo that.'

'Decided to call it through then, Colin?' Pete said, leaning back in his chair while he pushed the last piece of a Yorkie bar into his mouth, scrunching the wrapper and tossing it into the bin. 'Goal!'

'CID took it.'

'They've got to be quiet,' Pete laughed. 'Who's on it?'

'DI Blake.'

'Watch out, baddie,' he said, grinning, 'you're going down.'

The coffee machine spewed out a plastic cup and a white coffee drizzled into it. DI David Blake tore the corner off two sugar sachets and poured it into his drink. He swished it around with the stirrer then tossed it into the bin. His phone pinged a message. It was from his partner, Sarah. He'd reply later. He took a slurp from his coffee and walked over to his office on the far side of the department's floor. He twizzled the blinds on the internal windows and watched as his team milled about their desks. He flicked his computer on and waited while his screen lit up and prompted him for his password. He moved his coffee cup away from his keyboard and typed. On the other side of the room, DS Andy Prior received an email, and opened it: my desk.

He closed his screen and took his tea with him. Blake beckoned him in.

'Guv?' Prior said, closing the door behind him. The blinds rattled in the slight draught.

'We've got a visit to make,' Blake said, scrolling through the notes made by the police operator.

'Burglary?'

'Suspicious sighting of a child with a male.'

'Isn't that uniform, guv?'

'Huge RTA on M20, all uniform called in. We're quiet, we'll take a look. Notes say the caller wanted to remain anonymous, seemed a little cagey himself. Detection of racial aggravation through witness's description. Might take a drive past the beachfront first. You ready?'

'Sure. What're we looking for?'

'Not a hundred per cent sure. Just a little covert police presence in the area, and then go pay our anonymous caller a visit.'

The unmarked car slipped out of the station's car park and crawled along the main thoroughfare of Deal. A few pedestrians milled about on the pavement, unaware of the surveillance. The car veered off in the direction of Seaview Parade, passing the turning into the road with its string of white houses overlooking the sea. Blake slowed the car before coming to a halt on a strip of double yellow lines.

'Nice houses back there, worth a million or more. Might retire there,' he said dryly as he adjusted the collar of his jacket, loosened his tie and pulled his belt up. A traffic warden made his way over, already noting the time and number plate, Blake flashed his badge. The warden navigated a puddle in the kerb and walked around the car, thinking the better of putting a ticket on it.

'Police or not, it's a double yellow,' he muttered to himself.

The officers squeezed past the bins to the side where an old red Ford Cortina was parked outside the RNLI station. 'Nice car if it was looked after,' Blake said, tapping its roof then drying his hand on his jacket. He rapped heavily on the door. Then he pulled at his already pursed lips and waited.

Prior flicked his wrist up; it was 8.30 a.m. 'Out on practice, d'you reckon, guv?'

'Nah, there's somebody in, the boats are still on the slipway.'

'You already saw that?'

'See everything,' Blake winked, taking a step back and tilting his body backwards to look up to the first-floor window. 'Light's on.' He twizzled the knob on his radio, 'Oscar, Radio 5, our location's the RNLI station, Seaview Parade. Can you give an affirmative?'

'Radio 8, Bravo that, affirmative,' came the reply.

'Looks like our anonymous caller's playing hide and seek, Andy. Might take a look round the sides. Knock one more time.'

'Could be in the lav, guv.'

Blake shrugged.

The concertina door rattled as Prior rapped his knuckles hard against it again. The two men waited.

A stocky, red-headed man teased the door open, his face weatherbeaten from the sea air, and dressed in a pair of yellow waterproof dungarees and blue t-shirt with RNLI in red stitching in the top right-hand corner.

Blake flashed his card, 'DI Blake and my colleague, DS Prior. Mind if we have a word?' The man stood silent for a few seconds, and a tinge of colour flushed across his face, clashing with the redness of his hair.

'We're responding to a report made earlier this morning of a suspicious sighting.'

'Not sure what you mean,' the man stuttered. 'I've just clocked on for my shift. Been at home all morning with me missus. She can vouch for me.'

Blake raised his eyebrows, 'And your missus is?'

'Debs. She works in the hair salon down Parlour Lane,' the man rambled.

'Anyone else inside?' Blake questioned.

'Yeah, Rob. Shall I get 'im?'

'If you wouldn't mind,' Blake offered a smile.

The crewman, sliding the door to a little behind him, left the officers standing outside.

Blake raised his eyebrows and cast Prior a look. 'It's already looking suspicious,' he muttered. They could hear the faint sound of voices in the background.

A few minutes later a well-built man appeared at the entrance, his face unshaven. He edged himself out in front of the door and pulled it across slightly, to block out the officers' voices.

'DI Blake and DS Prior,' Blake said as they flashed their cards. The crewman folded his arms. Blake scanned his eyes along the ink sleeve on the man's arm, where in the centre was *Forever Britain* and a bulldog.

'You here about the call?' asked the crewman, pulling the door further along; it squealed as it ran along the runners.

Blake pulled his jacket forward a little. 'Did you make the report this morning?'

'Yeah.'

'Can we come in? Ask a few more questions?'

'What's wrong with here?'

'It'd be easier if we came in. It's not exactly sunshine skies out here.'

'We've only the main crew area, and like I said, I don't want no trouble, I want my name left out. Prefer to keep it private.'

Blake pursed his lips. The water in the overflow pipe from the roof gushed down and washed away down the side. Blake stepped back and raised his eyebrows. 'The report we have is a sighting of something that seems suspicious. Is that correct?'

'Yeah, like I said, not one of our type. Told that to the bloke who took my call. Just it ain't right. I do what I do, but this ain't right. Sick of it, I am.'

'Sick of what, exactly?' Blake asked, taking out a notebook from his inside top pocket.

'I do this job, but now it ain't the same. Used to be fishermen caught in storms, local people in distress, the odd kid not being too smart on a hot day, you know. Now it's nothing but *them.*'

'Them?' Blake mused.

'Yeah, you know what I mean. I pay my taxes. I done my bit. But why should I risk my life when they shouldn't be 'ere anyway?'

'Sorry, I'm not with you. The call we're responding to is a suspicious sighting,' DI Blake interrupted.

'Yeah exactly. That boat that was washed up a few months back would have been full of 'em. But we found no survivors, risked our own lives ... but it's not what it seems. Rescue attempt was called off by the coastguard. All we found was a few bloated bodies, drowned. You know what I mean.'

'Can't say I do. What are you reporting? We've got a suspicious sighting of a boy,' Blake pushed.

'Yeah that's right – they ain't all dead's what I'm saying.'

'But a moment ago you said they'd drowned,' Blake flicked his notebook back, 'your words, to be precise, were "all we found was a few bloated bodies, drowned". Charming, if I might add to your way of putting it.' He flicked the page back.

'Yeah, right – but that ain't right. The boat washed up, didn't it?'

'The boat?' Blake questioned, his eyes wandering through the slight opening of the door, where he could just about see the red-headed crewman sitting at a table ensconced with his phone, intermittently slurping on a steaming hot mug of tea. He'd seemed a little agitated by the initial police presence.

'Yeah the boat full of all of 'em, all reported dead – drowned at sea – but that's not what I've seen. Saw 'im with my own eyes, with a white man from them big designer houses. Not going to keep saying it. He weren't our type.'

Blake allowed his mouth to drift into an almost cynical smile, he nodded his head several times and pushed out his lips; *he weren't our type* he said out loud while he noted it in his book. 'You realise I'll have to caution you if you keep describing what you've seen in that way, don't you?'

'You're joking, right? Caution me, arrest me, and *they* get into the country scot free and take everything.'

'I've made no mention of arrest,' a semblance of a patronising smile crossed the DI's face. 'But a caution will be applied if you continue speaking with a racist tone. We'll certainly look into your report, but a small child who you're suspecting has managed to survive a sinking boat isn't what I would describe as getting into the country scot free and taking everything. Would you, DS Prior?'

'No, guv.'

'Probably scared out of his life, if I'm honest.'

'You saying it's right?'

'I'm not saying anything, just advising that you keep your personal feelings in check. I'm responding to a report. You say the designer houses? Do you mean Beach Top?'

'Yeah those are the ones, recognise the man, think he had something to do with the project when the land was developed. He's always out running early in the morning. Saw 'im this morning at around six when I clocked on. Seen 'im a few times now with the kid. Always running.'

'So why are you clocking on? Thought you were on standby with the RNLI?' Blake questioned. 'Thought it was all voluntary.'

'Used to be that way, but ever since the boats kept coming in, we've had two of us 'ere, full time. I'm the chief coxswain.'

'Chief cox …' Blake noted out loud.

'Swain,' Rob finished.

'Right, sounds important. Well, unless we have something more than that, we'll just add this to our log and if there's anything further reported then we can do something. I think that's about all for now. Thank you for your time, Mr …?'

'And that's *it*?' Rob snarled, moving forward.

'For the moment, yes. We've got all the information we need for the time being. Rest assured, though, it's never just *it*.' He took out a card from his inside pocket, 'If there's anything else, you can call the department.'

Blake and Prior left the RNLI station and walked back to their car.

'What do you reckon, guv? Anything in it?'

'Not sure. Small child, no shoes, could be anything. Nothing too significant in a child on a beach with bare feet, sounds pretty normal to me. Keep an eye on that one. Look up who the chief coxswain is, thinks he's being smart not giving his name.'

'And the guy with the boy?' Prior asked.

'I've got a hunch; description fits someone ... you know who worked on that development project?' He stopped for a moment whilst he turned the ignition on. 'Tom Edwards.'

'An important lead, guv?'

'Could be, he was the architect behind it all. And you know what else?'

'Nope.'

'When the houses were being built, he was in the news not just for that, but about his brother out in Africa. Don't you remember the news coverage on it? Kind of became something else rather than the huge development news and the protests from the locals. Something happened out in Africa with his brother.'

'Oh man, yeah, I remember now. He was reported missing, wasn't he, not sure whether he was ever found. D'you reckon the kid's linked?'

'Who knows? Kind of feel like we need to leave it.'

'And the report?'

'We followed it up. Now just close it down.'

'Our jobs could be on the line, though, guv.'

'Yep they could, but I kinda feel like we turn a blind eye. Keep schtum; if it's anything to do with his brother then something says we're doing the right thing, Andy. Sometimes there's a reason why a kid survives at sea, and sometimes you let sleeping dogs lie.'

'I didn't know you had such a soft side, guv.'

'Yeah, well I know what loss feels like, and I'm not about to stir up the past or have some kid thrown into the lion's den with social care. You know, whatever the government says, there's a reason why these people flee, and if a kid's safe then let it be.'

'What about our anonymous RNLI bloke?' Prior asked, loosening his tie and undoing the top button of his shirt.

The corner of Blake's mouth turned downwards. 'Didn't take a liking to him, and his mate seemed as shifty as hell. Just keep an eye on him. Let's take a drive up to the Top. We'll let this one simmer for now, and then I'll decide. Keep it as CID, though.'

Chapter Eighteen

'Tom, I thought we could take the kids out to the shopping centre today. What d'you think? Amanuel's grown so much in the past few months and Abrihet's beginning to blossom into a beautiful girl now,' Kate said, tearing a piece of almond croissant and scrolling through her phone, stopping momentarily to browse at an Insta reel. 'I even thought I might get her enrolled in a school – she's a bright young thing. What d'you think?'

Tom pursed his lips and drew in his breath. 'I don't know.' He stopped. 'How do we explain it all?'

She looked up from her phone. 'Like we said before, they're the children of a great friend of yours and staying whilst their parents relocate on business. Nobody'll suspect anything now. Their English is almost fluent, and they look well dressed and well fed – and they really *do* need an education. I've got the day off today and I'm not on call, so why not?'

Tom drew his lips together with his fingers. He clicked his tongue against the roof of his mouth. 'You're right. Let's do the shopping centre and then make a few calls to the secondary schools. Is that what you do, call the schools? I haven't got a clue. It'll probably be easier if we home-school Amanuel though; he's still young … and social services would be on it, wouldn't they? Abrihet's more likely to slip under their radar at the moment, though, isn't she? I just can't let them down, you know that, Kate.'

'I know.' Kate smiled softly and touched his hand with a gentle squeeze. 'Let's have a chat with them today about it, see how they feel. They might not even want to. I'm going to take a quick shower then I'll call the children down. I think they're just playing Snakes and Ladders in their room. I should stay more often; your croissants are scrummy.' She hopped off the chair and wrapped the bathrobe tightly around her.

'Clean towels in the airing cupboard,' he called after her.

She left the room and called from the landing to the children before disappearing into the shower.

Tom flicked the television on, and the hackneyed theme tune of This Morning broke his somewhat peaceful morning. As the chipper, almost puppet-like, noise from the presenters rattled along in the background, Tom's eyes moved away from the screen and focused on the headlights in the blanket of drizzle outside. As he tilted the slats of the shutter, a pristine bullet-grey Audi slipped past the house. Two men sat in the front. Had he caught the eye of the passenger, he wondered, or was it just by chance their eyes had seemed to meet? Black equipment hung from the car's rear-view mirror. Then the Audi seemed to pick up speed beyond Tom's house. The tinted rear windows gave nothing away, the number plate was unfamiliar.

Tom directed his look back to the television where the host presenter cooed and bubbled over the puppy that sat next to her guest on the sofa. He drew his thumb and finger up to his bottom lip, pinching it gently as he wondered why what seemed to be a deliberately inconspicuous car had driven so slowly past the house. Perhaps there had been a break-in. He left the television burbling in the background while he wiped the almond dusting from the kitchen island with the side of his palm. The tray of the dishwasher's contents rattled as he added Kate's sugary plate and coffee cup.

'She always looks so good, doesn't she?' Kate said, glancing towards the television as she bounded into the room with the children.

'Who, Kate?'

'The presenter, whatever her name is – she's just like this Hello Dolly pinup for you guys, don't you think?'

'Yeah she's all right, but not my type, too much make-up and sugary cooing.'

'What's up, Tom? You seem a little on edge.'

'Nothing.'

'Okay, if you're sure.' She threw him a quizzical look. Something had rattled him, she could tell.

'Right, you two,' Tom began, switching the television off. 'Kate and I need to talk to you about something, see how you feel about it. No pressure, okay?' He tossed Amanuel a wink, 'Enjoyed your run this morning, buddy?'

Amanuel beamed. The two children sat on the edge of the sofa, Abrihet's hands held together, Amanuel's cupping his knees, their faces expressionless.

'Don't look scared, it's all good. It's just you've been here now for six months and we've barely been out.' Tom began. 'Your English is amazing, and … well … you look just great. You know when we said that you were going to be the children of friends from Kenya, well the time's come. You need to have a life here and we're going to have to live that story for you to have that. Do you understand what I'm saying?' He felt like he was rambling.

They both nodded.

But Kate felt the rush of anxiety sweep through the room from the two children and, slipping past Tom, she sat close to Abrihet, turning her body inwards and taking both her hands. 'What Tom's trying to say is that we both thought it might be good for you to … I don't know … make a life here, but gently, carefully. Abrihet, you're growing into a beautiful young girl and you need an education, don't you?' She lifted Abrihet's chin with her finger. 'You must have hopes and dreams and aspirations. Don't you?

'Yes,' Abrihet said softly, almost in a whimper.

'What do you want to be?'

'I always wanted to be like the kind doctor from my village. You see …' she stopped briefly, remembering the days when she had watched him, the days when she had watched Elisabet in the medical centre.

'Go on,' Kate urged gently.

Abrihet smiled softly and a slight sound came from that smile. 'I always wanted to be wise and kind and gentle, and read the magazine he read. To be part of the British Medical Association.' She said it forthrightly, as if a wash of pride had taken over her body. And she sat up straight, her head high. A slight twang of an African accent in her voice. 'That's what I want, those are my dreams, my asper…, asper…'

'Aspirations,' Kate smiled.

Tom wiped his eyes, and the hairs on his neck prickled his skin. 'You want to be like the kind doctor,' he said.

'Yes, I want to be like him. To study hard and to be the same. If it wasn't for him, I wouldn't be here, nor would my brother.'

Tom swallowed hard and fought back the watery liquid that stung his eyes. He offered a smile and turned his glance back to the window. The blanket of drizzle still hung around the street.

'Well,' Kate said. 'That's amazing! You'll make a great doctor. Which is why Tom and I thought it might be an idea for you to go to school and learn and find your way through life. We thought perhaps the school close to here, maybe a bus ride away? We could make a few calls.'

'I would like that very much – and what about Amanuel? Will he also go with me?'

Kate smiled warmly. 'Not to the same school, because that one's for girls and boys of your age and older. Amanuel, I think, will learn a little more at home with a tutor.'

'A tutor?' Abrihet questioned. 'Is that like a person who teaches. A person like ...' She stopped, and her eyes dropped to the ground. Then she looked up and took her brother's hand lifting her head high. 'Amanuel has never left me. We have always done things together. Is that not possible? Is England so different?'

'I'm afraid here in England it *is* different. Maybe in the bigger towns where you lived, they had the same, where the older children would study or maybe they all went to the same school.'

'Yes ... So when do I begin?'

'First things first, Kate replied glancing briefly over to Tom. 'We need to find the best place for you. How does that sound?'

'That's fine, I'll wait,' Abrihet said, rubbing her thumb against Amanuel's hand.

'But in the meantime,' said Kate, 'Tom and I thought we'd go shopping to the mall and have a day out, shop till we drop. Why don't you both get yourselves ready?'

The children pushed themselves up from the sofa and made their way to the door.

'Abrihet,' Tom said when the children had crossed the sitting room. She turned back, her hand placed on the edge of the door.

'Who were you going to say? You said a person like ...' he asked, trying to disguise his own urgent need to know.

'Elisabet, she worked at the medical centre. She was the nurse who sat by my bedside when I was very sick. But on a Tuesday morning she taught English to the children in the open hut in my village. She was lovely. She was beautiful. She was the warm beat to the kind doctor's heart.'

Everything the children were saying and had experienced seemed to be drawing a picture of the life Tom had once heard about. The village Amanuel had made from pencil shavings, which stood on the sideboard. The red pool on the edge of it was a depiction of the land where the sun fell into the water and lit up below the aquatic life. Where now the woman whose name he had heard in letters and phone calls was the woman that truly was the warm beat to the kind doctor's heart.

'She sounds like a wonderful person. Maybe one day you'll share the stories of her life in the village with me.'

She offered a smile and nodded. The two children left the room.

His gaze followed her, and he wondered what her life must have been like. *Could tragedy have brought fate?*

'So, are you going to tell me what's eating you, Tom?' Kate said, waving her hands in front of his eyes.

He blinked away. 'What d'you mean?' He moved across the room towards the kitchen.

'You didn't seem all that together when the children came in. Like you'd seen something ... What's going on? You know you can't hide anything from me. I can read you like a book.'

He drew his breath in and exhaled loudly through his nose. 'Dunno. I just think we need to be careful. I'm sure an unmarked police car went by earlier.'

'Right, and …?' Kate questioned, her eyebrows knitted.

'How many times do you see an unmarked car go past, Kate?'

'Well I haven't but that doesn't mean anything – and I wouldn't know anyway, *because* it's unmarked.'

'Maybe, maybe not. But it went past pretty slowly and I'm pretty damn sure it was police looking in. I just think we need to be careful. There's no reason for the police to be up here, unless there was a break-in – and if there was,' he paused, 'wouldn't they have knocked on our door and warned us, or asked us if we'd seen anything suspicious?'

Kate shrugged. 'Well, I guess so. But I think you're reading too much into it. We've barely been out. The only time you go out is with Amanuel for your early morning run. And like you said there's nobody about. When you found the children there wasn't a soul to be seen. So how on earth could any of what you think be even vaguely true? It was just a car, could have been anybody, someone visiting a friend, looking for a particular house. Going slowly past doesn't mean *police*.'

'It was different – too clean for one thing – and I could see some sort of contraption on the mirror. And yeah, nobody about who I've noticed – you're right – but what if there *is* somebody about and that somebody has seen me with Amanuel? What if that somebody has shopped me.? It's not like Amanuel could be my son all of a sudden. Everyone around here knows I'm single and don't have children, and he's not white.'

'I still think you're reading too much into it. It was just a car, and nobody's shopped you. I mean, look at it this way. Let's say for argument's sake somebody *has* seen you, don't you think the police would have knocked on the door, come with a search warrant, asked questions? They haven't, have they?'

'Yet.'

'Tom, seriously, stop. You've seen a car, think it's unmarked police, you're just speculating. The children have been here for months now, the game would have been over a long time ago, you're just overthinking it. And I guess with Abrihet mentioning Elisabet and wanting to be a doctor, well … well, it's just bringing it all back, it all sounds familiar. You know that as well I do. Knowing where these children are from.'

'So, you think it too?'

She sighed heavily. 'I think they're from the same village, yes. And that kind of breaks my heart. But maybe finding it's true will give you the closure you need, give *us* closure. I miss him too, you know. And maybe, just maybe, they have the answers. You think their kind doctor's Sam, don't you?'

'I don't think it, I *know* it is.' He brushed his hand against his eyes. '*I know it is.*' The words caught in his throat. His teeth clenched and his jaw twinged, his eyes awash with tears.

'But it could be coincidence too, you know. Elisabet's probably quite a common name out there. And they have community doctors and nurses all over Africa.'

'If it was just that, then maybe. But it's more than that. I've had my suspicions, just things the children have said, you know.' He paused. 'But today I *knew* it was, I just knew. I sat on the rocks with Amanuel, cos he had a stitch and he said, *He did that.*'

'He did what?' Kate asked.

'I was turning a pebble in my hand, ready to skim.'

She smiled fondly. 'Yeah, he *did* skim stones – taught me too, along the banks of the Thames on a romantic picnic.'

'But not only that ...'

Kate urged him a smile.

'He called him *Dr Sam*.' He stopped dead and looked at Kate. 'They knew and loved my brother, Kate.' He pulled his breath in and forced back the tears that were wanting to come, flooding his head, his body his eyes. He brushed past Kate, out of the room.

'Tom ...'

Kate heard the front door opening and the beep of the car unlocking.

Tom stood in the wet murk outside, the chill in the air seeming to release the tension in his forehead. And as the blanket of drizzle turned into large cold raindrops the tears fell from his eyes, his sobbing drowned by the pelting shards of rain.

Chapter Nineteen

Adi Ada, Eritrea

Weeks had passed since Sam had first met Elisabet's parents. The medical centre remained busy with the continuous flow of daily patients. Like Tim had said, there was an influx of cataract procedures after the first successful operation on young Abraham. Each week, Sam would be faced with a queue of new patients whose eyes he restored to more normal vision. Every week the Red Cross van would arrive with mosquito nets and supplies. Now the simplicity of a sheet of voile allowed the children to sleep at night away from the deadly bite of mosquitoes and malaria. The medical centre became a hub for simpler ailments and vaccinations, allowing the small school in the village to open once a week. There had never been any type of education within the community before and now the village seemed to thrive.

Sam's presence, as the doctor who healed the sick and gave life to the unborn, brought opportunities to a village that in spirit was alive but in ability had been dead. A village that had been blighted by disease, and that had needed the intervention of the first world's help. And that help had come in the form of Doctor Sam. Young men who before could barely see now managed the animals. Abraham saw himself studying hard enough to finally fulfil his dreams of being an engineer. Small pockets of dry land were cultivated. It was worked on by the women, and farmed and ploughed by the men who once had been lame or ravaged by some infection. No longer did the blackness of death wait in the corner of the room, stretching out his hand to take. No longer did the mother weep over another shallow grave where the poison of an insect had consumed a life. And no longer was tuberculosis a reason for fear.

A change had come since Dr Sam's arrival. Nothing could take away his determination to make a village that was rich in spirit become richer in what the people could give by learning English and being well.

Every Tuesday morning, the open-sided hut would house no more than twelve children, their eyes widening as Elisabet recited short nursery rhymes. The chanting of young African voices beating out the English alphabet in a rhythmic loudness was interrupted by the gentle roll of the blackboard as each side was filled with white chalk words. All of them English words. On the ledge of the hut's half-walls, Katumba would sit for a while, delighting in a somersault as he left. It was as if he too would learn the English being taught. When early morning break arrived and the sun beat down onto the roof of reeds, the children would rush to the open-ended truck where their mothers and grandmothers had assembled, their baskets and bags open and ready to fill with the fresh produce they'd buy from Jeremiah. Hessian sacks overflowing with the vivid yellow of turmeric and the crimson of the mixed spice, berbere. Small wooden boxes of ginger tumbled about. Crates on the edge of the buck overflowed with bunches of coriander. Sacks of chickpeas and lentils rested on the ground, with a huge scoop pushed deep into them. Chickens in cages clucked and squawked, waiting for their freedom to scratch the baked earth. The monkeys above viewed the scene below patiently waiting for a mischievous opportunity to snatch the carelessly dropped banana skin from a child. The scraggy dogs skulked around the smashed fruit that would tumble to the ground. They'd push their noses up to the crate of feathered birds, each chicken ruffling its feathers and clucking even more loudly at the black wet nose of a mangy inquisitive hound.

A handful of goats tethered to the back of the truck chomped on a bundle of coarsely tied grass, with the women babbling and hollering for the younger men to come and buy another goat each or some chickens to add to their smallholding.

From the veranda, Sam stood with his shoulder leant up against the pillar. Katumba sat close by on the veranda's ledge, his mouth smacked around the juiciest of mangoes. He looked up at Sam and cocked his head. Sam broke a smile.

'She's lovely, isn't she?' Sam's gaze fell upon Elisabet, in the small school hut across the way, as she rubbed away the words on the board. The tail of her headscarf fell across her shoulder and her large beaded hoop earrings swayed and jangled ever so lightly with the movement of her body. The chalky dust billowed into the air as she patted the rubber with her hand. She glanced over to Sam and smiled, wafting her hand in the air to brush away the tiniest particles of chalk that sprinkled about her face. Sam pushed himself away from the pillar, and the door of the medical hut closed behind him. He rested at his desk, poring through the notes of the patients he'd seen that morning. Until the afternoon he had little to do other than prepare for the trickle of patients who would visit.

The sound of the door closing. He looked up expecting to perhaps see Elisabet standing there, stealing a moment to chat with him before the children returned from their mothers' sides.

Yonas stood before him. 'Do you have a moment?' he asked.

Sam beckoned him towards the chair at the side of his desk. He sat down and rested his arm on the edge of the desk and removed his trilby-style hat. His fingers lightly grazed the felt edge. 'I'd prefer it that my wife slept in my bed and fed me once again,' he said.

'I'm sorry, I don't follow; are you feeling unwell? Is Haben sick?' Sam pulled his body nearer, his face etched with concern.

'Neither of those is the reason for me being here.' He placed his hat on the desk and brushed at the felt.

'Then what, Yonas? My clinic will be starting soon.'

'I was wrong.' He cleared his throat. 'Elisabet's my only daughter. And her happiness means everything to me.'

'I understand that.'

'I judged you, and that was a disservice to my daughter. She is a strong, intelligent, loving woman. And I can see how much you mean to her. But you too must understand that she means everything to me. Her life is different here. It's simple and traditional, and her faith is strong. And should you break her—'

'Yonas, you're right. I *do* love your daughter, and I've loved her since the first day I saw her, because of what you've said about her. It's as if it seeps out of her pores. I didn't come here to fall in love. I came here to write my papers, better the medical service, lessen the death rate from unnecessary diseases. But by fortune, and my greatest fortune, I was given Elisabet as my nursing assistant. And you're right, I have no faith, I don't believe – but as a patient's mother said to me in the first days of me being here when I saved her baby, she said that the wise prophet bore my name, Samuel, and it meant *God has heard*. I'm a doctor, and it's medical intervention that saved the life of a newborn baby, but it was her hope that kept her strong, her faith that believed in me, and that night I didn't change my own belief or values. But …' he paused and stared Yonas dead on. 'I *did* understand hers, and maybe God *had* heard. There's no part of me that would hurt Elisabet. I will protect her, care for her, and love her for ever. I promise you that. But I can't promise to believe in a God that I don't believe in. And you need to respect that of me too.'

Yonas's beady eyes stared into Sam's. The corners of his mouth dropped to his chin and his head gently nodded. 'In Africa, marriage is not about love. It is about family and procreation, building generations.'

'If that is true, Yonas, why do you only have one child? Have you not grown to love Haben?' Sam's leg shook beneath his desk.

'I have, but it's a different kind of love.'

'Maybe that's true. But when a man misses the woman he married in his bed at night, then as I see it your love and my love are the same. We simply reached it in a different way.'

Yonas nodded his head slowly. His fingers smoothed the rim of his hat whilst he pondered for a moment. 'Then, I give you my blessing and my Elisabet.'

The two men stood. Sam extended his arm, their hand grip firm. 'Thank you, Yonas, thank you for coming.'

That night the walk to the pool was cooler than other nights. And as they walked together, they talked of their day, about the patients who had come to the afternoon clinic and the morning school Elisabet had taken. Sam gently slid his hand into hers and held it until they reached the water's edge. The gentle sway of grey moved slowly towards the pool, and as the sun began to fall the herd of elephants drank from the water's edge, a few taking steps to wade in a little further to cool themselves from the heat of the day, their trunks filling with the coolness of the water before hosing the thickness of their skin down in a wash of water, the smallest of the herd deciding to roll in the muddy edges, the matriarch letting out a trumpeting sound to acknowledge the playfulness of their youngest, the twinkle in her eye watching, knowing and understanding the feeling of being young once. And on the other side of the pool sat Elisabet and Sam, his arm around the woman who had made his life so very complete in the wondrous world he'd found in Africa.

'Elisabet,' he said, as he pulled her in more closely. She turned to him. 'Elisabet,' he said again while placing his hand on the side of her face, his eyes fixed on hers, searching her face for the binding love he had for her. His fingers played gently with her earrings, and she tilted her head, brushing her face closer into his touch. His thumb grazed the side of her cheeks before the words fell from his mouth as a lyrical lament.

'Will you marry me?' His heart raced, a rush of nerves swam to his stomach and he felt it churn while he waited for her, every minute feeling like a time when everything stopped still. She smiled at him faintly, her hand cupped his and as she looked into his eyes.

'You want to *marry* me?' Her eyes searched his face, knowing that building a life with him would come with a flood of uncertainties. She moved away from his touch and pushed her bare feet back into her sandals. She walked to the edge of the pool and bent down, brushing her hands against the ripples of the water. A fish darted up from beneath and dived back into the depths. A gentle breeze moved through the fruit trees, releasing a murmur of rustling. She wrapped her arms around herself and rubbed her hand against the bare skin of her arm. She felt Sam behind her, bringing her to her feet. 'My father would never allow it,' she finally uttered. 'He'd never let you marry me; we're from different worlds.' She paused. 'Your life is in England and mine is here. African women are different, you must see that. Your life isn't living in a makeshift hut with a simple existence. But this is mine, these are African people, and this is how they live, how they've always lived. It won't ever change. I couldn't ask you to give up your life for this, for me.'

'I'm happy here, Elisabet, and the home I have is all I need.'

'For how long, though, Sam? There will come a point when you'll want to return home. And then there's your own family. I've seen your photos, the smiling faces – even the dog seemed to smile.'

Sam let out a sigh of happy nostalgia. 'Bruno, yep, a dog that smiled. But I lost him a couple of years ago. Old age got him. The thought of losing another dog was too great, it was just too hard to say goodbye to him, so I chose not to get another one. And the picture on my table is of my friends and my little brother. But there are planes; it's not like I won't ever see them again. Is that really a reason?'

'It's not a reason, it's a life. A life I don't want you to regret. And my father—'

'Your father has given his blessing, Elisabet.'

A look of bewilderment stretched across her face. She knew her father was a man of tradition, and culture, and she had felt sure that her marrying a non-Christian – or worse still a non-believer – would never be allowed. 'He has?'

'Yeah, today. He came to the clinic.'

'What, just like that?' Her face furrowed with uncertainty. She shook her head slowly.

'No,' Sam laughed. 'Not just like that at all. But your mother plays a hard bargain, it would seem.'

'My mother?'

'Yep, he said he wanted her to return to their bed and feed him again,' he chuckled.

The birds flew from the trees as Elisabet tossed her head back and roared with laughter, breaking the silence of dusk.

'Your mother's a good woman. A reasonable woman. A woman who can recognise love. She made your father see what was right. And he shook my hand and gave me his blessing So ...' He took her face in his hands once more, his eyes drawing her in for an answer. 'Elisabet, I've never felt like this about anyone. From the first moment I saw you my heart beat faster. If you need more time, I'll give you that. But my mind will never change how I feel. My heart will never stop wanting you.'

She held her hands against his. And the softness in her voice gave the answer he had longed for.

Across the pool the sound of the matriarch's trumpeting reverberated around the fruit trees. As if the love that sat on the bank of the pool that night had fluttered across the water and fallen onto the mass of swaying grey. As if that night there was an understanding between human and the great mammals that a love had been found and was everlasting.

'D'you think she knows?' Sam glanced across at the matriarch and his smile formed a broad grin across his face as he watched her trumpeting high into the air and her foot pounding the ground.

'Elephants know everything,' she whispered. 'They're like people. They see and they feel, and they mourn their dead, and they find it hard to leave them. A little like this village, when the happiness is broken by the carnage that comes sometimes, the elephants here know the people of the village. There's a gentle understanding between us. Our people try to protect the elephants from the men who hunt them down. And likewise, they try to protect us. This is something you'll learn. Here in this village it's not all that it seems, and sometimes it's worse.'

The leaves rustled in the fruit trees and from them a small monkey scampered down a trunk. It walked steadily across the ground until all that could be seen sitting at the water's edge were the silhouettes of an English man, an African woman and a monkey, and ahead a mass of grey that now swayed in slumber. The sky cast a black blanket around them, and a small fire shot through the starlit ether.

And Elisabet's words remained in Sam's head, quiet and still, but he would protect her.

Come what may.

Chapter Twenty

The chicken squawked indignantly as it ran away from its brood. Abrihet and Amanuel laughed as they ran, trying to grab it. Their arms were outspread as they pounced, each time missing it. The hen scuttled into the undergrowth. They scrambled back up again – but this time they stopped dead. They could hear the sound of unfamiliar men's voices.

'Shhh, quick – get down.' Abrihet pulled at Amanuel's arm and tugged him down to the ground. They crouched low behind the mango trees. Across from the pool two men in uniform stood in an open-top jeep. They spoke in Tigrinya, signalling to three men on the ground, their hands bloodied, their clothes drenched by the redness of what lay on the ground in front of them.

'Who are they?' Amanuel said, his voice even softer than a whisper.

'Poachers.'

The three men shifted around their kill, laughing triumphantly. One posed with his leg on the head of the mass of grey. He was not Eritrean. He held his bloodied machete in the air. The fresh, still warm, blood slid down his blade and along down his wrist.

Amanuel gasped audibly. The men turned around. They shouted out. One of the hunters moved towards the trees, his rifle ready. He brushed away the hanging branches. The children inched back, their breath held, bodies low to the ground, hidden by the vegetation, their hearts pulsating like the beat of a drum out of time.

'Come back,' hollered one of the men. 'We need to get out of here.' The man with the rifle scanned the area. He kicked at the earth where two sets of small footprints were still visible, and he spat at the ground.

The men hacked at the dead animal, stealing the ivory. They heaved it into the back of the jeep. Two of the men sat on the back, their legs overhanging their vehicle of death. The man with the rifle still looked behind, until he saw a flash of purple. Then he caught sight of a girl running from where they had been hiding, and a small boy's legs carrying him at speed. Running ahead of his sister, faster and swifter his blue shorts and red top visible to the man who had spotted them.

They had been seen.

The jeep sped away, leaving behind a grey mass of barbaric death. The edge of the pool that a sunrise and sunset turned into a liquid golden red was now a murky red, the sun-baked earth sodden by the bloody carnage that had ensued. Huge gaping holes beneath the eyes that had once held glances of a steady love that spoke to their family. And from the mango trees the others came and there they stood, their trunks sweeping over the lifelessness of their dead. The sorrowful groans of beasts as they tried to bring back their family. The smallest of them finding its way to the front, its trunk pushing at the matriarch's head, urging her to wake up. It raised its trunk silently as she lay still, her face hacked open, her eyes still, and beside her two more lay dead.

The elephants did not leave. They stood by the edge of the pool and then they circled their dead. Momentarily they rocked, and from the lacrimal glands near their eyes a liquid trickled down their faces. And then their rocking would stop, and they'd push their trunks against the bodies. Brushing them softly, their feet gently nudging against the lifeless bulks, urging them to shift a little. The darkness of the sky began to seep in around them, camouflaging the herd who stayed and slept with their once matriarch and their sisters. And from the moonlit sky the blackness of a hand took the souls and left only remains.

In a nearby farm Jeremiah's truck was parked outside his ramshackle home, a small barn-like building with boarded-up windows and a sagging foundation, which stored the grain and produce he would sell to the villagers over the coming days. From inside, the aroma of freshly ground coffee beans filtering on a fire-lit stove funnelled through the air, anchoring the rhythm of the day. A leather money pouch hung over the corner of the table, and a metal cup small enough to hold in a child's hand steamed with hues of aromatic brown warm liquid and a stretch of earthy foam across the top. A plate of spiced chickpeas and unleavened bread warmed by the stove.

A jeep veered up the track and swerved to a halt outside; its lights dazzled through the cracks in the building. Three men pushed their way through the battered wooden door and shoved Jeremiah up against the wall, knocking his coffee to the ground, the cup rolling about the floor until its tinny noise finally stopped.

'The village, Adi Ada, you know the people. Speak, man.'

Jeremiah quaked against the wall as the man clasped his throat. 'I don't know them.' He spluttered through broken breath, saliva dribbling from his mouth.

'You're a liar. Do you want to meet your maker?' The intruder held a knife up to his throat, the blade sharp against him.

'What d'you want? Leave the village people, they're good people.'

The man threw a punch into Jeremiah's stomach, and then another, and another.

'Good people, you say.' His face was bristly and unclean, his breath carried a rancid stale stench.

Jeremiah's body doubled over at the fourth punch into his gut. He spat out a mouthful of vomit. One of the men took a blow to his face from Jeremiah and spat out a tooth. His face pushed up to Jeremiah's; 'Stupid move, farmer,' he snarled. He turned and then threw the butt of his machete into Jeremiah's face. Blood spewed from a pulsing lip. The third man came at him. 'Tell us their names, the boy, the girl.'

'I don't know who they are. How could I know? I just sell my produce there. What boy and girl?'

One of the men circled the table, a machete in his hand, his fingertips soiled. 'No boy runs that fast, like a gazelle. Talk and we'll spare you your life. You'll get to see another day. The young kid and the girl. You know exactly who they are. Don't tell us, and you'll get to walk with broken legs and ribs.' He moved his body towards Jeremiah and gripped his chin hard.

'They're just kids, leave them. They've nothing, no good to you.'

'So you know them?'

'I know the children in the village, I supply to them. Leave them be, I beg of you. They're good people.'

The man butted the end of his machete into Jeremiah's face again. 'Finish him!' he hissed.

The men threw punch after punch until Jeremiah's body slumped to the ground, and then they kicked him hard in his gut, until his ribs snapped, and he bled from the inside out. They jeered as another boot smacked into his back and his stomach. Like a baby in a womb he scrunched himself up. He cried out at every blunt kick. The blood, the saliva, the bile spewing from his mouth. His eyes swollen and the smile from his golden grin gone. He lay on the ground, a crumpled man, choking on his own blood. Broken.

The small pot on the fire steamed and the coffee boiled dry. The lights from the jeep glared through the window and it sped off, kicking up dust as it veered away. Its lights wavered for a moment, then it was dark.

The morning school bell resounded around the village, its noisy clang a joyful sound to the children who ran from their huts waggling a pencil they had each been given along with a notebook. A small boy clung tightly to the bell rope as he leapt with each toll, his words carrying in his laughter. 'To school, to school,' he sang out, beaming from ear to ear.

'Joshua, come down from the bell now, the children are coming,' Elisabet called from the veranda. Joshua leapt from the rope, landed on all fours, dusted his hands off and ran with the other children.

Sam kissed Elisabet as she left the medical centre and made her way towards the small sun-shaded pergola-style hut where the children sat at the desks. Tim had been able to source some furniture through the Red Cross warehouse, which had worked perfectly for the children in their morning English classes with the lyrical chants of the alphabet reverberating through the small community. A huddle of women waited nearby with their baskets ready to be filled with spices, chickpeas and vegetables. The menfolk waiting in anticipation for another goat to add to their herd and maybe a couple more chickens. As one was culled for food another would be reared and would eventually meet the same end.

Sam watched as the children tugged at their mothers' clothes, impatiently waiting to be heard. But instead there was only the incessant euphonious babbling of women still waiting for Jeremiah to arrive, the high-pitched voices of the women telling the men to get more rope to tether a goat. The tutting from the grandmothers at the lateness – they had rugs to weave and dough to knead.

But Jeremiah wasn't late. He simply didn't arrive.

Katumba sat perched on the ledge, watching on with Sam. As Elisabet moved away from Sam's arms he stopped her, grabbing her arm and holding her back from leaving.

'Wait.'

'Sam, I have to go. I have morning school.'

'No, wait.' She could hear the change in his voice. There was an uncertainty about it.

'What is it?'

'The women, they're still waiting for Jeremiah. He's late, I mean he's *really* late. That's not like him. Something's not right.'

'Maybe he's got a flat tyre,' Elisabet laughed as she took Sam's hand from her arm. 'You've seen his truck, it's almost falling to pieces. I must go. I'll see you later in the clinic.'

'I'm going to take a look – something's not right. And if it is a flat tyre, well, he'll need a hand.'

'I'm sure everything's fine, Sam.' She watched him as he went back into the clinic to grab his keys and bag. Katumba leapt from the ledge and scampered across the ground towards Sam's hut. He perched himself on the bonnet of the old Defender.

'What're you doing, Katumba? Come on, jump off.' Katumba hurled himself over the windscreen and onto the passenger seat.

'Fine, but just don't go running off, I haven't got time to be looking for a lost monkey as well.' The dust kicked up from the Defender's tyres as it took the track past the women who were still waiting for Jeremiah, their voices a burbling loudness. He veered left past the well where a trail of women carried urns on their heads. A young herdsman walked slowly, beating a stick on the ground as he followed his cattle, their bones protruding from their hindquarters. Sam pressed his foot hard on the accelerator towards Jeremiah's farm. As he approached it the hens clucked about the arid ground. Their water bowl was bone dry, their beaks bashing against the metal sides in the eerie silence under the beating sun. Jeremiah's wagon was parked outside the barn, its buck empty of sacks. Sam viewed the area before climbing out from behind the wheel. He went over to Jeremiah's truck and shielded the light from the window with his hands as he peered through the driver's window. It was empty. He walked towards the barn and pulled at the door. Inside, it was stacked with hessian sacks full of grain and spices.

'Jeremiah,' he called out.

He walked towards the house. There was a silent quiet in the air. He knocked on the door and it pushed open with his touch. 'Jeremiah,' he said again, inching his body around the door. 'It's Sam.' He glanced at the table, an empty plate of what looked like chickpeas, some of it smothered on the table in a trail. The smell of strong burnt coffee sifted through the air; a pan sat on a small stove-like fire that was now just warm embers. And by it lay a man, almost drowning in his own pool of blood.

His face was an unrecognisable pulped mess, vomit mixed in with blood dribbled down his cheek and onto his chequered shirt. His eyes were swollen and closed. The only recognisable feature was the slight glint of gold in his mouth.

'Jesus Christ!' Sam rushed to his side and knelt down by him. He placed two fingers on his neck, trying to feel for a pulse. Anything? He gently eased the bloodied shirt away from Jeremiah's body; a large area of deeply purple skin had formed around the abdomen. His stomach and rib cage were badly bruised. Sam placed his hands gently on Jeremiah's stomach, it was swollen. He percussed his chest, it was hollow.

'Jesus Christ,' he said again. 'Who the hell's done this to you? You're a good man, Jeremiah. Stay with me.' Sam grunted hard as he lifted Jeremiah onto his thighs from a crouched position, and then he lifted him in his arms. Jeremiah's arm swung down by his side, his head lolloped over and a tooth fell from his mouth.

Sam staggered towards his Defender with the man's broken body in his arms; he kicked the latch on the tailgate, and it fell open. Katumba covered his eyes with his leathery hands – he recognised Jeremiah.

'This isn't good, Katumba … Stay with me, Jeremiah.'

The monkey cocked his head and swung into the back of the vehicle. He sat with Jeremiah's head resting against the warmth of his fur and his small spindly hands cushioned his head ever so gently, as if knowing that another knock or hard hit would kill him. The drive back to the village was no London ambulance ride, but a simple metal base with a half-dead man lying on it. There was no 999 call or air ambulance hovering with a crash team waiting on arrival. Just the uncomfortable back of an old Land Rover bumping across a dry, hard terrain in the baking sun with no way of notifying anybody of the seriousness. At the turning for the main track into the village, Sam saw Tim's Red Cross van ahead. Sam held his hand on the horn until the van slowed and pulled over. Sam eased his foot off the accelerator as he went to pass it.

'Tim, come to the medical centre, quick! It's Jeremiah,' he yelled from his driving seat. Tim, from the height of his cab, could see the figure of a man lying still, covered in blood, in the back of Sam's Defender.

He swore in Swahili and floored it behind Sam.

Sam held his hand down hard on the horn as he drove through the village. Elisabet looked up from the desk where she was hunched over a child reading. She knew from his frantic driving and incessant hooting that something was wrong. She stroked the young child on the head, clapped her hands and told the children to pack away until the next week. The women who had been waiting for Jeremiah had now returned to their work. They all stopped and looked up to find out what on earth was forcing Doctor Sam to drive so insanely. Sam leapt out of from behind the wheel. Tim pulled up hard behind him. 'We're gonna need a stretcher to get him inside.'

'Is he alive?'

'Just. He's been bludgeoned to a pulp. Swollen and purple abdomen. Internal bleeding without a doubt, bruising from a blunt instrument, punctured lung, his chest was hollow on percussion.'

Together Sam and Tim gently eased him on to the canvas stretcher and pulled it away from the back of Sam's jeep. Steadily yet swiftly the two men carried Jeremiah into the medical centre.

Elisabet was already inside, preparing a bed for him. 'What do you need, Sam? Will he survive?' Her voice was just a whimper, her own distress visible. She had known Jeremiah all her life, and now he lay mashed on a bed.

'Everything. Sterile dressing pack; sixteen to eighteen-gauge cannula, 50ml syringe, three-way tap. Have you got any emergency trauma supplies in the van, Tim?'

Tim nodded. 'What you thinking, Sam? 4ml Lidocaine, Oramorph, Fentanyl 25G orange needle and 19G green, 5ml syringe?'

Sam shot a glance at him his mouth dropped open. 'You're—

'Trained at UCH, specialised in surgery, chose a different path though. On three one, two, lift.'

Together Tim and Sam lifted the stretcher onto the bed. Tim removed the poles from the loops of the canvas and left to get the medical supplies from the van while Sam scrubbed up.

Elisabet wheeled the trolley to the bedside. She brushed her hands down her front, the plastic of her apron crackling, then rubbed her brow with the back of her gloved hand while she stared at Jeremiah. The tears stung her eyes. She blinked several times, trying to make them disappear.

'You okay?' Sam rested his hand on her arm and held it reassuringly. She nodded and passed Sam the scissors. With a steady hand he cut through the material of Jeremiah's shirt.

Tim returned with the necessary supplies and laid them out on the trolley. 'I'm scrubbing up too, fella.'

Sam inserted a cannula into Jeremiah's vein and administered 1mg of morphine.

Both doctors stood below the buzzing light, the ceiling fan rattled in its spin, their brows perspiring. Sam listened to Jeremiah's chest, but there were no breath sounds. 'We've no time, Tim.'

'Lidocaine?' Tim offered. Sam nodded. Tim handed him the syringe. 'This'll sting a little, Jeremiah, and then it'll go numb. You won't feel a thing. Slight prick coming.' The standard words of a doctor when a sharp object is pushed into a patient's skin; his words just fell from his mouth while Jeremiah lay unconscious. Sam pierced the skin and injected 4ml of the anaesthetic drug into the area. Elisabet held out a scalpel to Sam, but he motioned her to pass it to Tim.

'You're the surgeon, not me.'

Tim took the knife and sliced through Jeremiah's skin with precision, making a small incision. He then placed a cannula into the pleural cavity and drained it of air, allowing the lung to fix itself and inflate naturally. It was their only hope, that nature would take its course. Jeremiah was unable to take deep breaths himself. There was no knowing whether, even with his lungs fully inflated, he would survive this attack.

Sam bandaged him heavily around his abdomen to protect his bruising and the ribs that had been broken; they would take weeks to mend. The internal bleeding had ceased, and for a brief moment both doctors could breathe once more. Elisabet dabbed at Jeremiah's face, gently cleaning his fat lip. His eyes were so swollen that only the tips of his lashes peeked through. Sam sutured the gash to his cheekbone and temple, and then they lifted him onto a different bed and wheeled his battered body into the corner of the room with an oxygen cylinder and mask; its trolley had seen better days. Elisabet hooked a saline drip onto a stand for the fluid to run into Jeremiah's body intravenously. From the window ledge Katumba watched on. Sam stripped off his mask and peeled away his gloves, and threw them into the nearby bin. He took Tim's hand with a firm grip, and shook it. With his arm around Tim's shoulder he led him towards the door.

In the haze of the afternoon the door closed behind them and a ripple of applause floated through the village, Sam smiled in relief, and the applause loudened, until some of the villagers beat against a drum and the children clanged pans. There was hope.

The two men stood against the veranda's ledge and viewed the openness of the land. Sam could feel his loose shirt clinging to his back.

'You didn't tell me you were a surgeon.'

'That's what brought me here – time away from the theatre, the trauma, the bright white lights. Can you even *imagine* attempting in London what we did with nothing here?'

'Everything's basic here – even the drugs are out of date. D'you regret leaving?'

'I'm Kenyan, so being back in Africa can never be my regret. Leaving the medical profession and working with the Red Cross? Well, let's just say they've now got expertise on their team.' He grinned broadly. 'It was good to be holding a scalpel again – not good that it was Jeremiah I was doing it for, though. But no, Sam, I don't regret it. My life *is* Africa, you come to love it, accept it. But the pull back to the big London hospitals – you can keep it. You know what I could kill for right now ...'

'A cold beer?'

Chapter Twenty-One

As the days passed since the attack on Jeremiah, his battered body still lay unconscious at the medical centre. The women from the village would take it in turns to come and sit by his side, babbling away at him. They'd sing sweet African melodies, as their fingers worked quickly and nimbly, every once in a while smiling at him and holding his hand. And then in a peaceful quiet with a reassuring grip they'd tell him that God was with him. Watching over him, keeping him restful until he was ready to open his eyes. The children would come too, and read the rhymes and poetry they had learnt at English school during the week. Abraham would sit by his bedside and smooth his hand along Jeremiah's still arm, now seeing for himself a brutality he'd been saved from seeing before. Jeremiah was never alone – there was always a trickle of visitors willing him to be okay.

Tim would arrive with medical supplies for Sam, and on the days that he wasn't due to deliver elsewhere he would sit at Jeremiah's bedside. He'd hold his hand with both his hands and smooth his thumb across his skin. 'Come on, my dear friend. Don't stay away too long,' he'd say.

And then Sam would stand by him and make his observations, every day the same. The light that shone into Jeremiah's now non-swollen eyes showed no change; this was a good sign. The villagers knew he was sleeping – but not a sleep that you wake from and your day begins. Instead a sleep that one day they hoped he *would* wake from. Each day they prayed that that day would come soon. Sam had said that the villagers must visit, talk to him, let him know they were there. Their prayers alone were not enough, their hope would not bring him back. The sound of their voices, the need for his brain to somehow hear them, was what he needed. And the villagers began to realise that medicine and science were more than an equal to their faith and their religion, but their faith kept them strong and united and a place to be when science couldn't make it right, because life belongs to no man. And their hope was all they had. While death slunk silently in the corner, unseen, waiting to take out its dark hand and steal him away.

At night Elisabet would sit with him; she'd rest her hand on his bed, and her soft skin would brush against his. She would open her book and read to him, *Out of Africa*, a memoir written by Karen Blixen, recounting her seventeen years in Kenya, Sam had given it to Elisabet to read; perhaps its tone, the sounds of wildlife, the sunsets and sunrises would feed through to the ears that Jeremiah needed to hear with. Each night he'd lie silent, just the gentle rise and fall of his sheet across him. Sam would stand close by, listening to her reading.

One night she asked: 'Will he ever open his eyes, Sam?'

'I don't know.' He touched her shoulder and squeezed it. 'But we can't give up while there's a glimmer of hope. When you find a man who has fought to stay alive after what he went through, you can't just give up. He's got a fight in him – it's still early days.'

'Does he even *hear* anything? Can he hear me reading to him?' Her voice was tinged with a hopelessness he'd never heard before. A woman whose faith had kept her strong was now beginning to doubt. He wondered whether she in herself was giving up.

'I don't know.' And that was the truth. Not even the most experienced physicians knew what a person in a coma could hear. But the medical world's belief was that you should talk, just keep talking, to them.

The door pushed open and Tim poked his head around it. 'How's he doing?'

'No change, Tim. It's been a week and not a sign. His pupils are equal, and constricting on light, so there's no brain injury at least.'

Tim exhaled. 'It's still early days, Sam, you know that. You've heard about the elephants, right?'

'Yeah, makes me feel sick to the core.'

'It looks like Jeremiah might have witnessed the poachers, looks like they came back for him, paid him a grisly visit – that's what it's pointing to.'

'But that doesn't sound right. It doesn't stack up at all. How could Jeremiah have seen anything? It would have been in the daytime, and everyone knows he's selling from his truck at that time. It's just not even possible.'

'The poachers are a pretty barbaric band of men, Sam, and if he didn't witness it he'll know who did, so he'll have paid a heavy price for protecting them. What doesn't add up, though, is why would a man take a beating so severe that he's lying in a coma, simply for another man.' He sighed heavily. 'He's a good man, Jeremiah. Always with a golden smile.'

'Unless it wasn't for a man? Unless it was for a ...'

'A woman? Maybe, but the women are busying themselves. He can only be protecting someone here in the village. And if it's not a woman, then a child. And they'd have to be from this village, because the elephants are the elephants of Adi Ada. The children don't roam to the other villages.'

'D'you think the poachers'll be back to finish the job? I mean, we need to find who did it.'

'Without a doubt we need Jeremiah to wake up, to at least try and tell us what happened. It's critical he wakes up.'

'Then we all need to remain vigilant,' Sam said as he began to close each window. For now, Jeremiah was safe, and the medical centre would be locked at night, in the hope of keeping away any intruders. Sam took up his bag and placed his arm loosely around Elisabet, then turned and locked the door, pulling down on the handle to check it had shut securely.

Tim made his way back to the Red Cross van.

Sam walked with him, his hands in his pockets. The night had cooled and a breeze meandered through the trees. 'How bad is this, Tim?' he asked.

'As bad as it gets. A village has been taken down before now. These men are corrupt and ruthless – they'll kill, they'll rape whether you're young or old, male or female. They don't care. It's not all about wars, you see, when people flee; it's about this. This life where the barbaric acts of greed dominate, the corruption, the transnational organised crime. The Vietnamese are big players in it, too. If there are children that need protecting, we need to know like ...' he exhaled, 'like *now*, and get them the hell out of here.' Tim turned the key in the ignition and the engine rumbled. 'We'll talk tomorrow.'

He cranked the handbrake down and drove away, his rear lights disappearing into the night. Sam kicked at the dusty tyre tracks and idled his way back over to where Elisabet was standing. She looked different that night; her face seemed to be shrouded in an unease he hadn't witnessed before.

'Hey, you look like you've the world's troubles on your shoulders ... come here.' He pulled her into him, and she nuzzled her face up against his chest, grappling at his cotton shirt. She felt safe in his arms, but she knew his arms could never fully protect her. Sam eased her away from him. 'Hungry?'

She nodded. He wrapped his arm around her shoulder and walked her in the direction of his hut. Katumba leapt high above in the trees whilst the stars fell through the spaces of each branch and the moon cast a silvery shadow over the village of Adi Ada.

'What were you talking to Tim about?' she asked, settling into the hammock, her back resting against his chest.

He sighed. 'The men who battered Jeremiah half to death, their reasons for it.' His hands gently massaged Elisabet's arms.

'It's a problem here, all over Africa, the illegal wildlife trade. Eritrea's responsible for crimes against humanity and systematic crimes, and the poaching levels have soared,' she said.

'But what about the government? Surely they come down hard on the traffickers.'

'You'd think that, right? But when ivory's a privately-owned stockpile under government management and it's known to have been entering into illegal trade, you stand no chance. And when the traffickers are caught by the *non*-corrupt officials, then the networks just regroup, reorganise. They're capable of that. They're clever.'

'How far will they go, Elisabet?'

'They'll massacre a herd of elephants, and if they need silence on their crimes, they'll do the same to a village. They don't care. Money, greed, organised crime, that's their drive. Murder, killings, that's just their hobby.'

'So, Tim wasn't joking when he said whoever they were after needed protecting.'

'No, he wasn't joking. They'll be back for whoever saw them. Nobody's safe here. I told you by the pool, d'you remember? I said sometimes it was like a nightmare. Now you'll see, you'll live the nightmare.' She turned her head into him, her hands cupped against her lips. She lay still whilst she felt the touch of his hands brushing her headscarf as if soothing the fear that now manifested itself inside her. Her stomach rumbled softly.

'Come on, you're hungry – and then I should go back and stay with Jeremiah for a while.' Sam tipped himself out of the hammock, helping Elisabet to clamber out.

On the far side of the pool the moon shimmered high in the blackness and threw silvery spears through breaks in the leaves onto a pool of black. The silhouettes of the herd steadily returned, their huge grey mass moving in a gentle harmony around the carcasses, the young bull curiously moving what appeared to be a dried-out ear, shifting it gently along the ground. In less than a week, the massacred beasts had fed hyenas, vultures and other animals, and now there was barely anything left but their skeletons. Yet there was still the powerful need of their family to return, to not leave, but to grieve.

They circled the bones of an elephants' graveyard to protect.

Always to protect.

Chapter Twenty-Two

Fourteen days had passed since Jeremiah had been found. The stitches had been removed from the gaping holes across his face, leaving two crude scars on his cheekbone and temple, while antibiotics still steadily trickled into his veins. Sam moved around his bed and placed two fingers on Jeremiah's wrist as he took his pulse once more, and noted his blood pressure using his watch and a stethoscope, before gently laying his arm back down beside him and resting his own hand on Jeremiah's for a moment before turning to write his observations in the file. He leant across Jeremiah and shone his light into his eyes; his pupils were still equal and they constricted from its brightness. Then as Sam moved away Jeremiah's finger twitched. Sam touched his arm and the finger twitched again, twice this time.

'Elisabet.'

'What is it?' she said, putting some clean folded sheets on the chair by the linen cupboard, and turning to Sam.

'He's just moved his finger.'

Leaving the cupboard door ajar she hurriedly made her way towards Jeremiah. They both stood at the bedside, their own hearts racing.

'Jeremiah, it's me, Sam.'

Jeremiah lay still and his hand didn't move. But his head moved slowly from side to side and his eyes flickered.

'Pur – gaz,' he mumbled through dry, blood-cracked lips.

Sam took his small light again and peeled back Jeremiah's eyelid, his pupils constricted on its dazzle. 'He's beginning to wake.'

'Purp – gaz – el,' said Jeremiah incoherently.

Sam dabbed his lips with a damp cloth.

'Gaz – elle,' Jeremiah rambled.

'What's he trying to say?' Elisabet questioned. 'I read to him about the Kenyan animals from my book, is that it?'

'Boy, run, gaz – elle,' a rambling of words came from Jeremiah's mouth.

Sam took his arm, 'Jeremiah, it's Sam. Can you hear me?'

Jeremiah's arm jerked; his hand moved across the sheet away from his body. He touched Sam. 'Gaz – elle, protect him.' His breath was laboured. 'Protect gazelle.'

'Protect the gazelle, what d'you mean?' Sam pulled in closer to him and held his hand. 'Jeremiah, squeeze my hand if that's what you mean.' Jeremiah's hand remained still.

'Pur – ple ...' he laboured. 'Chil – dren. Run. Gazelle.'

Sam shook his head. 'I don't understand, Jeremiah.'

Jeremiah's eyes fluttered until they slowly began to open. 'Protect children,' he stuttered. 'Please, protect children,' he winced.

'Which children? We'll protect them. Stay still, Jeremiah.'

Jeremiah nodded slowly.

Sam dabbed a wet gauze against his lips, removing the crusted blood from the corner of his mouth. Fresh blood began to weep from his split lips, and Sam applied a little pressure. 'Here hold this in place, Elisabet.' Sam left to get 2mg of morphine and an infusion solution. He removed the cannula's cap and slowly administered the morphine, allowing it to flow into Jeremiah's body and ease the pain.'

Jeremiah's hand quivered from the chill of the liquid flowing into his vein. It was the first time he had reacted to show any form of feeling.

Then his head began to shake from side to side, becoming stronger with each movement. He gazed at the blurry image of the woman beside him and he grasped her hand. 'Please, Johanna, tell him, the children, tell him – Johanna, tell him.'

Elisabet pulled herself closer to him, took his hand and rubbed her thumb across it. Then with her other hand she smoothed his forehead, dispelling his fear. 'It's me, Elisabet, Jeremiah, it's Elisabet.' She pressed her hand against his brow. 'Can you see, it's me? You're in the clinic. Do you see my face, it's me?'

He turned his head towards her, and a tear trickled from the corner of his eye. 'Elisabet,' he murmured.

Sam drew in his cheeks. 'Johanna,' he said, 'the children – d'you mean Amanuel and Abrihet? Were they seen?'

'Save children.' Then he stared up towards the ceiling, his eyes moving independently of themselves as he tried to focus.

'The boy, Amanuel, he runs like a gazelle. Is that what you're saying? Johanna's children are in danger, is that it?' Sam asked. 'It can only be Amanuel, he always kept up with you and your truck. That's it isn't it? Amanuel and Abrihet saw the poachers! Oh, man ...'

Jeremiah's head nodded slowly. 'Protect, protect, prote ..., pro ...' His eyes closed.

From inside the medical hut the sound of the Red Cross van could be heard. The door opened, and Tim stood with a box of mosquito nets. He cast his glance to the bed where

Sam and Elisabet were still standing. 'I've got more nets for you, thought I'd drop them now and see how the patient's doing,' he said, heaving the load onto the chair by the desk. 'Everything okay? Is Jeremiah okay, Sam … Sam?'

Sam moved away from the bed.

'Sam, is everything okay?'

'Jeremiah woke briefly, it's the children. The poachers are after the children.'

'Whose children?' Tim questioned.

'Johanna's.'

'Johanna's? You mean Amanuel and Abrihet? Why? What did he say?'

'It was just ramblings at first, then he called Elisabet Johanna. Kept saying *gazelle*, *purple*. Just words. And then he said *protect them*. That was it.'

Tim's face dropped. 'Amanuel's known as the little gazelle. Ever since he first ran, he was like lightning, nobody could keep up with him.' He sighed heavily. 'It's going to happen again. We need to find Johanna. We need to tell her, and we need to get the children away from here without anyone knowing. Nobody can know.'

'What, to the next town d'you mean?'

'No, Sam – we need to get them the hell out of here. They're not safe, nobody's safe. We need to get them to a different country.'

'A different *country*? How the hell do we do that? They won't have passports. Can't we just report this, tell the officials about the attack on Jeremiah and the children?' Sam rubbed his forehead frantically.

'Sam,' Elisabet took his arm. 'The officials are in on this. That's just it – Tim's right – we need to get them away to safety. Stop, wait, Jeremiah's stirring again.' The three went to his bedside.

Jeremiah's eyes flickered open and closed, open and closed. The three figures stood as a blurred outline in front of him, he held up his hand as if to fight them off to protect himself from another blow.

Tim spoke in Tigrinya: 'Jeremiah, Jeremiah, it's me, Tim. You're safe, we have you. The children are safe, we'll protect them. Now rest.' He held Jeremiah's arm steady. 'Now rest, my good friend.'

Elisabet pulled up his bed sheet and smoothed it down, then gently lifted his head and plumped the pillow a little, and laid his head back down onto its cushioning softness. With a damp cloth she dabbed at his brow, then adjusted the saline drip and left him to sleep.

Tim led Sam back to the desk, and as he did Sam looked over his shoulder and watched as Jeremiah tossed his head in his sleep, perhaps reliving the night where he'd remained silent; silent to protect two children who he now knew were wanted by ruthless men. A nightmare that Abraham's mother had begun to share when she'd said she could have wished her son to be as before. Only now was Sam beginning to realise the meaning of it all.

'So … when do we do this, when do we steal them off into the night, when do we start this clandestine operation? I mean that's what it is, isn't it? Moving the children illegally and secretly.' Sam's voice was hushed. 'How do we tell a mother and father we're taking their only children? Tell me that much, Tim, 'cos I sure as hell don't understand any of it.' He sank his head into his hands and rummaged his fingers through his mop of hair, pulling tightly at the strands. He wanted to scream out loud, but instead with a calm quiet he said, 'I saved both her children from dying and now I have to tell her she's going to lose them anyway.' He screwed his eyes shut and held his breath briefly. 'You know, I ...' he paused. 'I don't understand how men can do this. What world do we live in? ... Do I need to go *now* and tell the children?'

Tim nodded. 'We have so little time.' The three stood in the clinic, the rattle of the fan slicing through the sombre silence, just the intermittent sounds of a restlessness from Jeremiah. They were together in a clinic that served the people. But a community that was now thriving was about to be thrown into a fireball that was hell. All of them were thinking the same thing: if it was an adult the task would have been easier, but it being children had changed it all. A surreptitious operation to remove small people from a village where they lived and to try and keep them shielded and move them to safety was something that would come at a price, and that price was not the exchange of money. The price was two innocent young lives.

'Shall I come with you?' Elisabet reached out to Sam and he felt the lightness of her touch against the tension in his forearm. His hand clenched, he replied, 'No, stay with Jeremiah. He may wake again.' The door closed silently behind him.

Katumba followed in the treetops until Sam reached a hut where a dim light flickered inside. Johanna was preparing the dough for the next day. Sam knocked on the edge of the wall where a beaded curtain hung in the doorway.

She turned quickly, startled by his presence.

'Doctor Sam?'

'Good evening, Johanna.'

'Would you like some coffee?' She hurriedly moved her needlework from the chair and beckoned to him to sit down. 'Please forgive me, I wasn't expecting anyone, Elijah isn't here.'

'Are the children asleep?'

'Yes, but please sit. Coffee?'

Sam took a seat, his leg trembled. 'Johanna …' he began, then stood up sharply.

Johanna stopped pouring the coffee. 'What is it?'

He inhaled and then exhaled slowly as if to sound out the words that were racing in his head. 'It's the children.'

She stared at him, her eyes moving from side to side, searching his face for more.

'The children, do they need more vaccine?' she finally said. 'Please …' she beckoned to the seat once more. She passed him a small cup of strong black coffee.

Sam sat down again and with a calmness that didn't echo the turmoil of his gut, he responded. 'They saw the killing of the elephants, and not only did they see it, but they were *seen*. The brutal beating that put Jeremiah into a coma was because the men had gone to find them.' He paused. 'They're not safe here. You know what I'm saying, don't you? You know what those men are capable of.'

She stood deadly still, her eyes fixed on Sam's face. 'They?'

'Amanuel and Abrihet.'

She showed no emotion. If it wasn't her child it would be another's. And God had been kind and given her the years she'd had with them. But she also knew that God would protect them, he wasn't taking them for her to bury in a shallow grave but instead he had let Jeremiah live to warn them; to warn her of the atrocity that was coming.

She swallowed, and the words stuck in her throat: 'I understand. How long do I have?'

'Tomorrow night we must leave. I'm so sorry, Johanna, I'm so sorry.' His voice broke.

'You've been a good, kind man, you've saved my children once, and you will again. Do not be sorry. God will be with them, I have that to hold onto. I will have them ready for you when you want.'

Sam left the hut and walked back to the medical centre, but instead of going inside he drew up a chair on the veranda and slumped into it. A mosquito buzzed around him until it left a blood-splattered mark on his white cotton shirt. Sam flicked its distorted body from his arm. Katumba sat nearby on the ledge and watched. Inside, Sam could hear hushed voices coming from Elisabet and Tim. He bit at the skin on the side of his finger until it bled. The door opened; Tim stood there with a bottle of Jack Daniels in his hand and two glasses.

'How was it? Did you speak with Johanna?'

'Yeah, I spoke to her. The children were sleeping. She was preparing tomorrow's bread.'

'How was she?' Tim asked pulling up a chair.

'Surprisingly calm, I mean a weird kind of calm. That calm that comes when there's a patient sitting with you in the privacy of your office and you've just thrown them a curve ball. D'you know what I mean, Tim?'

'Like a death sentence calm?'

'Yeah.' Sam grazed his bottom lip with his teeth. His eyes fixed ahead on a cloak of darkness speckled by a white, fluorescent dot-to-dot within an innocence of peaceful hush. He turned the glass in his hand and took a sip. 'It's when you'd expect them to crumble, fall apart, cry, do something and yet they sit there, unemotional and say *right, okay, well I've a school run to do now, thank you Doctor.'*

'It's the shock, it's the unknown being dealt to them, the unexpected. So, they normalise it,' Tim replied.

'But it was more than that, like she was grateful for the time she'd had with her children. Like they were a gift and she just had this unequivocal acceptance of that.'

'Remember what I said to you – African women are different. And maybe, Sam, that's the same answer as *right, I have a school run to do now.* The removal of emotion, the need to be strong, and yet inside we're crumbling.'

'D'you mean Elisabet would do the same, give up our children?'

'Is there something you're not telling me?' Tim nudged Sam.

'No – just I don't think I could do that. Have the strength to say *take them.* Does that mean Elisabet could?'

Tim sighed and took a large gulp from his bourbon and swirled it around in his mouth before swallowing it. He leant forward, his legs astride, then swirled his drink once more and watched as the amber liquid trickled down the edge of the glass. 'Africa's different, the people's faith is strong, their belief even stronger. They lose their families to all manner of atrocities, famine, disease, corruption – and it's not that they become hardened and desensitised to it. It's just that they accept that the children were never theirs to *keep.* They're different to us, my friend. They see their children only ever as a gift, that one day they'll give them back to a greater life, to an everlasting life.'

'But you're African. Don't you see it that way too?'

'Yeah, I was born here. But I went to school in England, trained as a surgeon at UCH. I had a privileged upbringing.

But the people who work on my parents' reserve are not like your parents and mine – they're looked after well, but they live a different life. It's not the same.'

'How do we even *move* the children, though? They won't have passports or any kind of travel papers. They barely speak English. They don't stand a chance.'

'Through the night we can get them across Eritrea and into Sudan, and then from there, they'll have to make their way towards the Mediterranean.'

'Tim, they're *children*! I can't leave them to cross countries on their own in some vague hope that they might manage to find their way to a boat setting out from ... where? Some coastal town near Tripoli – and then across the Med in, what, a rowing boat? They'll never make it; they'll die of starvation if nothing else.'

'The people here are used to hardship, they're used to walking. Before this clinic opened they'd trudge kilometres to have their children seen at the mission hospital. They're not like English people or even Europeans. They live just to survive.'

'Kilometres, Tim, not countries—'

'It's their only chance. Believe me, they have more chance by seeking asylum than by staying here. If they stay here, Johanna'll be burying them. That's the brutal truth. I'll stay here tonight with Jeremiah; you can't sit with him every night. You get some sleep. Got the keys?'

Sam gave him the keys and Tim finished his bourbon, and as he took the steps down from the veranda he turned and said, 'I'll be back early.'

Chapter Twenty-Three

The white cotton sheet lay in a crumpled mess over Sam as his body tossed and turned through the night, a small bedside fan rattling chaotically beside him. Red eyes glowed at him, white teeth snarled at him, closer, closer it came— 'No!' he screamed.

He sat bolt upright, breathing hard, his torso soaked in sweat, his sheet clammy and damp. He drew his fingers through his hair and breathed out heavily. Pulling his sheet into his waist and turning the edges of it in his hands, taking low slow breaths to calm him, he leaned over to the side for his watch. It was 1 a.m. He sighed heavily and padded across the floor to the kitchen area. The fridge light flashed on and off, and he blinked several times from the immediacy of its brightness. He took a bottle of water from it and placed it against his face, rolling it over his cheeks and holding it to his forehead before opening it and glugging its contents back.

He pushed the latch down on his door, opening it. Pushing aside the beaded curtain, he stood for a moment. The blackness wrapped itself around the village with a warm air. He breathed in; there was different smell to the night air. He struck a match from the box on his window ledge, and it fizzed and smoked, giving an immediate smell of sulphur. He lit the flame on the torch and blew out the match, placing it back in the box the other way up from the unlit ones. He laughed inwardly as he remembered how frustrated Kate would get when he used to put the dead matches back in with the others. He remembered how she'd dig her fingers in, trying to find a pink-ended one to light the now bum-sucked cigarette hanging from her mouth – a bad but cool habit they had both given up halfway through their first year as young and aspiring medical students. Neither of them had touched a cigarette since.

He climbed into his hammock; its slight sway brought a breeze across his naked chest. The torch flame danced high and low, attracting flying insects to its glow. A moth dared to flit too close and the delicateness of its wings was scorched by its intensity – it fluttered to the ground like a fallen leaf caught in the autumn wind. He breathed in heavily and slowly exhaled, closing his eyes momentarily as he did. From the mango groves echoed the haunting 'whoop whoop' of a scavenging hyena skulking around the elephants' graveyard on the other side of the pool. A bat darted low, and Sam raised his arm, spilling some of the water. He let it trickle across him before drying it in with his hand. Two bright eyes lit up on a branch above and moved away beneath the leaves. A mosquito whined and then stopped.

His mind churned over and over, thinking about the massacred elephants, Jeremiah's beating, the vileness of the poachers, Johanna's formidable courage, Amanuel and Abrihet not knowing what lay ahead – all of it swamping his head with a pressure that felt like it would explode while the incessant clicking of cicadas echoed in the stillness.

How would the children ever survive out in the wilderness? Not be terrified when exposed in the open to the sounds of the night? He couldn't just leave them, he knew as much, but he also knew Tim was right: in the village they stood no chance. Jeremiah was lucky to have survived, and even now nobody knew what his quality of life would be. Since Sam's arrival everyone had allowed themselves to hint at something bad, but frustratingly had never given him any more. His fingers scratched through his hair. He kept hearing Tim's words, *young or old, male or female. They don't care. It's not all about wars, you see, when people flee, it's about this.*

'About *what*, Tim?' he had almost shouted. Now he knew. And then there was Bamidele, Abraham's mother, saying *I would wish for my son to be as before. He was protected from the brutality that has been here. The sights hidden from him.'*

He remembered how Anbessa had gently silenced her, stopped her from continuing. And then Elisabet, his own beautiful Elisabet, her words by the pool – *Now you'll see, you'll live the nightmare.*

'Now I'll live the nightmare,' he said out loud. His eyes stung, and he wiped them. 'I don't *want* to live the nightmare,' he murmured, 'I don't want to see or live it, I want to see Kate trying to find an unused match in a matchbox again. I want to see normal again. I don't want to see this.' His head fell into his hands and he cried. Above in the treetop two bright eyes glowed in the dark, watching him silently. He brushed his eyes and wiped away the wetness from his face, then tipped himself out of the hammock, placing his bottle on the upturned barrel before going back inside.

The flame-lit torch gave the room a warm glow. He took his bag from the sofa and rummaged at the bottom of it for his pen, and his writing pad from the pocket. He pressed his mobile on and cursed at the intermittent 3G signal it gave him. He googled "travel on foot to the Mediterranean from Eritrea" and waited. A rainbow-coloured kaleidoscope icon whirled in the centre of the page like a multi-coloured lollipop on a spinning wheel. The screen went blank: no results found. 'Well, there's a surprise!' He tried again, this time typing "map of Eritrea to Libya", and the icon spun once more until a map came up.

'Bingo!' he said.

He stretched his thumb and middle finger across the screen, enlarging the map. He snorted at the sheer size of the terrain, and quickly, before losing signal, sketched the map on his pad, and then on each border wrote the name of the neighbouring countries. At the bottom he wrote *Eritrea* and circled it, and then from the most southerly point, Adi Ada, he drew dotted lines up to the next point and wrote *Sudan,* then *Libya*, circling them again, and then *Ajdabiya, Tripoli.* Then he drew a boat and waves, and scribbled in the waves *Mediterranean Sea* and on the other side of the sea he wrote *Italy* in capital letters. Just as he finished that, the screen went blank; his sketchy signal had petered out to non-existent. He wasn't too fazed by the lack of a European map, as he knew it from his days of cycling through most of the countries as a medical student for charities and skiing in the Alps and the Pyrenees from an early age. He drew Europe in, with a dotted line going north to Switzerland then north-west, another dotted line to France, and the penultimate dotted line to the northern coast where again he drew a boat and some waves, and penned across it *English Channel*. On the other side of the water he wrote *England*, underlining it, and beside that he wrote, *where Manchester United are from and cricket is played: the Land of Hope.*

He looked at the map, tracking his finger along the dotted lines all the way from Eritrea to England, and then he carefully tore it away from the pad's spine. He tucked the pad away in his bag along with his pen. Pushing himself up from the sofa, he went back outside and slid back into the hammock, leaning across to retrieve his water. He guzzled it down while holding the map up, viewing the countries Amanuel and Abrihet needed to traverse, as if a picture made it easy and a dot-to-dot from country to country really was just a walk in the park. If they ever reached their destination, they'd be at least a year older and have a tale to tell. 'If they ever reach their destination,' he murmured. He pressed his fingertips on the ground to push the hammock and then he lay in it watching the galaxy above as the stars danced and a fireball shot through the blackness and hearing the 'whoop whoop' of the hyenas slinking about in the still warm darkness. The gentle back and forth of the hammock's rocking slowly allowed Sam's mind to rest and fall away into the night.

It was the cacophony of shrill squawks from black-winged lovebirds that caused Sam to peel open an eye. A cockerel crowed from the rooftop of a hut, reminding the village that daybreak had come. Katumba swung in the treetops before resting above the hammock, his spindly hand nudging the top of Sam's head. Sam flicked his arm up. The long, soft tail of the young monkey brushed across his face as he scampered back up the trunk and into the tree where he perched, his mouth smacking around his fruity breakfast. Sam rubbed his eyes. The torch had burnt itself out and the sky was glowing a warming crimson. He blinked several times and rolled himself out of the hammock, and as he did so his paper map fell to the ground. He bent down and picked it up, dusting it off, and went back inside, the beaded curtain swaying and rattling behind him. He placed the map inside one of his medical magazines on the table while he ground a handful of coffee beans, the rich, smoky fragrance tickling his nose. He poured fresh water from a bottle into his percolator and left his coffee to percolate on a low flame.

In the shower his boxer shorts dropped from his waist. The cool water splashed against his face as he leaned his head back, allowing himself to let the calmness take over, the feeling like a warm summer rain on his face and body. The coolness of the water eased the angry itchiness of the many small bites he'd garnered from sleeping under the starlit sky – a cool sultry night without a mosquito net came with consequences. He lathered the soap into his hair and stood beneath the rose, rinsing his hands through his head until no more suds ran down his body, he stretched over to the small ledge for his toothbrush. He could stay in its tranquil cocoon all day but the aroma of coffee and the bubbling from the pot's spout and the clanging of the percolator's lid was his alarm to end his cooling shower. He turned off the lever and wrapping his towel around his waist as he made his way back to the bedroom, he expertly latched his boxers onto his big toe and, bringing his knee up, he high-kicked them like a football into the laundry pile – goal!

Turning off his bedside fan he pushed the mosquito net to one side, shaking out his sheet allowing it to billow and fall onto the mattress, the protective netting falling back around the bed. He took his watch, strapping it to his wrist, then he padded into the kitchen and poured his coffee, a deep treacle liquid with a smooth creamy top steaming in the colourfully hand-painted coffee cup. He flicked his wrist up; it was 4.56 a.m. After savouring every last drop from his cup, he grabbed two bananas and some unleavened bread, dolloping a sweet fruit preserve onto them and in a clean cup he poured another coffee. He tucked his medical magazine into his bag before leaving to make his way to the medical centre, trying not to spill a drop from the cup.

Katumba followed high in the branches until he reached the same destination, then lobbed himself over onto the generator and rested while Sam opened the mesh door and unlocked the main door with Elisabet's keys.

The stale closeness of the air hit him, and an immediate sweat formed on his brow. He left breakfast on his desk with his satchel and went to retrieve the coffee he'd left on the veranda ledge whilst he had opened up. The fan hummed, its blades whizzing tirelessly while Sam flung open the windows, allowing cool air to circulate and give some relief from the clinic's suffocating heat. He glanced over to the corner, Tim's head was drooped, his chin almost on his chest, and two large patches had formed in the pits of his T-shirt with what looked like a map of a country as a perspiring imprint on the front of his top. His face glowed with tiny pops of perspiration while he snored gently.

'Hey, Tim,' Sam nudged him gently until he slowly opened his eyes. 'It's morning; I can take over from you. I've brought you some breakfast, and more importantly a coffee.'

'Sam' – Tim blinked several times – 'what's the time?' He stretched his shoulders back until they clicked and then pulled out a handkerchief from his pocket and mopped his brow and cheeks. 'Man, it's like an oven in here.'

'I've opened the windows to let some air in. It's just gone five. How was Jeremiah through the night?' His voice was low, so as not to wake Jeremiah, ironically.

'Yep, not too bad,' Tim said, taking a generous mouthful from his cup. 'Aww, that's good, Sam, that's really good,' taking another gulp. 'Got to hand it to us, we grow the best coffee,' he smiled with a wink. 'Yep, Jeremiah, he did okay, slept through pretty much, tossed and turned a little, held his ribs a bit. I administered 2mg of morphine at about 1 a.m. – it's all in his notes. He called out a few times, for Johanna mostly, and shouted, *Run, boy, you gotta go*. He's beginning to sound more coherent, not so garbled. I'd say he'll start to properly come around over the next twenty-four hours.'

'Twenty-four hours too late, right?'

'For the children yes – we can't chance it. Abrihet wears a purple skirt, and a boy who runs like a gazelle, there's only one and that's Amanuel. *Run, boy, you gotta go* kinda says it all for me. They need to be gone by early evening; I can hold the fort here if you drive them.'

Sam went back to his desk and took the magazine from his bag, grabbing the bananas and bread as he did, and pulled a chair up next to Tim.

'Here's breakfast!'

'Nice! Fruit jam. Who made this? Bamidele I'm guessing, looks like hers.'

'Yep! It's not bad, is it?' Sam said, as he shook the magazine a little until the map fell out. 'I drew a map last night – well at one in the morning to be precise. I just couldn't sleep, so I googled the countries the children need to cross to get anywhere close to Europe. If I can get them near the border of Sudan by car, or even across it, that's at least one hurdle of God knows how many eliminated.' He trailed his fingers up the dotted lines and patted the tip of his finger on the page. 'Then they'd need to walk until they reached the Libyan border – that alone's about 2,000 km – and then, depending where they end up, they'll need to navigate their way across the country to get to Ajdabiya and then Tripoli, on the Mediterranean coastline – God, this sounds insane! I've worked it out that crossing Libya alone'd be about 3,350 km and that'd take them over six hundred hours.'

'What's that? – about twenty-five, twenty-six days?'

'Yep that's full on, no stops and at an adult's pace.'

'So, we can triple that easily. Three or four months for them,' Tim said.

'Something like that – and that's not even thinking about dehydration, exhaustion, blisters, ill-health, fear, hunger, whatever else can be added to this nightmare of a journey. Three or four months, maybe longer. From Tripoli they'd need to get a boat somehow, and if they do make it to that point then they could be in Italy. They'd be over halfway to the UK. But they don't have any legal papers, they don't have anything.'

'They have faith, Sam. And I know you're not a believer, but it will force them on, trust me. I know the African mind; we don't give up. And Sam ...'

'Yes?'

'When you leave this evening take the Red Cross van. You'll get further in it and you're less likely to be stopped. Take your medical papers and identity cards, passport – the children can be hidden between the medical supplies. You'd never make it across the border in your Land Rover – the children would be spotted immediately – but if you're in a charity vehicle, Border Control are less likely to search you or even ask questions. Plus, it doesn't look suspicious; you're a medical practitioner working for an independent humanitarian organisation. We're impartial to conflict, not government-funded, so it's probably the best cover for you to get them out of Eritrea unseen.'

As the two men talked Jeremiah stirred in his sleep: 'Boy, run, like gazelle, you run ...'

'Right,' said Tim. 'I'm going to get out of here. I stink like a man who's slept with the pigs! The children'll need just the basics. I'll be back later.' He pushed himself up from the chair, patted Sam hard on the back and left. 'Thanks for the coffee, my friend.' The door closed behind him.

Sam pushed the chair to the side of the room and took up Jeremiah's notes from the end of his bed. Tim's writing was as bad as his own. He moved round to the side of the bed and took Jeremiah's hand, 'Hey, Jeremiah, it's Sam just doing your blood pressure. How ya doing?'

Jeremiah squeezed Sam's hand.

'Good, so you're doing okay, that's good. And the pain, how's the pain? Squeeze hard for bad, and not so hard for not too bad.'

Jeremiah gripped hard.

'Bad huh? Want something to help?'

Jeremiah squeezed again.

'No worries, I'm just going to shine a light into your eyes – it's coming just about now.'

The light dazzled; Jeremiah flinched a little.

'Pupils still equal and constricting,' Sam said out loud. 'That's good, Jeremiah, really good.' Sam teased out 2mg of morphine and administered it into the cannula; Jeremiah's hand moved uneasily. 'Feels a bit cold and weird as it goes in, doesn't it? I'm just going to flush it through, it'll feel the same … there, all done, that should ease the pain.'

Sam moved to the end of the bed and wrote up the observations and drugs administered. He left Jeremiah's bedside and sat at his desk poring through his clinical notes.

Elisabet arrived, and Sam flicked his wrist up; it was 7 a.m. He scrolled down the list of vaccinations to administer and went to the drugs cupboard, counting through the vaccines; he'd need more. He took out the yellow sharps bin from the bottom shelf and placed it on a trolley ready for the morning's jabs.

'Coffee good,' Jeremiah mumbled.

Sam turned and looked over to him. 'Jeremiah?' Sam moved swiftly over to him. Jeremiah's eyelids fluttered, and slowly, slowly his eyes opened, then he closed them again slowly and opened them again. He did that several times until they remained open. He could see a blurred outline of a figure standing beside him; he blinked as it came closer and moved further away from him, back and forth. A tear fell from the corner of his eye, and then the blurriness stayed at the same distance and the outline of it became clearer, the fuzziness surrounding it began to move away – and then there it was, a clear image of a person.

'Doctor Sam,' he uttered.

'Hello, Jeremiah.' Sam crouched down by the bedside and smiled.

'Good coffee.'

Sam snorted through a smile, 'You're right. You sell good coffee, damn good coffee, my man.'

Jeremiah broke a smile, the first smile since before the attack, and the tiniest hint of gold peeked through.

'You're back, Jeremiah, we've got you back,' said Sam, burying his head on the bed, holding Jeremiah's hand tightly and the tears ever so slowly trickled down both their faces.

He left Jeremiah briefly, allowing him to come around slowly. He'd feel disoriented, confused for a while, and would need a little space to bring himself back.

Sam opened his bag and pulled out his mobile: *He's woken up*. As the text was sent to Tim's phone, the door opened and Elisabet stood in its frame, a pale blue cotton dress flowing over her body, a turquoise scarf tied around her head.

'Sleep well?' she asked as she slipped past him to the medical cupboard, to leave her basket that only ever carried her book in it. He touched her hand as she did.

'Yes,' he lied – she didn't need to know – 'Look over there,' he swiftly continued, gesticulating with his head towards Jeremiah's bed.

'What is it?' She turned and gasped. 'Jeremiah!' She made a noise as she took a sharp intake of breath. 'Oh my!' She rushed to his bedside, her dress swishing like a waterfall as she did. She took his hand and leant over and kissed his forehead, and with the delicateness of her touch she smoothed the softness of his beard that was slowly beginning to hide the bruises, tracing her fingers lightly across the crude scarring on his face. 'Welcome back, Jeremiah,' she cried softly into her smile. He took his arm up to hers and his own smile was golden.

Sam rested his hand on Elisabet's shoulder, 'I have to go back to Johanna's now, to support her. Can I leave you for a while? I'll be back in time for the vaccination clinic.'

She nodded.

'See you later, Jeremiah, don't go anywhere,' Sam said as he patted his shoulder and winked.

From the veranda, Sam stared out, letting his eyes take in the view of the huts once more, and Katumba edged its way along the ledge copying him.

'Hey little fella, he's awake.'

Katumba cocked his head and clapped his hands then chattered while delighting in a somersault.

'Right; now I'm going back to Johanna.'

Every day, Sam had walked this walk it was no more than a few hundred yards, yet today his feet dragged as if he was carrying weighted bags of stones in his shoes. With her husband Elijah away from home, tending his sick mother in another village, she had nobody else to console her.

As Sam neared their hut, he could see Johanna washing the plates and setting them out to dry in the sun. She looked up from the bowl, and a knowing smile formed on her face. A smile that wasn't really a smile because her eyes said something else. It was a smile that acknowledged the sadness.

She stood up and dried her hands on a cloth. 'Please,' she said and ushered him into her home.

Sam shook his head and chewed at the side of his mouth; his palms felt clammy, and he clenched and unclenched his fists.

'How long do I have?'

The words stuck in his throat and his eyes welled with a liquid that would not relent. He gritted his teeth, his jawbone flexed, and he drew in his breath. 'Until six o'clock.'

She nodded once. Her eyes flicked about the room, and she swallowed, 'Will you take them to somewhere to begin ...' she stopped, her voice trembling. She allowed herself to breathe, closed her eyes, took another breath and opened her eyes again, 'to begin their journey?' she finished.

'Yes, Johanna, I'll take them.' Every inch of his body wanted to let the tears fall, but he couldn't, not when he stood in front of a woman whose world was being ripped out from her body. Whose heart was breaking over and over again, and yet she stood in front of him with a courage that ripped at his own heart. Knowing that what she had given life to was being taken from her in the cruellest way possible. At least with death she had the comfort of her maker keeping them safe, watching over them eternally. Instead, she was giving them to the unknown, leaving a grief unfinished, still open, still scarring her daily until the day she would finally be called. He stood in front of a woman who would no longer hear the call of her offspring's names, the joy in their laughter, the chants of their English. She stood strong in front of him.

'Shall I bring them to you?'

'Yes, to the medical centre, just with a light bag, something warm, a blanket maybe,' he stuttered.

'I'll be there.'

Sam offered a smile, one that he knew was helpless and pathetic, and could never change what was happening to Johanna or her family. He touched her arm as if to say *it will be okay*, knowing it was far from that, and then he left.

The same way he'd leave a family in an over-lit hospital corridor hung with signs to different departments (or 'suites' to sugarcandy their name), where unused trolley beds sat stationed at the side. Where he'd be faced with the relations outside a room sitting on blue plastic chairs, where the powerful pong of disinfectant hung heavy in the air, hands gripped, turning on themselves, the endless pinging of mobiles waiting for news – still waiting for news, any news … And when that news finally came and the faces changed from an anxious exhausted look to a nothing, a face that didn't cry, didn't move, stayed still as the disbelief of the words fed through their ears and then smacked them in the gut. The silent closing of a door and hushed shake of his head to say *We did all we could.* That overwhelming feeling of uselessness and the awareness of the dark shadow that lurked in the corner wanting to get its way, waiting to take out its hand. That feeling of walking away remained.

The beaded curtains of Johanna's door swayed behind him – and that was when he heard an African woman break, a keening, howling wail that only comes from grief from a daughter, a wife, a friend and a mother, always a mother. He didn't see her crumple to the ground – but he knew, and his own tears fell.

Chapter Twenty-Four

Sam glanced up at the clock. It was 4.49 p.m. He watched as the second hand ticked around the clock's face and then the minute hand almost quivered into place.

'What time are the children coming?' Elisabet asked as she packed away the last of the vaccine syringes into the cupboard.

'Six o'clock.'

'And Tim?'

'He should be here any minute. Can you hold the fort while I get a few bits for the journey?'

'Sure – and Sam …'

He turned.

'Nothing. Go, it can wait.'

Leaving his bag on his desk he quickly made his way back to his hut, the leaves in the trees above rustling as he did.

The beads of his door rattled as he pushed them aside. He wafted his shirt from his chest and brushed his sleeve across his brow.

He knelt down and waggled a cane under his bed to pull his rucksack out; grabbing it, he brushed it down. In the kitchen his shelf seemed to jump out at him like a conveyor belt on some televised games show. 'What do I need, what do I need, what do I need?' he muttered. His eyes swiftly scanned the shelf: packets of nuts, dates, dried fruit, a bunch of bananas, two mangoes, a packet of chocolate-covered biscuits, a tin of travel sweets. He stuffed them into his bag, scooping up the *injera* and the unleavened bread, wrapping it several times in a muslin cloth and nestling it down the side of packets. 'What else, what else, what else?' He rummaged through the small cupboard and found a packet of Jacob's cream crackers and box of Weetabix. He'd found some in the supermarket in Asmara when he'd first arrived, and ever since then had returned to buy a few of his home food comforts, crackers one of them. The children could eat the Weetabix dry. He left the empty cereal box on the side. Marmite? He tilted his head from side to side, his eyes creased at the corners; he put it back. The seal of the fridge door eventually came free with a sucking noise, and five hand-sized bottles of water rolled out. He rejigged his bag and placed them at the bottom so as not to squash the food, along with two bars of Cadbury's Dairy Milk. They'd stay a little chilled there, at least.

He rolled a lightweight blanket into a tight sausage and stuffed it into the top of the bag. With one tug on the toggle he closed his rucksack and the clasp snapped shut. He went back to his room and opened a wooden trinket box at the side of his bed, turning out a silver chain with a locket. He held it up, letting it dangle in the air; the locket spun, dancing shadowlike crystals on the wall as the spears of light caught its prettiness. He snaked it into his palm and tucked it into his pocket, then left.

Wafting his shirt as he sped across the baked ground, he smiled at the women as their melodies funnelled into the suffocating atmosphere. He raised his hand at the men as they sat listening to Abel, the aroma of coffee filtering through their huddled bodies.

'Hey, Doctor Sam!'

Sam looked up, shielding his eyes, and waved to Anbessa, who was repairing his roof. In the treetops, Katumba followed along on his skyline pavement. He tossed no fruit today, as if he understood the urgency of Sam's footsteps. Sam took both steps of the veranda in one stride and pushed the door open. In the corner Jeremiah was now propped up and sipping a glass of water through a straw. Sam heard the engine of the Red Cross van pulling up and the excitement of the children as Tim got out of it.

The mesh door opened, it was 5.40 p.m. 'Are you okay?' Tim asked, mopping his brow with his handkerchief.

Sam shook his head.

'You've got this,' said Tim. 'I've brought you a road map to get you to the border, here.' He spread it out on the desk. 'You need to get yourself onto the mountain roads; that way, if you get into any danger you can hide in villages, and you won't be out of place there. You're going to be heading north. Here, take this.' He handed Sam a compass. 'About an hour before you reach the Sudanese border, hide the children between the supplies and the boxes; the roads near the borders are notorious for police and spot checks. When you get to the border, if you're questioned simply tell the border control officers you're heading to the South Sudan Red Cross refugee camp and you're part of the medical convoy for the camp there, to aid with the contaminated water crisis. They'll go with that. There's a huge problem at the moment with waterborne diseases, vulnerable lives, young children dying ...'

'And then?'

'Once you've cleared the border, get the children as far north as you can – and then ...'

'And then I have to leave them,' Sam's voice trailed off.

'And then you have to leave them.'

'Have you got food supplies?'

'For them? Yes.'

'Medical?'

'A small first aid kit – the basics, plasters, creams.'

Sam looked up at the clock. It was 5.55 p.m.

'How are you feeling, Sam?'

'Sick. How I'll always feel about this. It'll never go away, will it? Like Johanna and Elijah, I'll be empty inside, not knowing whether they made it, whether they found refuge or whether running got them away. Which fear is worse? Dying violently, or knowing it'll happen anyway? Excuse me a moment.' He left Elisabet and Tim, and the toilet door closed behind him. The sound of him hurling violently into the loo bowl could be heard, then the rush of water spurting from the tap. Sam returned, wiping his mouth and face with a paper towel. Nobody said anything – the fear, the dread, the deep sickening feeling, was felt and understood by all of them.

The door opened slowly; Sam swallowed. 'Hey,' he said, 'Johanna.'

Two young children stood in front of him, Abrihet wore a simple cotton skirt and top, and Amanuel his red top and blue shorts. They stood silently by their mother's sides, her hands cupping their faces, her body rocking.

'Do they know what's happening?' Sam asked.

'Yes, I've explained it to them. They know how far they must go to be safe, to always follow the north star.'

Sam took the map inside his magazine, crouched down and began to show them the dotted lines that meandered through each country. He explained how they'd need to get across the sea, and that they'd have to hide on the boat each time. He told them how he had packed a bag for them, that would give them nourishment and water to sip, for a little while at least, along the way. They looked down at the drawing and watched as his finger followed the line to each border. They watched his hand as it moved like the sea, as he told them *this* was a good place to reach. And then his finger trailed through Europe and dipped up and down as if they were crossing the rugged terrain or the snow-capped mountains of the Alps where they would find shelter in the outbuildings for animals, and where the water running down the mountains would be fresh and clean and good to drink. And then, when they finally reached the north coast of France – because they *would* reach it – there they would see the greyness of the sea that was known as the English Channel, and their need to stow away on a boat was even greater.

He explained that the sea would be different, and that there would be many big boats, but it would be a smaller sea to cross, and the journey would be short. And once they had crossed it, then they would be safe – they would have reached the land of hope.

And they *would* reach it.

From his wallet he took a wad of banknotes and tied them together with an elastic band. 'Look after this. It will help you.' Abrihet noticed the picture of a woman with a crown on her head. Sam gave them Tim's compass, and then from his pocket he took the silver chain and locket. He opened it; inside was the tiniest fragment of a mango leaf and a sprinkle of cinnamon bark. On the front of the locket was an imprint of St Christopher, the patron saint of travellers. He proffered it to them.

'Here, this was my mother's. She loved to travel when she was younger, and she too believed just like you, maybe it will guide you too, just like the north star. There's a little piece of mango leaf inside to remind you of home and the mango groves where the elephants drank and stayed cool by the pool where the sun sinks beneath its surface to light it up for the fish below – and here, smell …' He lifted it to the children's noses.

'It smells of home,' Amanuel said in Tigrinya.

'It does, doesn't it? – and of the sacks on Jeremiah's wagon, too. Keep it safe with you. Here …' He lifted Abrihet's braids and put the necklace around her neck. He looked at the clock. It was 6.10 p.m. 'Are you ready?'

'We ready,' they said.

'Johanna, are you ready?' Sam asked.

Her face held an expression of calm stoicism, her eyes filled with unfallen tears, 'I'm ready,' she said.

She bent down to her children and her arms embraced them both. Then she held her son's face and traced her hands across it, outlining every part of it, and pulled him into her body, with her hold on him as tight as she could ever hold him. She brushed away his tears and kissed his wet cheeks. And then she took her daughter and pulled gently at her beaded hair, letting every bead gently run through the palm of her hand to the end of her fingertips, then she smoothed the line of her daughter's face, cupping her hands in hers and pulling her into her body and breathing in the smell of her child. And with both arms she held her children, with every hold inhaling their very essence, reminding her for ever of her children, until Sam gently eased her away.

His hands rested on her shoulder until he uttered the words no mother wants to hear when she's letting her children go, unsure of their own safety and into the wilderness, where the nights would be dark and long and the journey everlasting. Her face remaining strong pretending everything would be okay yet her heart breaking silently with pain.

'We must go,' he said.

Johanna nodded and handed a small bag to him. Elisabet stepped forward and hugged both the children, then held Sam. He brushed her tears away and kissed her softly. From the corner of the room, Jeremiah smiled at the children, his smile broad and golden. 'You be safe, Little Gazelle, and keep going, Abrihet.'

Sam led them out onto the veranda with both bags on his shoulder towards the Red Cross van. Tim followed, shook Sam's hand and embraced him hard, and lifted both children in a bear hug. On the veranda, Johanna stood and watched as her children turned one last time to see their mother, her hand to her lips, the other held up to wave.

And then it happened – the blaring of horns, the shooting of guns, the sounds of screams, the jeering as the invaders rampaged through the village with terrifying violence, torching the roofs of homes of the villagers where before a calm silence had been. The branches of the fruit trees swayed manically as loud shrieks came from the troop of monkeys, leaping through the branches as the poachers chased and shot their rifles high into them, flames reaching upwards, licking the leaves of mango trees, before the branches became engulfed. The men kicked over the pots that had been boiling water to be clean enough to drink, dogs howled and whimpered as heavy boots kicked them aside. Chickens squawked and ran everywhere, unsettled by the noise. Women screamed as poachers barged into their homes – a home where each woman was violated whilst the filth of the other poachers watched, undoing their trousers ready for their turn.

Katumba leapt from branch to branch, throwing himself onto the back of a man who had grabbed a child. The handle of the man's machete beat it off, and Katumba whimpered with the bluntness of the hit. Sam crouched low at the side of the medical hut, the children huddled into him; they hid, terrified, crouching low behind the generator, surrounded by the mad, disgusting noise of men with machetes and firearms, hungry for barbarity. Villagers ran to their huts hiding with a trembling fear. Women were grabbed by their hair and pushed up against walls, their clothes ripped from them. Tables, chairs upturned. Savage brutality – children ran screaming towards Elisabet and Johanna, who rushed them into the medical centre for safety, Elisabet's eye catching Sam's as he hunkered down low behind the generator with Abrihet and Amanuel silenced in his arms. His finger went to his lips. *Look after them all in the clinic* he telegraphed. Johanna nodded, and with her arms outspread made a frenzied attempt to push the small children into the clinic and lock the door.

Sam waited for the madness to pass him, and then he lifted both children, one on his back and the other in his arms, and inched his way around the generator to see the Red Cross van nearby. Tim lay beneath it. Then, without a moment to lose, Sam stood up and ran towards it, the children gripping onto him. A man who had a woman by her throat, holding her down, ready to perform some horrific act on her glimpsed the red t-shirt from the corner of his eye. He spat in her face, and turned – he looked like a Vietnamese. He shouted out and his men came running. Katumba flung himself on the man's back, screeching and pulling at his hair. The man grabbed Katumba's fur and threw him off, and another man came at the monkey. Katumba whimpered again. The man shouted another order and a crate covered Katumba, and then the man shouted more, saliva drooling from his rotten mouth, his eyes thin, his nails black. A gun fired. Sam groaned in pain and grabbed his leg, the children clung to him, Tim slid out from under the vehicle and opened its door ready, another shot came, and Sam stumbled, Katumba shrieked and rattled at the crate's bars. Then another crack from the rifle reverberated around the village. Sam, still running, blocking out the pain, threw the children with the bags into the vehicle, another shot came, and as he slid down from the open door a wetness ran down his leg.

'Get out of here, Tim, get them out of here,' he shouted, thrusting a crumpled, blood-stained map into Tim's hand. The engine roared and the gears ground as Tim slammed it into first, the tyres spun, and the van screamed off, away from the onslaught. Tim watched from the rear-view mirror as another shot took Sam. He lay still.

The vehicle wavered for a moment and then it was gone. The man who had shot at Sam shouted more orders, and two of the men took the crate and threw it into a jeep.

The terrified crying of children, hidden, unsure whether it was safe to come out. The lifeless body of a man who'd come to live and help the village.

And from the mango groves a mass of grey came, feet kicking the dust, ears flapping, trumpeting a warning – a warning that their killers did not heed – and so it happened; they came with formidable power, with might, and a need to protect. Their feet thunderous on the baked earth, they did not move in the gentle sway the village people knew – they came in force, their ears pinned back, their trunks curled under, their ivory tusks held ready to spear as they charged, charged at the men who had massacred their family, charged at the men who had raped the women, charged at the men who had stolen happiness, their trumpeting blasting the air as their feet crushed those who did not care. And when those men had fallen they charged the man whose sickening laugh enjoyed the killing of beast and man, who stood firing his bullets until his trigger just clicked. And from a few metres away from him the youngest of the elephants came to a dramatic stop, the smallest elephant who would wallow in the edges of the pool, who had urged the matriarch to wake, finding its way to the front, flinging his trunk towards the man, kicking the dust in fury. The man fell back, trying to run, trying to scramble to his own wretched feet, and as he did the feet of the elephant stamped on his body, crushing his ribs as Jeremiah's had been crushed, and its tusks impaled him.

The elephants had come to protect because they were the elephants of Adi Ada.

Chapter Twenty-Five

The viscid layer of smoke that had draped itself over much of the village had slowly begun to dissipate. The raging fires that had blocked out the sun, casting an apocalyptic orange hue over the village, had subsided, now just leaving a heavy dust. The women sat in silence, the vibrant colours of their clothes and scarves seeming to carry a heaviness. Bright yet dull.

The children helped their fathers clear the charred debris and start to rebuild huts for those whose homes were now just piles of ash, some of them still smouldering. There was no noise about the village. The smiles and happiness had been stolen by the sick men who had come. Yet now once more the villagers would rebuild their lives. The troop of monkeys made weird, melancholy noises as they searched for their youngest. Johanna would visit Elisabet daily in the medical hut, where their silence could be heard, their own sorrow tearing at their hearts, ripping them apart.

Elisabet sat rocking in the wicker chair, a notebook by her side with a page torn out and pen beside it:

Falling in love. Perhaps the most beautiful part of two people's very existence. When the heartbeat can be heard outside my own ribcage. The sound of your name catches each time in my throat. Warm and soft. My dreams each night with you in them. So real, so vivid, so strong. Like the rush of wind through my hair. Like the burning sun on my face. A warm glow in my life. And then when I wake you are there. You stroll into the room. The hinge of the door breaks the silence. The slight crease around your eyes when you smile. The soft touch of your hand. And your voice, different to mine. You brush past the beds, and the comfort of you is present. How did I receive such a gift? A love so hard. My lips are wet. My eyes are full. To brush my cheeks is to brush away you. The tears that fall. Unstoppable. You are gone.

My faith will keep me strong.

Back and forth, back and forth. Her legs scrunched up to her ribcage, her arms swaddled around her knees. The inner door swung on its hinge, a man in uniform stood at it. Jeremiah from his bed glanced over to the door.

'Elisabet Sebhuto?'

She looked ahead hearing the sound of her name. 'Who wants to know?'

'We need to ask you some questions.'

She blinked and a tear fell down her tear-stained cheeks. She looked up and turned her head towards the door.

'Some questions?' she said.

'The men who did this. We need to ask you questions about it.'

'Men?' She turned away and stared ahead. The chair rocked in the dull silence, the only sound of the cicadas and the rattle of the fan. She looked over to Jeremiah.

'The men who took the lives of innocent people,' she said. 'The men who had stripped the ivory from the elephants and left them dead, their faces hacked open. The men who raped the women and the children who have fled. The men who beat my friend to a pulp. The men, the men ...' Her voice shook as she tried to say the words that choked her. 'The men who killed ...' she stopped, her words stuck in her throat – the name she loved, the man she loved, now his name jammed in her throat. 'Men? Is that what they are?'

The officer inhaled and breathed out. 'May I sit down?'

Her eyes directed him towards the desk. 'Not there. Not that chair. Please don't sit in that chair.' He removed his hand from Sam's chair.

He pulled up a metal chair from beside the desk; it scraped across the floor. 'Did you see them? Can you tell me anything of what you saw?' he asked.

'Five days have passed, and you come *now*? You come now to ask me what I saw? I saw a barbaric thirst for poisonous money. I saw a man I loved killed.' She made her hand into a gun. 'Bang, bang, bang! Have you ever seen an innocent man killed, shot in the back whilst he runs, unarmed, carrying children? Have you ever seen a woman savagely beaten and raped? Have you ever seen two children escape for their own safety, terrified, alone? And a mother crumple to the ground, watching them go? Have you ever seen a man battered half to death? And you ask me what ...? Did I *see* anything? My head is filled with what I've seen, what I will always see, what you and your men protect because you're as corrupt as them, you *are* them. Get out! Get out! Get out!' Her head fell into her arms and the chair rocked.

He didn't move.

'You heard her.'

Elisabet looked over to the door and squinting through bleary eyes she tried to make out his silhouette. 'Please leave,' the man said, and moved aside while the man in uniform brushed past him. She squinted again, wiping her eyes, for a moment she thought it was ... For a moment she thought it had all been just a terrible nightmare and that *he* was still here. She smudged the tears from her face and the slime from her nose that slid down over her lips.

'Tim!' She ran towards him and he caught her in his arms as she collapsed to the ground, the sound of her sobbing uncontrollable and raw as he rocked her in his arms. 'He's gone,' she cried, 'he's gone.'

'I know.' He held her head in his chest, and his own tears fell.

Chapter Twenty-Six

Deal, Kent

In the time that the children had been with Tom, they had become accustomed to their new lives; they also knew that to protect themselves they had to live secretly. They believed Tom and Kate, and the promise they had made to keep them safe.

Tom would still run in the early hours with Amanuel, leaving Abrihet at home asleep. Tom and Amanuel would sit and talk on the rocks they'd first sat on.

'Tom?'

'Yep, little fella?'

'Why no elephants come here?'

'What d'you mean?'

'Every day we come here, and I never see elephant. Do people not like elephant?'

Tom smiled. 'We don't have elephants like you.'

'You don't?' Amanuel's eyes widening. 'Why you don't?

'Because our country doesn't have that kind of wildlife. We just see them in zoos or on television.'

'Like tiger?'

'Yeah, like the tiger.'

'But that's not their home.'

'No, it's not – but it protects them. Maybe it's wrong to keep them like that, but if they weren't protected then we'd lose them.'

'You think they happy?'

Tom sighed and tried to smile in response to the inquisitiveness of this small boy who now sat daily with him as though his own son, with a need and hunger to know. 'I don't know.' And that was the most honest he could be; he didn't know. 'What do you think? D'you think they're happy?'

Amanuel snorted and puckered his lips. 'How can they? In my country, our land is their land. You know, we share. They must miss their families.'

'Their families?'

'Yes, their brothers and sisters and mothers and fathers. They must cry.'

'I think you're right … come on, let's run back, my bum's gone numb.' Tom nudged Amanuel.

'We go – I win, you know.' With a glint in his eye Amanuel had already run ahead. 'Come on, Tom, I win.' His words carried in the wind, his laughter like an echo around them, as his body pelted ahead of Tom, his arms in a running position his red top pushing backwards, swift and agile past the beach huts, past old Bert's boat shed, past the Crab Shack, past the RNLI boats on the slipway and back to Beach Top.

He stood grinning at the end of the driveway, waiting for Tom.

'I win,' he beamed.

'You sure did,' Tom panted.

Tom took the front door key from under the plant pot and opened the door.

Down the road, the RNLI's external light automatically switched on as one of the crew members made his way to the door for his shift. He pursed his lips and drew hard on his cigarette before flicking it over the harbour wall. He snorted and spat the contents from his mouth.

'Ain't right,' he said under his breath. 'You don't belong 'ere.'

Amanuel sat perched at the kitchen island, his legs dangling from his seat, munching on a piece of toast and peanut butter. From the kitchen, they could hear Abrihet surfacing then making her way downstairs.

'D'you fancy cereal or toast for breakfast, Abrihet?' Tom asked.

'Toast, please.'

'Thought we could watch *Two Brothers* tonight for our Friday night movie?' Tom said as he popped two pieces of bread into the toaster.

'*Two Brothers?*' Amanuel frowned.

'It's a film about two tigers who get separated as cubs. Kate will be over too, so how about we do pizza and popcorn?'

'Like tiger in zoo?' Amanuel asked.

'Not quite like the tiger in the zoo.'

'How they lose?'

'Well, little chap, let's watch the film and find out. But until then, I need to crack on with my work and make a few phone calls.'

The children finished breakfast and disappeared back upstairs, leaving Tom to work.

He took the piece of paper where he had jotted down the numbers of the local state schools, but as the morning passed it became progressively more and more depressing, everyone saying the same thing: they were full to capacity and the local authority would need to be contacted to add the child's name to a waiting list. Tom sighed with frustration as he put the phone down.

A message from Kate pinged into his mobile:

Hey, you, how's the school hunt going? x

> *Rubbish, all the schools are full which means going through the council and being put on their waiting list.*

Bummer x

> *I know, we can't go that route, I've got one more school to try and then I draw a blank, and we can't hide them here forever…*

What are you saying? x

> *They're not ours to keep…*

And what about Alcatraz, Tom? We promised them. x

> *I know, but I'm running out of ideas.*

I need to get back to work. I'll pop over about 7ish, chin up. x

Tom reread Kate's message, then leant back in his chair and pushed his hands through his hair. 'Alcatraz, damn it! Come on, schools, one of you has to have a space.'

He googled again this time, pushing his radius out to ten miles from Deal, hoping that at least one school that he hadn't already tried would come up. He waited while the icon swirled on the screen: St Benedict's RC Secondary School, Ebbsfleet, near Ramsgate. He stared at the screen, reading the school name over again until he finally clicked on the link. He read through the details. Everything seemed perfect – it was only nine miles away, towards Ramsgate, an area he knew well, as a few clients of his lived that way. He dialled and waited.

'Good morning, St Benedict's School, Wendy speaking.'

'Oh, hi, good morning, I wonder if you can help me?'

'I'll certainly try.'

'Right, okay. I just wondered whether you had any places in your school for new admissions now?'

'New admissions, for the September intake d'you mean?'

'No, I meant like *now*.'

'Are you local to the area?'

Tom sighed as if resigning himself to the reply, 'About nine miles away, if that's local.'

'Right, that shouldn't be a problem. What year group are you looking at?'

Tom gulped; he hadn't ever got to this part of the conversation before, and he wasn't entirely sure of Abrihet's age. He took a punt. 'Twelve.'

'Okay, so that's Year Seven. Let me have a look.'

Tom waited. listening as she mumbled to herself.

'Well, it looks like you're in luck. We have one space. Sorry, what did you say the name was again?'

'Abrihet.'

'Abri?'

'Abrihet,' Tom repeated, and proceeded to spell it out.

'And, sorry to ask, but is that a male or female?'

'She's a girl, she's staying with me for a while."

'That's fine, and your name is …?'

'Tom Edwards.'

'And your address, Mr Edwards?'

'It's Cove House, Beach Top, in Deal.'

'That's perfect. So what I need to do is to fix up for you and Abrihet to come in and meet the headmaster, Mr O'Connell, just to chat to Abrihet and show you around the school.'

'Right – and that's it? You don't need anything else?'

'No, just the address where she'll be living, and her birthday. So, how does ummm, let me see …' she flicked through the diary, 'how does Monday the 16th of April sound, at ten o'clock?'

'Sounds great! Do we need to bring anything?'

'Just a proof of your address – a utility bill, driving licence, something like that, and that's it. And we'll look forward to seeing Abrihet Edwards, on the 16th. Pretty name, Abrihet.'

'Perfect. Thank you, thank you, thank you so much.'

'My pleasure. Have a lovely day, and we look forward to meeting you both.'

Tom closed the call and fist-punched into the air. 'Yes!' He picked up his mobile and messaged Kate:

She's in, well almost, they've got a space at St Benedict's near Ramsgate, got to take her there on the 16th. Just one problem…

Fab! What's the problem? x

They think she's my daughter!

Huh? x

The receptionist woman called her Abrihet Edwards and I couldn't correct it cos I don't know her surname or even if she has one?

I'll swing by later are we doing a movie tonight? x

Sure are!

I'll grab popcorn x

Tom left his desk and from the bottom of the stairs called up to the children to come down. Amanuel and Abrihet stood in the sitting room.

'Guess what?' Tom said grinning.

They turned to each other then looked back at Tom and shrugged.

'Come and sit down, both of you, I've got some news.'

Abrihet and Amanuel perched themselves on the sofa.

'So, you know I said I had some important calls to make.' They both nodded. 'Well it turns out that one of the schools that I called has space for you, Abrihet, and they'd like to meet you and show you around,' Tom beamed. He watched them, Abrihet's eyes looked a little vacant. 'Abrihet? Is everything okay?'

'Is the school big?' she asked eventually.

'It'll be quite big, yes.'

'Oh.'

'Abrihet, in England and other European countries we have a surname.'

Abrihet frowned, 'I do not understand.'

'When you travelled here the countries you travelled through, some of them, would have been part of Europe, like Italy and France and then here.'

'Yes, I see, people were white.'

'Yep, and also we have a family name. I am, Tom Edwards. And, you?'

'My father is Elijah.'

'Right, but after his name he has another name.'

'Yes, it is Abraham.'

'So you are, Abrihet Abraham.'

'No,' she said assertively. 'I am not that.'

'Right, um … so what *are* you?' Tom asked.

'I'm Abrihet Elijah.'

'And Amanuel?'

'The same,' she said puzzled by Tom's difficulty in understanding. 'He's Amanuel Elijah.'

'Right, so you take your father's first name?

'My father's Elijah. Why you ask?'

'For the school. I'll need to give them your full details.'

'When will I go?'

'Next week, on Monday at ten o'clock.'

'And me? What about me?' Amanuel chirped.

'Let's do this first, and then we'll concentrate on you.'

'So, my feet run still.'

'Yes, you'll still coming running with me, Amanuel,' Tom smiled.

'Good,' Amanuel beamed.

'Tom, do you work today?' Abrihet asked.

'Yes, why?'

'Can I go for a walk to the beach with Amanuel?'

Tom bit his lip. He hadn't let the children go out on their own before. Although they'd been to the zoo and the shopping mall, and Amanuel ran daily with him along the beach, Tom had always felt nervous about them going out. But now that he was getting a place for Abrihet in a local school she was as good as legal.

'Okay, but remember if anybody asks you're from Kenya and your parents are friends of mine.'

She nodded and took Amanuel by the hand to get their coats and shoes from the hallway. Tom gave her the key to the front door. 'Don't be too long,' he said.

Together Abrihet and Amanuel walked down the steep incline of Beach Top and towards the steps that led to the seashore. The bleakness of winter was passing, and the sky with its richly marbled greys took on a hint of blue mottled by cottonwool-like puffs in the sky. The nakedness of the trees was now dappled in green, some with a sprinkling of candy floss of pale pinks and whites. Abrihet noticed how the flowers waved in the breeze like a smile to the sea, and she let her eyes flow from each of their pretty white heads. Fresh sunlight illuminated the water and the slight seaside chill in the air felt like it had a touch of magic about it.

Amanuel's arms swung by his side, still holding his sister's hand. They cut through by the side of the RNLI station, illuminated inside, with the red Ford Cortina parked outside. They veered to the left of it, taking the steps down to the beach. Then the children stood still, holding hands, and let the salt breeze brush across their faces, gasping as they swallowed its chill brininess. Amanuel rubbed his eyes as the breeze turned a little harsher, making them water. With Tom he had always walked across the lifeboat slipway to the other side then run past the beach huts and towards the Crab Shack, but today with his sister he turned left, to a bit of the beach that he had never returned to until now.

Abrihet looked back towards the steps and the delicateness of the snowdrops which had now pushed their heads up, welcoming the spring; they seemed to wave their own gentle smile, pushing the children to walk further along the beach.

Amanuel held Abrihet's hand tighter as a seagull wheeled in the sky, darting low and circling the beach. It screamed through the air until it dived down and stole a beakful from a discarded bag of chips. They walked further along the beach, breathing in deeply and allowing their lungs to fill with the salinity of the air.

'D'you ever remember?' Amanuel asked in Tigrinya as he turned to face the sea.

'Yes,' Abrihet replied holding his hand a little tighter.

'D'you ever cry?'

'Yes.'

'D'you ever want mama and papa?'

'Yes.'

'D'you think they cry?'

'Yes.'

'D'you think they'll come too?'

Abrihet said nothing, just stared into the sea and watched as the waves swirled further out and a fishing boat carved its journey across the foamy chop with a trail of seabirds following its course.

'I don't know,' she replied, brushing the braids away from her face amid the sting of tears.

'I remember the noise in my sleep,' Amanuel said, wiping his eyes.

'What noise?' his sister asked, blinking as the early spring breeze whipped around her face.

'All of it,' he paused, 'the man who laughed with the bad teeth, the screams of our people, the gun. Why did he shoot so much? Why did he shoot Doctor Sam?'

'Because ...'

'Doctor Sam was a good man, and Elisabet must be crying, because I was crying. And I want to not cry. I want things to be the same as before.'

'I know,' she squeezed his hand in hers. 'Try not to think about it, Amanuel.'

'What if people shoot *Tom*? Then what'd we do?'

'They won't. It's different here.'

'But why don't people like us?'

She sighed, 'I don't know, but I'm going to school soon and our life'll be different. We'll be okay – Tom and Kate promised us.'

'I don't want to lose Tom; I like him so much. He can't run as fast as *me*, though,' Amanuel smiled and picked up a pebble, turned it in his hand and then crouched down low, flicked his wrist back and counted as the pebble skimmed the water before it disappeared. 'D'you think he's up there, Doctor Sam?'

'Yeah, I do,' Abrihet said, pulling her arms in around her and tugging at her brother's arm. 'Come on, let's go back, it's getting colder now.'

'Why doesn't the sun come here? Maybe it doesn't like this place either.' Amanuel turned to walk back, then stopped and looked back at the sea, its greyness uninviting and cold. 'I remember this place so well. I remember the cold – I thought my body would be eaten by the sea.'

'I remember it too.' Abrihet turned back to him.

'D'you think Tom found us for a reason, like an angel to look after us?'

'I think so, Amanuel,' Abrihet smiled.

'You think he'll always look after us, for ever?'

'I hope so.' Her voice was just a whisper.

'You know what I think?'

'No ... What d'you think, Amanuel?'

'I think he looks like Doctor Sam, a bit. I like that. It makes me think Sam's in my heart still. So I won't forget. I'm scared in case I forget all their faces.'

'Me too.'

The gulls screeched above, soaring down into the waves, one of them snatching at a fish that swam a little too close to the surface.

On the slipway four men walked towards the RNLI boat, and a tractor hitched itself to the boat's carrier while the men embarked. The children watched as the tractor's engine rumbled, a red door slammed shut and a man drew on his cigarette before flicking it to the side. As he did, he caught sight of the children, then stopped and stared at them as they ascended the steps before turning up the hill to Beach Top. His gaze followed them until they were out of sight. He breathed heavily, cleared his throat and spat the contents of his mouth onto the ground.

'Come on, Rob; I know it's only a practice run, but we *do* need to get the boat on the water.'

'Yeah, all right, I'm coming,' his stare still on Beach Top.

'Ah you're back,' Tom exclaimed, looking up from his drawings. 'Go anywhere in particular?'

'Just to the beach, but a different way. The place you found us,' Abrihet said.

'How was it? Was it okay?'

'I think it was okay,' she replied.

'Good. Hungry? Fancy some lunch? Kate's coming over later and we can order a pizza.'

The children nodded.

'Perfect. How about cheese on toast?' Tom swivelled himself off his stool and made his way to the kitchen. 'Gosh I can feel the cold on you,' he said as he walked past them. 'Was there anyone about?'

'Just the men in yellow with the boat.'

'Ah, the RNLI.'

'What do they do?' Amanuel asked.

'They help people at sea, rescue people when they're in difficulty.'

'So, they help us?'

'They would have been out looking if they'd known boats were coming in, yes.'

'They kind people, then?' Amanuel asked.

'Yeah, they're kind people,' Tom said, taking the cheese from the fridge. 'Really kind people.'

'Good. I like that, Tom.'

Chapter Twenty-Seven

The scenery was plain. It could have been anywhere as they drove along past the terraced houses until the road opened up and then the road seemed to wind higher, almost like a mountain track but smooth with gentle curves. The children gazed out of the windows as they passed beautiful architecturally designed houses with sharp angular lines, rendered in a clean white finish. The walls were punctuated by huge great windows that spanned the façade of each upper floor, with a terrace-style balcony for the inhabitants to sip on their freshly poured cappuccino while taking in the seascape. The houses were similar to Tom's, only bigger.

The pit of Abrihet's stomach churned a little, and she played with the hem of her skirt. Kate had bought her some new clothes, and for today she wore a pretty miniskirt dotted with the tiniest of blue flowers, with a simple grey top. Although it was spring now, the days were taking their time in adding a little heat to them, so Abrihet wore a pair of plain navy tights too. It had taken her a while to adjust to this type of clothing as in Africa her legs had never been covered to keep them warm.

The road seemed to wind high above the treetops until the car bumped across a level crossing before reaching open countryside. On either side of the road the fields stretched for miles until they almost seemed to reach the sky marbled with clouds.

They drove past a tall sign that read *Finglesham* in huge gold letters, Abrihet tried to focus on it, craning her neck to see the word again and sound it out in her head. The houses seemed different to the houses along the seafront; they weren't attached to each other. Amanuel leaned forward as if to get a better look as they passed slowly through the hamlet. The houses' walls were painted white, and evergreen plants trailed up the front of them and around the windows and doors. The roofs were covered in what looked like reed, just like their home, only thicker. He looked at Abrihet as if to tell her the houses reminded him of home, the roof he would climb onto with Elijah his father. Abrihet smiled at him and rubbed her hand on his head.

They drove on and the children gasped as they crested a hilltop and saw the sea once more, with stretches of golden sandy beaches and, in the distance a harbour that was bustling with life and boats that weren't crammed with people. And then they saw a building with a huge great sign at its entrance: *St Benedict's Secondary School, RC*. Tom indicated right and turned into the crammed car park.

'We're here,' Tom said as he pulled into a space near a blue sign, Visitor Parking. 'Are you ready?'

Abrihet wiped her hands on her tights and unclicked her seat belt. They had ten minutes before their appointment with Mr O'Connell. The building looked vast around them. The car beeped as the central locking clicked. The three of them got out, and walked to the double doors and entered through them, and after Tom rang the bell in the empty reception area, they waited a moment until a grey-haired woman came from the office. She wore moon-shaped glasses and her hair was tied back in a bun. She pulled her cardigan across her, and smiled at the three faces on the other side of the desk.

'Good morning. How can I help you?'

'Good morning, I'm Tom Edwards, and we've come to look around the school.'

'Ah, yes, that's right – and it's Abrihet. isn't it? Such a pretty name.' She smiled at Abrihet as she pulled out a visitors' book. 'If you could just sign here, that'd be lovely.' She looked over to Amanuel who stood transfixed by the goings on. 'And you must be Abrihet's brother?' She peered over her glasses.' He nodded. 'That's lovely. If you'd just like to take a seat, I'll let Mr O'Connell know you've arrived.'

Tom ushered the children to a row of brown plastic chairs above which hung a notice board adorned with announcements and club timetables. Next to the board was a collection of photographs of all the teachers, each with their name and title beneath it, within a glass frame. While they waited, Amanuel's legs swung back and forth and Abrihet held her hands tightly together, staring ahead at the picture of a bearded man in a robe holding a bell, and the blackest of birds next to him. Above the picture in a semi-circular layout were the words *Pax, Ora et Labora*.

'Ah, Mr Edwards, I'm Seamus O'Connell. Please come through. Would you like a tea or coffee, Mr Edwards?'

'Coffee, white, no sugar, thank you,' Tom replied.

'And would you two like some orange juice?'

The children nodded.

'Wendy, perhaps you could bring it all through to my office when you've a moment.'

Seamus O'Connell led Tom and the children down the main corridor before turning left into his office. 'Please take a seat,' he said ushering them towards a round table and chairs. 'So you must be Abrihet?' he said, taking the typed-up notes Wendy had given him ahead of the appointment. Abrihet nodded, turning her hands in on themselves under the table.

'And who are you?' said O'Connell, smiling over to Amanuel. 'You can't be ready for senior school just yet.'

Amanuel puckered his lips and shook his head.

'This is Amanuel, Abrihet's younger brother,' Tom interjected.

'Great names, and with such wonderful meanings. Marvellous!' He caught sight of Abrihet staring at a copy of the picture of the man with the words above his head.

'Peace, prayer and work,' she whispered.

Mr O'Connell cast her a look, then turned: 'So tell me, what has drawn you to the school, Mr Edwards?'

Tom shuffled in his seat a little and placed his hands on the table in front of him. 'The children are staying with me for a while. Their parents are relocating at the moment and in the interim, well, I thought it would be good for Abrihet to go to school.'

'Absolutely, absolutely, couldn't agree more. And, umm, Abrihet, where do you normally live?'

She swallowed. 'Kenya.'

'Wow, that's some country, I went there for my honeymoon, amazing. So, here's a little different.'

'A little different, yes,' she replied.

'And how are you finding it?'

'It's cold.' A slight smile crossed her face.

He chuckled, 'Yes it certainly is, to be sure.'

'So, at present you're living in Deal – is that correct?' Mr O'Connell asked.

Tom looked at Abrihet for a moment and then answered. 'Yes, that's correct, they're living with me, I have the proof here of my address, if you'd like to see it. Oh, and Abrihet's surname's Elijah, not Edwards.'

'That's absolutely fine, Wendy will sort all that when you leave – if you like the school, of course.'

The meeting was interrupted briefly while Wendy brought the drinks into the room and placed them on the table.

'So, I guess you'd like to hear a little bit about the school, wouldn't you?' Mr O'Connell said, taking a sizeable slurp of his coffee. 'St Benedict's is obviously steered by our motto, which you may have seen in Reception; it's about developing wisdom, compassion and resilience through prayer and work.'

'Right,' Tom nodded.

'And the majority of the children here are from Catholic backgrounds, I'd say ninety-eight per cent of the children are from a Christian upbringing. Can I ask what your religious belief is?'

Tom looked across to Abrihet and smiled. 'I believe in God,' Abrihet said.

'That's great to hear. So, what can I tell you about St Benedict's?' He cleared his throat and took another mouthful of his coffee. 'As I said, we have a very strong ethos here, and I pride myself on the students who have gone on from here having learnt great things and becoming aspiring and inspiring human beings. We have a three-form intake and have thirty children in each class, with many of our pupils going on into the sixth form. As a school, we pride ourselves on the kindness and tolerance of all our pupils and do not allow behaviour that does not match our values. The school day begins at quarter to nine with registration, and finishes at three thirty. We have a number of school clubs, including sports and the arts, which are financed by the local authority. Do you have any interests, Abrihet?'

Abrihet stared at him and looked over to Tom and frowned.

'What do you like doing? Tom said.

'Oh, I make rugs,' she said.

Mr O'Connell's brow furrowed. 'She means she made tapestry-style rugs with her mother, they wove baskets together, that kind of thing.' Tom interjected.

'And fish swimming,' she added quietly.

'Sounds wondrous.'

'Yes, it is, in the red pool, we swim and catch fish with our hands.'

'Enchanting, simply enchanting. Do you have any questions, Abrihet, before we look around?' Mr O'Connell asked, pushing his empty cup to one side.

Abrihet shook her head.

'Right, well, I'm sure you'd like to see the school and what we can offer you.' Mr O'Connell shuffled the notes he had made and guided the three of them to the door. The corridor was long, and the smell of overcooked vegetables sifted through the air. He pushed open the double doors that led into the school's main hall. A wall was flanked with a cargo climbing net and ceiling-high windows. In the far corner blue plastic gym mats were stacked in two towers, and on the wall in green writing was the school's motto and a crucifix. Along another wall gym benches were doubled up and rows of stacked plastic chairs.

'As you can see, this is the main hall. It becomes the canteen at lunchtime, and we also use it for prize day and assemblies, Year Eleven and Thirteen exams, and all school productions. We also have gym in here, and after some lunch periods it's used for badminton and dance club. It's most versatile, as you can imagine.'

The two children stared at the room open-mouthed. They'd never seen such a huge space, and the floor looked similar to Tom's; wooden, but with the floorboards joined in a zig-zag pattern. Abrihet looked up to the ceiling expecting to see a fan, but all she saw were long strips of tubular lights.

'It's big,' she whispered.

Mr O'Connell looked at her and a smile eased across his face, empathising with her unease. 'It's a little daunting, I suspect, isn't it?'

She hadn't understood his words, but his face almost told her what she thought he might have meant.

'Come on, let me show you the classroom.' He led them back through the double doors and into the corridor, stopping at a blue door with a window he peered through before knocking and opening it.

'Miss Humphrey, I'd like to introduce you to Mr Edwards and Abrihet; they're interested in starting here.'

'Welcome,' she said, turning from the whiteboard where numbers and signs were scribbled across it. A murmur of voices bubbled with curiosity. '7D, could we have a little hush? Please put down your pens.' The children did so and stared back at the three faces.

'It's lovely to meet you, Abrihet. I'm Miss Humphrey, 7D's maths teacher. Their maths is always in this classroom, but for other subjects the class will go to different classrooms. This, though, is where the day starts, for morning register and for afternoon register, too. Archie, perhaps you'd like to introduce yourself and explain what we've been learning today.'

Archie shuffled his bottom on his seat. 'Yeah, umm, well, I'm Archie, and we've been doing geometry, measuring the angles of a triangle and learning that the sum of the internal angles is equal to a hundred and eighty degrees, Miss.'

'Thank you, Archie.'

'And have you all got your geometry sets?' Mr O'Connell asked.

'Yes, Sir,' the class answered.

'And how are you enjoying it, Alfie?' he asked, turning to another pupil.

'Yes, Sir, it's kind of really interesting.'

'That's splendid.'

'Bethany, perhaps you could tell Abrihet about some of the other subjects.'

Bethany tucked her hair behind her ear. 'English is with Miss Richardson. She's really kind. We're reading poems at the moment, and looking at the pacing of them.'

'And what's your favourite subject, Bethany?' Mr O'Connell asked.

'Drama. It's ace! Mr Roberts is like really cool, just lets you do what you want so you can express yourself. Kinda dead nice teacher.'

Abrihet gazed at Bethany; her hair was blonde yet her eyelashes almost jet black.

'And are you doing anything in particular in drama, Bethany?' Mr O'Connell asked.

'Yeah, Sir, we're doing *The Face* by Benjamin Zephaniah and Richard Conlon, which tackles prejudice, disfigurement and drugs.'

'And how are you finding it?'

'It's kinda hard, Sir, cos it's about kids like us and what goes wrong and changes your life.'

'Sounds impacting, I look forward to seeing the production, Bethany. Thank you, Miss Humphrey, we'll leave you to it.' Mr O'Connell closed the door behind them and led them back towards Reception. 'I hope I've been able to give you a good idea of the school, and as you can see the children are engaging with their subjects. As a Head, I think it's really important to be on the same level as the pupils to get the very best out of them. How did you find it all, Abrihet?'

'I like Bethany.'

'Did you like the drama and the play?'

She nodded. Although she didn't know the play, its meaning resonated with her.

'There're certainly many plays that make the pupils stop and think about the bigger picture, about life and what can change your life. And, Mr Edwards, if you feel this school's the right fit for Abrihet, then we'd like to welcome her. I'm happy to offer her a place. The local school uniform shop's on the high street, or online if it's easier, and if you'd like her to start this week, perhaps the 18th, then she'd be most welcome.'

'Thank you, Mr O'Connell, I think I need to go home and chat to Abrihet about it, and then perhaps I could confirm with you this afternoon. Would that be okay?'

'Absolutely. I'll leave you here in Wendy's capable hands – and Abrihet, it was a pleasure meeting you, and you too, Amanuel. Have a think about it when you get home, and just phone the office to let them know of your decision. Once again, it was lovely meeting you all.' Seamus O'Connell shook Tom's hand and left him to sort out the administrational side with Wendy. Then Tom and the children headed back to their car.

'So, did you like it, Abrihet?' Tom asked catching sight of Abrihet in the rear-view mirror.

'Yes, I did.'

'Was there anything that you particularly liked?'

'I like the girl.'

'Wasn't her name Bethany?'

'Yes, I like what she say, I like her story.'

'Ah the drama, I think you'd like drama.'

'Can I go, Tom?'

'Of course, you can. Let's sort the uniform when we get home, and I'll call the school to let them know you'll be going there.'

Chapter Twenty-Eight

Abrihet stood a little haphazardly in the sitting room wearing a blue pleated skirt, white shirt, navy-blue knee length socks and shiny black leather shoes, in her hands she held a blue and grey striped tie. She knew from seeing the pupils in the class that she needed to wear it, but wasn't at all sure how to put it on.

'Here, d'you want me to do your tie?' Tom asked, taking it from her hands. 'Lift your chin up.' She lifted it while he turned the shirt collar up so it stood starchy and hard around her neck. She peered down, almost going cross-eyed, as Tom's hands looped the tie in and out before pulling a perfect knot and turning her collar down again. 'There,' he said. She craned her neck a little from its discomfort. 'You look very smart,' he said, handing her a new black rucksack which contained a pencil case, geometry set, calculator and a piece of fruit. 'Are you ready?'

She nodded.

'Come on, then, let's go.'

Her stomach churned as she sat in the back of the car, Amanuel took her hand and held it, then looked up at her and smiled. But there was an unrelenting feeling in her tummy that comes not from excitement, though at first it appears that way. There was an element of relief, some fear and a profound amount of grieving for a place she'd left, they'd left – and all of a sudden it came at her like a powerful whoosh of anxiety. They'd made it to the place of hope where Manchester United were from and cricket was played, and now her journey was continuing without the love of her mother. But would this new place be accepting of her? Would it be like the promise made? And would she fit in, be wanted? Ahead was the unknown. She'd become accustomed to Tom's house and reading in the quietness of the four walls that cocooned her, the laughter, and the films with Kate on a Friday night with popcorn and pizza. A simple existence unmarred by noise, destruction and fear.

The indicator clicked as the car turned into the school car park, and that's when Abrihet really knew her next journey was about to begin. Tom had been told to let her make her own way into the school itself, because sometimes the guardian or parent being there makes the separation so much harder, Wendy had reassured them, *we'll look after her, she'll be fine.* And so Tom and Amanuel watched the lone figure walk into the building, with her own thoughts of *I'll carry on* drumming around in her head.

The classroom seemed warm as she entered it, a noise of chatter surrounded her. She paused in the doorway, her toes crinkled up in the hardness of her shoes. Her eyes roamed the room before anyone noticed she was there. A boy with blond spiky hair barged past her, and she dropped the water bottle that she'd been clutching. It clanged to the floor and rolled back and forth. He turned back at her and the corners of his mouth tilted down to his chin, unapologetic. She stood still and silent. The clouds billowed high in the sky and a vape trail fractured the blue marbled ether. She had crossed terrains that had frightened her, heard noises that were so unfamiliar to her and her younger brother, and now she was faced with a different kind of fear. The shouts of a class moved into a low hum around her, and her grey eyes cut a glazed stare beyond the faces, until she heard nothing. The clouds morphed into a silhouette, the outline of her mother's face and moved in an undulating kind of way in the blueness, and her thoughts returned to another time …

The mountains soared up like they wished to challenge the sky itself, they dominated the horizon in every which way they looked back. To look back wasn't an option, their homes already burned down. Sometimes they'd stumble on loose ground. Would there ever be the fragrant smell of cinnamon and love again?

Suddenly her destination was known and unknown all at once. Her water bottle still rolled on the floor; the room fell silent.

'Hey, come and sit here … ignore Johnnie, he's a pillock, everyone knows it. What's your name again?'

'Abrihet.'

'I'm Bethany.' She bent down and picked up Abrihet's bottle, smoothing her hand over the slight dent on its shiny surface, before leading Abrihet to the desk beside her. Abrihet paused at the chair. Suddenly, she felt lighter, and a smile spread across her face as if it belonged there. She recognised the kind girl. So many friends she might have in one place; perhaps that's why her smile had such staying power that day. The cacophony escalated before the morning bell clanged, an alien sound compared to the melodic ringing of her village bell. Abrihet held her ears. A paper ball hurtled its way through the air and hit her in the head. She put her hand up to her braids and turned to see Johnnie sniggering at his desk. He puckered his lips and flared his nostrils. She turned back away from his unkindness.

A woman walked in and closed the classroom door behind her.

'Settle down, please. I'm sure you all heard the bell above this din. Can you take out your poetry books and turn to page five where we will be looking at Khalil Gibran's poem 'On Pain'. But before that can I have a little hush for the register? She looked up from the desk and glanced around the classroom.

'Abrihet Abraham,' she called.

'You say *Here, Miss,*' Bethany urged.

'Here, Miss,' Abrihet said softly.

Miss Richardson looked up from the register. 'Ah, Abrihet, welcome to class 7D and St Benedict's. If there's anything you need just shout. I see Bethany's helping you.'

Abrihet nodded and smiled.

'She probably needs some bananas,' Johnnie sneered under his breath.

'Johnnie, did I call your name?'

'No, Miss.'

'Another comment like that and you'll find yourself in after-school detention. Do I make myself clear?'

'Yes, Miss.' He slunk down in his chair and snorted.

Miss Richardson rattled out thirty names. 'And finally, Zack Williams.'

'Here, Miss.'

'Right, lovely, so can we all now turn to page five – and perhaps, Bethany, you'd like to read the first verse.'

Bethany cleared her throat and moved the book in between herself and Abrihet.

　'Your pain is the breaking of the shell that encloses your understanding.

Even as the stone of the fruit must break, that its heart may stand in the sun, so must you know pain.

And could your heart in wonder at the daily miracles of your life, your pain would not seem less wondrous than your joy;

And would you accept the seasons of your heart, even as you have always accepted the seasons that pass over your fields.

And you watch with serenity through the winters of your grief.'

'Lovely. Thank you, Bethany,' Miss Richardson smiled. 'Abrihet, perhaps you'd like to continue,'

'Me, read?' Abrihet murmured.

'Please.'

Abrihet trailed her finger under the words, her stomach churning. She swallowed.

'Much of the pain is self-chosen.

It is the bitter po, pot … pot …'

'Potion,' Bethany helped.

'Potion by which the phys …'

'Physician,' Bethany whispered.

'Physician within you heals your sick self.

Therefore trust the phys … phys … physician …

'That's right,' Bethany whispered with a smile.

'Therefore trust the physician, and drink his remedy in silence and tran … quil … lity:

For his hand, though heavy and hard, is guided by the tender hand of the Unseen,

And the cup he brings, though it burns your lips, has been fash ... ioned of the clay which the Potter has mois ... tened with His own sacred tears.'

'Thank you, Abrihet, and well done. So, class, what is the speaker asking us with this poem? What is the pain, and why do you think the analogy of a stone is used?'

Bethany raised her hand.

'Yes, Bethany?'

'Is the speaker saying to accept pain as it is?'

'Yes, he is.'

'Abrihet, how did you find the poem?' Miss Richardson asked.

'The stone of the fruit is forced open ...' said Abrihet.

Miss Richardson smiled, 'Go on ...'

'To meet our pain,' Abrihet said, glancing out of the window. She swallowed once more. 'To trust in God. It is curious, I think. To trust it, we cannot avoid it. It is for us to know the full force of our reality, and we can meet it, stare it in the eye and not be taken and pulled under by the tides that will eat us.'

She continued to stare out of the window, and Miss Richardson watched on, moved by the child's words, the depth from whence they came and the obviousness of her knowing what pain truly was. The hairs on her neck prickled her skin, and she smiled softly at Abrihet. 'Yes,' she said. 'Yes.'

And so the lesson continued, until the clang of the bell came again.

'Right class, before you pack up I'd like you to take the poem home and analyse it. What's it teaching us? Why do you think the fruit stone has been used? All your work is to be handed in for marking tomorrow. Class dismissed, and go quietly, please. No running.'

'Come on, we have break now and I'll show you the tuck shop,' Bethany said, stuffing her books into her bag and grabbing Abrihet by the wrist. 'Have you got any money?'

'No, I have no money.' Abrihet's forehead furrowed.

'Ah don't worry, I have lots, I'll buy yours. I'll look after you and if pillock Johnnie says anything else, just come and tell me. I'm not frightened of him or his dad.'

'Abrihet,' Miss Richardson called from her desk. 'May I have a word?'

Abrihet looked at Bethany sheepishly.

'Go on,' said Bethany. 'I'll wait for you. She probably wants to tell you how you nailed it today, I mean, you were awesome.'

As Abrihet pushed past the chairs, Johnnie barged past her, his backpack cracking her in the side. 'Oh, *sorry*, I didn't see you there,' he mocked.

'Abrihet, come,' Miss Richardson beckoned. 'The poem, I just wanted to say what you said was beautiful.'

'Thank you, Miss.'

'So, where in Africa are you from?'

Abrihet paused and remembered what she should say, what Tom and Kate had said. 'I am from Kenya.' Her voice was strong.

'And did the poem mean something to you?' Miss Richardson asked.

'Like what?'

'You seem to recognise the pain and God, and you talked of the tides.'

'It is the poem.'

'Yes, it is. You're right, I look forward to seeing your analysis. Don't worry too much about the English or the spelling – just put what you think. Just like you did in class.'

'Yes, Miss.'

'Come on, Abrihet. I'll show you the tuck shop and the loos and anything else you need to know. D'you like dance and drama? And street dance …' Bethany pulled Abrihet along chatting and smiling as she pointed everything out to her.

The day seemed to fly by, and Bethany stayed right by Abrihet's side. When the school bell rang for the end of the day, a myriad of backpacks pushed through the corridors until the pupils spilled out into the playground like a herd of Ninja turtles. Some ran to the school buses and others dawdled down the street chewing gum and hitching their skirts a little higher.

'Oi, don't forget the zoo's open for you,' Johnnie hollered across the tarmac.

'Oh shut up, Johnnie, go play with the traffic or something,' Bethany said sliding him a look of disdain.

'I've already been to the zoo,' Abrihet smiled.

'Good for you. See you tomorrow, don't forget money for tuck,' Bethany called as she clambered onto her bus.

Tom stood beaming by the car. 'So, how was school?' he asked as he held the door open for Abrihet to climb in.

'It was good, I made a friend, she's nice.'

'What's her name?'

'Bethany.'

'Ah, the girl who loved drama,' Tom replied as he turned out of the car park.

'I also met an enemy,' Abrihet said.

'An enemy?'

'Yes, I don't think he likes me. But it's okay, I don't think people like him. So maybe he has many enemies.'

'Probably. And if he gives you any more bother, just tell me, okay – promise?'

'Promise.' As the car sped down the lanes the long day encouraged Abrihet to close her eyes until her head rested against the window and her tiredness consumed her.

Chapter Twenty-Nine

A string of pretty terraced cottages lined the country lane of Ripple Vale, a quaint coastal village about five miles from Deal. In the heart of the village the Plough Inn boasted traditional cask ales and wholesome country grub. Tubby, the landlord, stood behind the bar with his hands gripping the beer pump.

'What'll it be, Sarah?' he grinned broadly, his tummy resting on the beer trays.

'Just a Merlot, thanks, Tubby – and can you put a beer in for Dave. In fact, could you just add that to a tab?'

'His usual? No probs, beautiful. I've popped you and Dave in the corner, specials are on the board. The steak and Guinness pie's a corker.'

Sarah sat at the bar, waiting for Dave to arrive. She had been 7D's form teacher for five years and was St Benedict's English teacher as well, although she'd chosen a school that gave her a little distance from her private life. The fire crackled in the corner of the pub, and the flames licked about the log, dancing up high. The doorlatch lifted, and Dave strolled across the pub floor.

'Hi, gorgeous – sorry I'm late.'

'IPA, Dave?'

'That'll be good, Tubby. It's been a bit of a day.'

'Catching the bad guys? – come on, you know you love it,' Tubby laughed as he let the froth of the beer overspill and placed the pint on the bar.

'How was your day?' Dave asked, squeezing Sarah's leg.

'We had a new girl start today,' she said taking a sip from her glass. 'From Kenya.'

'Sounds interesting. How did she get on?'

'Yeah, she did okay. She read from a poem that we're analysing and when I asked her what it meant to her, she just blew me away, like a child who'd experienced something that I couldn't quite put my finger on. There was an emotion that stirred up inside me as if there was something more.'

'Like what, Sarah?'

'I don't know, really. Shall we go sit by the fire? Tubby's reserved our table.' They left the bar and moved onto their table, and Sarah adjusted the seat cushions. 'It was just strange,' she continued. 'She made reference to the tide swallowing her or people, and to almost look pain and fear in the eye.' She paused. 'Like ...' She bit the inside of her cheek and took another mouthful of her wine. 'I dunno, I've never heard a child speak like that or take that kind of meaning from poetry. I mean they're *twelve*-year olds, yet she seemed to have an experience of a lifetime. And then I had Johnnie, who's this right little shit, mock her.'

'Mock her, how?'

'Oh, he made some comment about bananas. He's always been an unkind boy, probably always will be, and if I spoke to his parents they'd do nothing, you know – those kinds of people who just shouldn't exist.'

'They exist, hun. I came across one not that long ago. Some guy made an anonymous report about a black kid on the beach.'

'You didn't tell me.'

'Well, you know I kind of haven't told anyone, but me and Andy went to a job – not normally a CID matter, but uniform were dealing with a huge RTA on the M20 so we took the report and paid the caller a visit.'

'What happened?'

'Nothing. I took down the details, but I didn't like him or what he said. So I filed it.'

'Why didn't you like him?'

'I've worked with the force for a long time, and you know when you're dealing with an unsavoury character. Might not have broken the law, but you can do without them.'

'And the child?'

'Some kid on the beach running with a white guy.'

'But didn't you have to file the report?'

'Yeah I filed it and left it there. So, what about this Johnnie kid?'

'Well, if he does it again he's got a detention. It's just tricky, because I know the dad definitely won't like it.'

'What do they do?'

'Not sure about the mum, but the dad works for the RNLI. He's got a bit of an attitude –probably where Johnnie gets it from.'

'The RNLI? In Deal?'

'Yeah, why, d'you know him? Covered in tattoos. He was the one who came to the parents' evening and gave me a hard time, asked me if I was qualified to teach. Don't you remember me telling you?'

Dave pursed his lips, 'Yeah, I do remember. What's this Johnnie's surname?'

'Spencer. Why?'

'Just got a hunch, looks like I've found my anonymous caller's name.'

'Hey, what're you thinking? You going all Clouseau on me?'

Dave made a clicking sound on the roof of his mouth. 'Umm, I think I might be.'

'Are you going to let me in, seeing as I've given you some of the information?'

'Might need to reopen this file. The new girl, you say she's from Kenya?'

'That's what she said. But I don't know ... there was something quite deep about her, it just didn't strike me as Kenyan. But then what does *Kenyan* conjure up? I don't know, it just felt like she knew pain, like she'd experienced something traumatic.'

'And you got that just from a *poem*?'

'You'd be surprised what you can get from a poem. So, what are you thinking?'

'Has she got brothers or sisters? D'you know where she lives?'

'Seamus O'Connell said she had a little brother and they're living with Mr Edwards, a family friend in Deal.'

'Edwards?'

'Yeah, why?'

'Tom Edwards, the architect?'

'I don't know about him being an architect, but yep, it's Tom Edwards.'

'Hmmm,' Dave flicked his beer mat back and forth. 'Interesting, Johnnie hasn't fallen far from the tree. I think I might have got my man.'

* * *

A stack of dirty plates piled up on the counter next to the sink. 'Oi, Johnnie,' Stacy Spencer hollered from the kitchen, 'Your dinner's ready. Go call your dad, he's on the drive fixing the car.'

The three of them sat on the sofa with a plate of beans and oven chips and an anaemic brown burger that dribbled grease. Johnnie slopped his beans up and then licked his knife.

'So, what you learn in school today, son?' Johnnie's dad asked.

'Not much, some stupid poem.'

'Poem, what ya talkin' about *poem*?' he said, stuffing a mouthful of chips covered in ketchup into his mouth and wiping his lips with the back of his hand.

'Dunno, just a load of rubbish, Beffany and the new girl read it, and Miss told us we had to write about it for our homework.'

'Well, have you done it?' his mum butted in. 'You've been on your Xbox since you came in.'

'I'm not doing it, 'specially when a girl like *her* read it. She couldn't even read it proper, bit thick and not right.'

'What d'you mean, Johnnie? Are you causing trouble?' his mum said, glaring at him. 'I ain't going up to that school again, you know. You need to sort yourself out, or you'll get a clip round the ear.'

'What, about this new girl then, why can't she read?' his dad asked.

'Well, she *could* read, just Beffany had to keep saying words for her.'

'Like what?' his dad asked his mouth full of food.

'Well I dunno, just words. She ain't one of us, told 'er she needed some bananas.'

'You told 'er *what*?' said his mum. 'What she want bananas for? I swear to God, Johnnie, I don't know where you get it from. 'Ave you been feeding 'im your crap again, Rob?'

'I ain't said nothing, girl, I'm just eating my dinner. But 'e's got a point. Who is she, and why can't she read?' Rob slurped his tea and let out a belch. 'What d'you mean, ain't one of us? Where's she from?'

'Africa, and she can't read, Dad.'

'Right, is that so? I *knew* it,' Rob sneered under his breath.

'What did you know, Rob? Leave the poor girl alone, 'ow would you like it, she ain't done nothing to you. And, Johnnie, if I 'ear you say one more thing like that, I swear to God you'll wish you 'adn't. Now get up those stairs and get your homework done, and while you're at it you can bring me your Xbox. You ain't 'aving that, d'you 'ear me?'

'Dunno why you're sticking up for 'er.' Johnnie kicked the door as he left the room.

Stacy glared at Rob; her upper lip seemed to snarl.

'What? What you looking at me like that for, girl?

'You're feeding our son with a load of shit, and I won't 'ave it. I ain't no racist, and I won't 'ave you make my son one, d'you 'ear me?'

'Well, it's all right for you to say. *You* ain't the one on a boat looking for 'em, putting your own life at risk, when they ain't welcome.'

'What you talking about, Rob? You chose to work at the station, no one put a gun to your 'ead. And who said she's *that* anyway? And, to be 'onest, what if she is?'

'It ain't right, Stace,' he snarled through gritted teeth. 'It ain't right, and I know she's one of 'em, there's more than one, I've seen another one at the beach running, no shoes, with a white man. I already called the police once, and I'll be doing it again. They ain't staying 'ere, and she ain't staying in that school.'

Stacy stared at the man who sat in front of her, her eyes drilling to the back of his head. She bit hard on her bottom lip, and her breathing slowed – she could hear it as the air passed down her nose. She slowly shook her head and let her chest inhale and exhale at a steady pace.

Then she pushed herself forward in the chair, clutching the cutlery to the side of her plate. She didn't flinch. 'You make sick, you know that? Even as you wrap yourself in a false hero cape for the station.' She got up from the armchair, left her plate on the kitchen side, took her coat from the hook in the hallway. The letterbox rattled as the door slammed behind her.

Rob pushed his empty plate onto the coffee table in front of him, where it teetered on a small pile of gossip magazines. He took out his phone and wallet, and from the inside pouch he pulled out DI Blake's card.

He dialled the number.

'CID. How can I help you?'

'I want to speak to DI Blake, it's urgent.'

'Can I take your name?'

'Rather not.'

The line rang through to Blake's desk: 'Sir, I've a got a caller on the line, says it's urgent, won't give his name.

'Thanks, Jess, put him through.'

The line buzzed through. 'DI Blake.'

'It's me, I spoke to you a month or two ago about a sighting.'

Blake kicked his legs down from his desk.

'Ah, you'd be the crewman from the RNLI – Rob, wasn't it?'

'Yeah, that's right. I've got more information.'

'Really? And what might that be?' Blake flicked his pen in his hand.

'There's more than one – I *told* you something was sus.'

'You told me you saw a boy on the beach running with a man. What d'you want to add to that?'

'There's a girl too, I reckon she's one of *them*,' he sneered.

'One of who?'

'The type that ain't supposed to be 'ere.'

'What exactly is it that you'd like me to do?'

'I thought you were the police, I thought that's what I paid my taxes for, to get the people who ain't s'posed to be 'ere.'

'Perhaps you'd like to come to the station, to make a proper statement. That'll help speed things up. I can send one of my team down to give you a lift, or you can come in at your leisure. Shall we say tomorrow, midday?'

'If I come, I want you to get them *out* of this country, d'you 'ear me?'

'I hear you. I'll see you tomorrow.' Blake closed the line. He pursed his lips and his eyes narrowed as he pulled up the screen and a mugshot of Robert Nicholas Spencer, aged thirty-nine, glared at him, previous charges against him ABH and GBH, the victim was of ethnic minority, Spencer arrested in Paris at Le Parc des Princes football stadium for racial intimidation, violent threats, assault and hooliganism. 'Welcome to my world, Robert Nicholas Spencer. Welcome to my world,' said Blake under his breath. His chair swung back to the upright position and he took his mobile. A message pinged in; it was his partner, Sarah.

Grab a Chinese, it's been a long week, and a bottle. How was your day? x

Good, and tomorrow just got better. See you in a bit, beautiful. x

The following morning the CID department was buzzing as officers compared their notes on the reports they were following up. Blake opened his screen and searched through the profiles of British football supporters that had a tendency to generate trouble. He scrolled through the list of names and their pictures, resting the cursor on Robert Nicholas Spencer. He stared at the screen and the mugshot of his RNLI caller. He read through the French police's account at the football stadium in Paris and the mayhem that ensued. Spencer had spent two nights in French custody with two other men, Steven Hawkins and Gary Smith. The DI's internal line rung.

He pressed handsfree. 'DI Blake.'

'Sir, I have a gentleman at the desk. He says you'll know who he is.'

'I'll be right down, thank you. Oh, Jess?'

'Sir.'

'Is there an interview room available?'

The line went quiet while Jess looked. 'Room C's free, Sir.'

'Great, I'll be right down – and could you get the station solicitor in there too? I saw him beetling about this morning on our floor, pretty sure he should be free.'

Blake printed off the three profiles and left his office, glancing over to where Andy Prior was sitting. 'Follow me,' he said, 'we've got our RNLI man at the front desk.'

'Guv.'

The two detectives took the stairs to the ground floor, where Rob was waiting in the lobby.

'If you'd like to come this way.' Blake led him to the interviewing room where he ushered him to a seat across the table. The infra-red light of a camera ignited; Rob looked up at it. Blake took out his file and opened it. 'So, thought we could look into this report you've made.'

'Right. It's about time,' Rob sneered.

Blake allowed a dry smile to cross his face. The door opened and a short man entered the room and took a seat beside Rob. Blake nodded to Prior, who pushed the Record button on the tape deck.

'For the purpose of the tape, it's Friday the 20th April, twelve hundred hours. DI Blake and DS Prior are present with … could you state your name?'

'What for?'

'For the purpose of the tape and your report. Without your full name it won't be valid.' Blake made a sign to stop the recording.

'I thought you said this'd be simple.'

'Due to the nature of the report, it's best that we have everything recorded. Like I said, it's never just *it.*' Blake signalled for the recording to recommence.

'For the purpose of the tape, DI Blake and DS Prior are present, with station solicitor Mr ...'

'Eric Onodopolis.'

'And your name?' the DI threw a glance at Rob.

'Rob Spencer,' he growled, and kicked his leg out from under the table then slouched further back into his chair, his arms folded.

'Thank you,' Blake said as he looked through the file. 'On Tuesday the 2nd of March a call was made to our police operator at six fifty in the morning. The call came from a mobile ending in three, six, four. Can you confirm that as your number?'

'Yeah – and so what?'

'The report taken by the call handler states that you wanted to remain anonymous. For the purpose of the report, would you like to explain why?'

'Cos I didn't want no trouble, it was just a bit sus.'

'Sus, that's right,' Blake wrote down the word *sus.* 'So, this call – why would you choose to be anonymous?'

'Why are you 'aving a go at *me*? Shouldn't you be questioning someone else?'

Blake leant forward. 'Like who, Mr Spencer?'

'Like the ones who ain't supposed to be 'ere,' said Rob, pushing himself forward with both arms on the table.

'Ah yes, a small child of ethnic minority. We'll get to that.'

'Call it what you want,' Rob snarled, and sat back in his seat.

'Thank you. I'm just a little bit confused here. Why exactly would there be any trouble in making a simple report? DS Prior, do you have any ideas?' Prior shook his head. 'I mean, isn't it just a worthy thing to do, to look out for the community? Your job alone would suggest that. So, why anonymous? I just don't get that bit.'

'Like I said, I didn't want no trouble.'

'This is what's puzzling me. Why would there be trouble, Mr Spencer?'

Spencer shifted in his chair. 'Do I just answer *no comment*, like I'm the crim'?'

'Mr Spencer, have you ever been to Paris before?'

'What's this got to do with anything?' Spencer sniffed heavily and rubbed his nose with the back of his hand.

'Have you?'

'Yeah, why ... and? Hasn't anyone?'

'What, perhaps for a romantic weekend?' Blake offered.

Rob's leg shook under the table, he chewed at the inside of his mouth.

'Well, was it a romantic weekend, Mr Spencer, with your girlfriend, partner, wife?' Blake suggested. 'Maybe a day out at Disneyland Paris with your son or daughter?'

'I went to watch the football.'

'Ah, the football – so you must be an avid fan.'

'Not really, watch the odd match.'

'Not an avid supporter? But you went to Paris to watch a game. That would suggest to me that you're keen.'

'A few of my mates were going, just went for the ride.'

'And how *was* the ride, Mr Spencer?'

'It was all right.'

'Probably a memorable weekend, I'd imagine?' Blake pushed.

'Yeah, what of it?'

'Perhaps you'd like to explain, for the purpose of the tape, why it was memorable?'

'Like what? It was just football with the boys. Just a gang of us.'

'Just a gang of you. Gang, it always conjures up a bad image. Don't you think? Gang of youths, a gang hanging about. D'you know what I mean?'

'It was just football,' Rob Spencer muttered.

Blake smiled dryly. 'It was just football, you're right – although looking at your file it would seem it was garnished with a side order of ABH, GBH, hooliganism, and violence in a racial attack, and a man put in hospital with severe head injuries. You see, what I have here in my file is a report on your behaviour that weekend with other accomplices and a young boy.' Blake twizzled the file around so that Rob Spencer could see his profile picture and the report made and below in red capital letters, ABH, GBH and Racial Attacks in Police Custody. 'For the purpose of the tape, I'm showing Mr Robert Nicholas Spencer his profile picture and report. Mr Spencer, would you like to confirm that this is indeed you?'

A hint of red flushed into Rob Spencer's cheeks, and he pushed the file back.

'Yeah, it's me. But that was *years* ago. I ain't been in no trouble since, neither has my boy.'

'Did you often find yourself in trouble, Mr Spencer?'

'No – why would I?'

'Well, it just seems odd that a man who works for the RNLI would be the same man who'd physically attack someone because of the colour of their skin. You see, the picture I'm painting here is you didn't go to *watch* the football did you, you went to cause trouble with a minor, your son and the two other men named here in the report.'

'I don't need to answer any of this. I made a call, I saw something that wasn't right, and I reported it. What the hell! Like now I'm the *bad* guy, right?'

'You made an anonymous call,' Blake continued, 'which in itself is odd – unless of course you were afraid for your own safety, which would make it more plausible. But that's not the reason, is it? When you made the call you wanted no trouble because you *were* the trouble. Isn't that how it is?'

Spencer snorted.

'You see, when I look back at the notes I made, you said at the RNLI station *he weren't our type … they get into our country scot free.* Now anybody hearing that could only assume one thing: that you're xenophobic, that you'd go out of your way to make sure these people didn't come into the country. And the reason why you tried to remain anonymous is because you know we have a file on you. The tattoos on your arm tell me your political leanings – a bulldog with *Forever Britain* is almost the trademark of the National Front.'

'I can support what I like. *That's* not a crime.'

'It's not a crime in itself, but when your belief begins to aggravate, it becomes just that. Your son – Johnnie, isn't it …?'

'Leave Johnnie out of this. He ain't done nothing.'

'What school does he attend?'

'What's it got to do with you?'

'It's probably better that you cooperate, Mr Spencer.'

Spencer shifted his look to the station solicitor, who nodded.

'St Benedict's. But he ain't done nothing.'

'Are you sure, Mr Spencer?'

Spencer clenched his teeth.

'New girl in his class, isn't there?'

'Dunno.'

'Oh, I think you *do* know. Where's she from?'

'Dunno.'

'Is she white, Mr Spencer.'

'Dunno.'

'She's not, is she? – and why would Johnnie say she needs bananas?'

Spencer squirmed in his seat. 'I don't know where you're getting your information from.'

'Like I said, Mr Spencer, I'm a detective inspector. It's my job. And isn't it your job to save people at sea?'

'I do.'

'But you prefer to save just white people, would that be correct? People who belong here? Did you leave people in the sea to drown?'

'The coastguard called off the search. We done our job. The bodies we found were already dead.'

'I'm sure that's true, but what I'm struggling with here is why d'you want to *report* people who perhaps have survived? Isn't it a good thing that they've survived? I mean a boy you said was maybe seven or eight and a girl who perhaps is related, we don't know. But it would seem you and your son want a negative end. You see, like I said to you, surviving the sea isn't getting away with *anything* scot free, is it?'

'They got lucky,' Rob snarled.

'And your crew, Mr Spencer? Did you threaten them to keep them quiet?'

'The bodies were dead. I told you that.'

'Naturally. What are you and Johnnie planning? Is this girl going to be harmed by your son?'

'What my son does is his decision.'

'Is that a threat, Mr Spencer?'

'You're going to have to let me go, I've got a shift to do.'

Onodopolis interjected, 'Detective Inspector, unless you have further information and an arrest is likely, you'll have to let Mr Spencer go.'

'Not a problem, Mr Onodopolis. Interview suspended at twelve hours twenty-five. Mr Spencer, we'll be in touch.' Blake shuffled his file in order and left the room with Prior, closing the door behind them.

'What have we got, then, guv?'

'A dangerous man and his son.'

* * *

Back at the RNLI station, Rob Spencer sat in the main room. He turned DI Blake's card in his hand.

'Think you're *clever*, don't you?' he said under his breath. He pushed his chair back and rummaged in his pockets for his cigarettes and lighter and left the room. The sea pushed up along the slipway, and Rob drew hard on his cigarette, then googled a number on his phone and pushed the dial button on the website. The line rang, he drew hard again on his cigarette then exhaled a dense plume of nicotine smoke into the air. The call answered; he listened and then, with another drag of nicotine, replied.

'I want to report illegal immigrants living at Cove House, Beach Top, Deal. A girl and a boy hiding from Immigration.'

Chapter Thirty

A large marked van flew down the Deal seafront, passing the pier and veering off left in the direction of the RNLI station. It stopped at the lights, its driver tapping his steering wheel impatiently as the green man flashed, allowing the pedestrians to dawdle aimlessly across the main road. On the other side of the lights a bullet-grey Audi stopped. Its occupants watched as the van pulled away on the green light, and through the rear-view mirror the driver kept his eye on the van as it indicated left, towards the coastal road. The Audi driver turned left into a no through road, then turned back out again. A local dodged the illegal manoeuvre and hollered, giving him the finger. Blake pushed a button, and the grille of his car lit up in blue; from the back it flashed the same. The pedestrian looked sheepishly away.

'What're you doing, guv?' Prior asked.

'Something's not right.' Blake swerved out and put his foot down, then decelerated before going through the lights at red, and accelerated again, the scream of his siren cutting through the air as cars pulled over and pedestrians watched him speeding past. When he caught sight of the van he slowed, turning off the lights and siren. He tailed the van along the road until it indicated left to Seaview Parade. Blake followed. The van's tyres screeched around the bend and then it careered up the hill before pulling over with sudden a halt outside a white house on Beach Top.

'Seems to be in a rush,' Blake mused.

'Guv, you know where it's heading, right?'

'Yep, we'll sit and wait,' Blake said. He indicated and parked behind the van. The driver descended from the main cab and opened up the side of the vehicle where five men in uniform fell out one by one and like swat men ran up the driveway ready to swoop. The sides of the van were emblazoned in navy and pale blue check and above in capital letters IMMIGRATION ENFORCEMENT.

Blake watched on from the car as the intrusive mob hammered at the front door. From across the road the postman whistled merrily, turning back to see why an immigration vehicle had swerved up and parked outside Cove House. The lead officer banged again with a bludgeon on the grey front door, chipping it, and another of the men was getting ready to bash it open on a word. Residents began to congregate on the street, all slightly confused by the goings on over the road in an area that saw little excitement or trouble – or, indeed, immigration transport.

Inside the house, Tom flew down the stairs from the shower into the sitting room. Through the slats of his shutters he glimpsed the fluorescent checked vehicle and the low hum of people's voices from outside.

'Shit!' he said, grabbing his mobile to call Kate. The thunderous bashing on his door came again. 'Pick up, pick *up*,' he said in panic as he ran back up the stairs to the children.

'Hey, Tom,' said Kate.

'Get over here – Immigration Enforcement's outside. Hurry!'

'Fuck! – hold on, I'm coming.' The line went dead.

Tom stared at the children; amazingly, they were both still asleep. 'Hey, you two, wake up, you need to get dressed, it's important,' said Tom as calmly as he could.

'We go run?' Amanuel beamed through sleepy eyes.

'No, not today,' Tom said in a hushed voice. 'Just get dressed and stay here, don't say a word, just stay in here. Something bad's happening,' He was desperately trying to remain calm, although his heart was pounding through his chest and his hands shook.

'What is it, Tom?' Abrihet asked. She could sense the fear in his voice. It reminded her of the day she left the village.

'Hopefully we'll be okay – just get ready and stay as quiet as anything. Don't come downstairs.' As he left the children to dress and went back down the stairs, an ear-splitting crack came from the door, along with the booming shouts of the men who had forced it open. Tom froze in the hallway.

'Immigration Enforcement!' the first man shouted. 'Get down on the floor!'

Tom stood there. He didn't get down on the floor, just stood in front of the stairs, not moving an inch.

'Take the sitting room, search the cupboards,' the man ordered. Three men pushed past. 'Move away from the stairs,' he shouted at Tom.

'No.' Tom stood there defiantly. 'What are you doing here? You've illegally entered my house with force.'

'Move out of the way,' the man snarled, wielding a baton.

'I want to know what you're doing here. This is my *home*.'

'Seize him. Get up the stairs, you know what you're looking for. Find 'em and get 'em. I don't care how.'

'Stop this *now*. You've no *right*,' Tom shouted. 'Just leave us alone.'

The men barged past Tom as he was shoved up against the wall by another enforcement officer. From upstairs came the sound of doors being opened and slammed shut and rooms being tipped upside down.

Behind their as yet unopened door Amanuel and Abrihet sat on the bed, dressed. They could hear the horrible noises, the fear inside them overwhelming. Were they alone now? Had Tom gone?

The door burst open and in they came, mob-handed, four of them. Amanuel sat on the bed as still as a statue, and took Abrihet's hand. In his head he wondered if the elephants would come to protect them, to charge at the men. The men who frightened him. His small hand clutched the duvet cover, his other hand clung to his sister's. *Where are the elephants? Why do they not come?* One of the men pulled at Abrihet and she stumbled to the floor, hitting her lip. She took her hand up to her mouth, felt a crack on her back.

'Get up,' the man jeered. Then he seized Amanuel roughly, grabbing his wrist. The boy's small body shook with fear at the force.

'We've got 'em,' one of the officers bellowed. With an unkindness to two young lives they pushed them through the bedroom door, holding their hands behind their backs, carelessly frog-marching them down the stairs.

Tom broke free. 'Take your hands off them. They're just children,' he said, calmly moving away from the man who'd restricted him.

'Hold him, put him on the floor if he tries anything!' the lead officer ordered. Their wickedness emulated that of the men who'd beaten Jeremiah to a pulp, though nobody in the house would have known that.

'Leave us alone, leave the children, you're scaring them. What kind of people *are* you?' Tom went to run to the children, to protect them, but a baton from another officer went up, and another man laughed as he went to manhandle Tom to the ground ...

'I wouldn't bother doing that if I were you. You heard the man. Let go of him and the children.' A figure stood at the bashed-in front door.

'Get out of here,' said the immigration officer, sizing up the man in the doorway.

'Move away from the children, and let Mr Edwards go,' said the man, undeterred by the smell of hate that permeated the hallway.

Tom looked at the man, perplexed; how did he know his name?

'Move out of the way; they're illegal immigrants and this man's been harbouring them,' the immigration officer spat out. He grabbed Amanuel by the wrist, Amanuel wincing with pain, then pushed him towards the stairway. Amanuel hit his head on the banister and a trickle of blood ran down his temple.

'Let the children go, and take your hands off Mr Edwards, *now.*'

'Look, mate, get the hell out of here. We don't need the likes of superman without his cape,' sneered the enforcement officer.

The man in the doorway looked around him and smiled dryly. 'CID, Detective Inspector Blake.' He moved forward, undeterred. 'Let the children go, and take your hands off Mr Edwards.'

Amanuel stared up at the man in the doorway. Blake's walkie-talkie crackled, his radio reminding Amanuel of the men who'd found his bear at the zoo.

'Oscar, Bravo Radio 5, we have an incident at Cove House, Beach Top. Send two units down on blue lights. A child support officer and a paramedic are required at the scene as well.'

'You can't do that. This is *our* job, *our* patch,' said the enforcement officer, rounding up towards Blake.

'Watch me,' said Blake wryly. He signalled to Prior. 'Children, come over here.' Prior moved towards the crew of unsavoury-looking men. The men threw a look at their boss and then back at Blake. They took their grip off the children, who stood silently with tear-stained cheeks, then Amanuel ran over to Blake.

'You okay?' Blake said as he crouched down to Amanuel's level. He took his hands and turned his wrists; they had large red burn marks on them and the skin was slightly broken. There was a gash on his head from when he'd hit the metal of the banister. Blake inclined his head towards Tom, and signalled for him to move away from the men and stand with the children.

'You don't have any authority over me,' snarled the lead enforcement officer at Blake. 'Don't listen to him,' he spat at the band of men who'd forced their way into Tom's home. 'Get the children back,' he snarled. But only one man went forward, and Blake walked slowly and deliberately towards the brutish bully, pushing the children back and towards Tom. Prior covered him. Blake stood in front of the leader and, with an unwavering commitment to justice, reached into his inside pocket and took out his badge.

'Steven Hawkins, I'm arresting you on suspicion of assault. You do not have to say anything. But it may harm your defence if you do not mention when questioned something which you later rely on in court. Anything you say may be given in evidence.' He turned to Prior. 'Cuff him.'

Blake bent down to Abrihet. 'Which man did this to you?' She stared across at the man who'd pushed her so that she'd split her lip. He raised his eyebrows and the corners of his mouth tilted down to his chin. 'Gary Smith, I'm arresting you on suspicion of assault. You do not have to say anything. But it may harm your defence if you do not mention when questioned something which you later rely on in court. Anything you say may be given in evidence.' Blake took out a set of cuffs and handcuffed Smith.

'You won't get away with this, you know that. I never said my name,' Hawkins hissed.

'You didn't need to. I never forget a face – or, should I say, a mugshot on police records? As for getting away with it, neither will you, Hawkins, or indeed your ringleader, Robert Spencer. You see, as I said, I never forget a face, and I saw yours at the lights this morning, familiar as the mugshot I saw on my files yesterday – three racist hooligans in Les Parcs des Princes. In fact, both your faces' – he glanced over at Gary Smith – *'all* your faces are etched in my mind. Three men who caused trouble in Paris and put a man in hospital, your intent was to cause racial intimidation, aggravation and harm. And my hunch this morning is Robert Spencer tipped you off, because what's happened here shouldn't have happened, as you well know. This isn't your patch. These are minors, and we both know this falls into the Department of Social Care, not Enforcement. Like I said, I always get my man – and it never is just *it.*'

From outside, the sirens screamed up the road, and uniformed officers entered the house.

'What've we got, guv?'

'Illegal entry without a warrant, and they're being charged with GBH, with photographic evidence of the children to follow. Take them down to the station and take a car and two officers to the RNLI station. I want Robert Spencer arrested and brought in, with intent to cause racial aggravation and harm to two minors. Detain them all.'

Kate hurtled up the road to see two marked police cars leaving the house. She tried to look into the windows, but the cars drove away too quickly for her to catch a glimpse. *Oh God,* she murmured, trying to control the tears flooding her eyes. She pulled up, and ran the last few yards to the house. Tom was sitting on the stairs with his arms around the two children.

'Tom, Amanuel, Abrihet,' she flung her arms around them. 'I saw the police and thought you'd gone, I was too late. What's happened to your head, little man, and your lip too, Abrihet? What've they done? Oh my God, you poor things.' She brushed her hand tenderly above Amanuel's gash. 'I need to see to that; it needs stitches.'

Blake stepped forward. 'Miss …?'

'Doctor Kate Glover. Sorry, you are …?'

'DI Blake, CID.'

'I need to sort the children, Detective Inspector, before you do anything, before you take them,' her voice was shaky.

'It's fine, they're fine, Doctor Glover, and of course please see to their injuries, I just need to take a photo of them before you do. Then the station's children's support officer here will speak to them. Perhaps we could use your sitting room for that, Mr Edwards – it'll be a little less frightening for them, and they've been through a lot.'

Kate nodded. 'Yes. Tom, take them through, I just need to get my bag from the car.' She wiped away the tears that stung her eyes and brushed her hair behind her ears. 'I'll come straight back.'

Tom led the children into the sitting with the support officer and solicitor. Blake and Prior following. Kate came back in from her car with her medical bag and closed the front door to the world that had watched on.

Epilogue

A year later

The towering chimneys of Battersea Power Station loomed above the River Thames, whose slow passing currents were caught like a sprinkling of flawless diamonds across its surface. A red double-decker stopped in the bus lane, allowing a huddle of tourists and London folk to climb on board and others to disembark.

Amanuel sat with his nose pressed up against the black cab's window, his view of the immense towers of the industrial building momentarily obscured by the bus. He crooked his neck, trying to gain a sight of it once more, until the bus pulled away. 'Will we see tiger?' he said, turning from the window.

'Maybe.' Kate squeezed his hand.

They drove on for a while, then, 'You can stop just here,' Tom said, leaning forward to the cab driver. 'We can walk the rest of the way.'

'No worries, guvnor, that'll be fifteen pounds, enjoy the sights. Hope you see that tiger, little chap, you'll definitely see the lions at Trafalgar Square,' he winked at Amanuel as he handed the card machine to Tom.

Amanuel's eyes widened further, he turned to the cab driver, 'Lions …?'

'Four of them,' chirped the cabbie. 'They prowl the streets at night.'

The door clicked to unlock, and Tom, Abrihet, Amanuel and Kate bundled out.

Kate linked her arm into Abrihet's. 'How ya feeling?' she said as she nudged into her.

'Good. London's amazing. It's more than I imagined.'

'Yes, it is. I've lived here most of my life, went to medical school here too – in fact I spent many a time having a picnic along the embankment, learning how to skim stones. Being back here feels like I never left.'

'Why *did* you leave?'

'I had an opportunity to work in a practice near Deal, and I took it, and my best friend was leaving too, so it all worked out. Best decision I ever made.'

'Why?'

'Because I got to meet you and Amanuel and become a part of your lives. Come on – let's catch the boys up.'

Amanuel slipped his hand into Tom's. 'You all right little fella?' Tom asked, ruffling his hand on the boy's now bouncy afro.

'Yes, I am' – he moved aside as a jogger ran past him – 'and oh, he has running feet like me, Tom,' he said, with a slight skip in his step.

'He does – but not as fast as yours.' Tom pulled him in and laughed. 'Right, we're here.'

A flight of stone steps spanning the width of the building led a myriad of museumgoers to its open doors. Amanuel stood, his mouth gaping, as he gazed at the rooftop where a lion sat on a plinth on the left-hand side of Britannia above the pediment. It was carved from stone and sat on its haunches with its front leg planted on the ground, its paw resting on a shield and its head looking towards the river. Behind

Britannia a Union Jack fluttered in the breeze that carried across London. Amanuel's gaze moved to the other side and he tilted his head out of curiosity of the animal that stood on the right-hand-side. It looked a little like a gazelle, yet its horn seemed to suggest it could not be a gazelle. He had never seen such a creature, one with a single horn in the *middle* of its forehead. At the top of the steps to the building, twelve huge pillars stood as if to support the building, and at the front an enormous red banner hung down with *Tate Britain* across it. Dappled light sprinkled confetti-like shadows on the pavement as the sun shone through an avenue of trees.

'Ready?' Tom said, turning to the three of them.

'Absolutely,' Kate replied.

They took the steps up to the doors and entered. The huge hall was decorated with the latest pieces of artwork and sculptures. The children took a breath.

'It's pretty special, isn't it? But there's something even more important. Come on.' Tom led them to the reception desk where a cheery lady greeted them.

'Hi,' said Tom. 'I'm Tom Edwards and we have an appointment with Mr Barratt-Smith, the head curator for *Kids' Art*.'

'Of, course, Mr Edwards, we've been expecting you. If you'd like to just wait here, I'll page him.'

They moved to the side and waited until a booming voice echoed across the main hallway.

'Ah, Tom, so good to finally meet you, I'm Lawrence. And these two must be my VIPs, and *you* must be Amanuel.' He crouched down low to Amanuel and shook his hand. 'I have to say I've been super-excited to finally meet you. Please come this way.' He led the four of them through two beautifully

310

decorated art-filled rooms until they reached the Kids' Art hall. A crowd of people stood blocking the main centrepiece.

'Please ...' said Lawrence, spreading his arms out to encourage the audience to fan out, and as they did so a ripple of applause began to carry around the room. The two children looked at the smiling faces that lined their path and as they neared the centre of the room the applause got louder and louder until that was all that they could hear.

And then there it was in front of Amanuel's eyes. He held his breath whilst his gaze rested on the sculpture in front of him. It was lit up by spotlights above and to the sides, and under it was a plaque that read:

Amanuel Abraham, HOME

Tom stood behind Amanuel with his hand on his shoulder, then nudged him forward. 'Go take a closer look,' he said in a whisper bending down to him. 'It's *your* work.'

As Amanuel walked tentatively forward a hush fell in the immense hall. He stood silently, his small hand sweeping across a coloured board of browns and greens, and a crimson pool with ripples of orange flowing through it. Where the artwork of his elephants stood, and their eyes seemed to catch his with an unwavering sense of love and protection. And the teepee-like shavings adorned the ground on matchsticks glued together to form the walls of the homes of the community he had once been part of. The miniature construction of a medical centre, and beautifully made trees where the tiniest of papier-mâché mangoes hung like peach-blushed lanterns. Every detail picked out. Over the time spent with Tom the intricate miniature model of his village in Adi Ada had been completed.

'So this is your work,' Lawrence finally said.

Amanuel nodded, taken aback by it all.

'Ladies and gentlemen, boys and girls, it gives me the most profound and greatest pleasure to welcome and present Amanuel Abraham, our youngest artist at the Tate Britain. An artist who has, along with his sister, faced an experience in life that we could only ever read about in the newspapers or imagine. Together they have travelled across countries on foot without their parents to guide them or shelter them. They have fled danger, and crossed seas that have taken the lives of those who have been forced to see the perilous open ocean as their friend, safer than their homeland. A journey that took them over a year to complete, and more than 5,700 km travelled, and by the grace of God were found by Tom Edwards, a cutting-edge and prominent architect who's designed many of the wonderful buildings we see in London today. Two young children who were clinging to their own lives on the shores of the English coastline the day that Tom took them in to be safe. Amanuel has shown a talent and a gift for art that is beyond exceptional, and it is here that we have the greatest pleasure of exhibiting his work, his village, his community, his home. Ladies and gentlemen, Amanuel Abraham.'

Rapturous applause reverberated around the great hall, echoing through the building, and a boy who came from a simple life, a simple community stood, overwhelmed by the sense of welcome, overwhelmed by the faces that smiled at him, faces of all nationalities. And there he took his sister's hand, and together they stood, in the country where Manchester United were from and cricket was played. And by their sides were two people who had promised to look after them, to keep them safe and let them aspire to the greatness they would achieve. Amanuel, a talented young artist and his sister Abrihet, who would one day fulfil her own dreams and become a doctor and belong to the British Medical Association.

Full guardianship had been authorised for these two children, with the help of DI Blake and the CID. Information had been collected from the Home Office and the country they had run from, and over their many months of being in care with social services, because the British government *did* have a duty of care to two minors. And when Tom and Kate finally won their court case and became the children's legal guardians, they learnt of the sadness and grief that had fallen on the village and that the people who had given them their chance to run had now gone. One day the children would return to their village and grieve, just like the elephants who still returned from the mango grove to the place where their family had once lain.

But what the children did learn, and kept in their hearts, was that the elephants had indeed protected the villagers, and they learnt that love and fate run hand in hand. And although their lives had been tinged with an overwhelming sense of sadness there was a brilliance for their future. And they would learn, too, that fate came in the form of a pebble that could be skimmed across the water wherever that water was, and that Doctor Sam, wherever he was, would always be a part of their lives because his brother Tom had found them.